The Coffee Girl

by

SHANNA HATFIELD

The Coffee Girl
Copyright © 2012 Shanna Hatfield
All rights reserved.

ISBN: 1479151270
ISBN-13: 978-1479151271

Shanna Hatfield
shanna@shannahatfield.com
shannahatfield.com

This is a work of fiction. Names, characters, businesses, places, events and incidents are either the products of the author's imagination or used in a fictitious manner. Any resemblance to actual persons, living or dead, or actual events is purely coincidental.

Books by Shanna Hatfield

FICTION

The Coffee Girl

Learnin' the Ropes

QR Code Killer

Grass Valley Cowboys Series
The Cowboy's Christmas Plan
The Cowboy's Spring Romance
The Cowboy's Summer Love

The Women of Tenacity Series
The Women of Tenacity - A Prelude
Heart of Clay
Country Boy vs. City Girl
Not His Type

NON-FICTION

Savvy Holiday Entertaining
Savvy Spring Entertaining
Savvy Summer Entertaining
Savvy Autumn Entertaining

*To those who encourage and support others
in their dreams.
You are so appreciated!*

And to Colleen - the perfect Coffee Girl!

Chapter One

Listening to the rain pelt against the windows of the coffee shop, Brenna Smith held back a long-suffering sigh as she impatiently waited in line.

Knowing how busy the shop was early morning, she should have skipped the coffee or left the house five minutes sooner. If the line didn't start moving a lot faster than its current snail-like speed, she was going to be late for work at her office in Portland.

Being late wasn't an option.

Skies the color of cold gunmetal coupled with the frigid drizzle of rain didn't help her dreary state of mind. Unwilling to think about what the day would bring, she rolled back her shoulders, closed her eyes, and took a deep breath.

The delicious scent of cedar wood, warm musk and, not surprisingly, rich, dark coffee filled her senses. Taking another deep breath, she opened her eyes, fastening her gaze on the back of the man in front of her.

It was him.

Brenna first noticed the man in the coffee shop weeks ago. She could always smell his unique, outdoorsy scent before she saw him. How had she not noticed he was standing right in front of her today?

Seeing him dressed in a canvas coat, jeans, work boots and a ball cap brought the hint of a smile to Brenna's face.

The guy wasn't movie-star handsome, but he was ruggedly good looking and from the way his coat stretched across his broad shoulders, she assumed he would be fit. Standing around five-ten, Brenna liked his easy smile and the way laugh lines framed his bright hazel eyes. She guessed him to be around her age.

While he placed his order, Brenna tried not to stare too intently at his back or listen too attentively to the deep cadence of his voice.

Turning around, he handed her a cup of coffee with a wink and a smile before walking out the door.

"Thank you," Brenna called to his retreating form. He waved a hand in response as he strode out of the coffee shop.

Brenna's thoughts tumbled around the man while she took a sip of her coffee. Biting back her grin, she wondered how he knew she always ordered a Chai latte.

Rushing out the door, she stepped off the sidewalk only to be splashed by a car speeding through the parking lot.

Staring at the car with something akin to murderous fury in her eyes, she dashed across the puddle-ridden asphalt and got in her car grumbling. Her momentary euphoria at having the cute guy purchase her coffee was quickly dissipating.

"Just perfect," Brenna muttered to herself as she merged onto the freeway, heading north into Portland.

Putting her foot down on the accelerator, she kept her speeding just shy of going over the point that would get her a ticket.

Letting out the sigh that had been building since she got up that morning, she gripped the steering wheel in frustration.

She hated this rush to work every day. Hated her job. Hated pretty much everything about her current existence. In a few weeks she was going to turn thirty and this was not how she pictured her life as she hit that dreaded milestone.

Pulling into the employee parking lot at Harchett Industries where she worked as a research analyst, Brenna found a space in the sea of other vehicles belonging to coworkers. Hurrying inside, she tapped the toe of her high heel at the elevator, anxious to get to her office.

Working long and hard to make it to a management position, Brenna's job no longer held any joy for her.

Racing down the hall past the receptionist, Brenna threw her rain-splattered trench coat on the rack just inside her office door, grabbed notes and a folder from her desk, and hurried to the early morning staff meeting. Sliding into her chair with two minutes to spare, she took a breath, closed her eyes, and tried to center herself.

Her hotshot boss came swaggering in five minutes late sporting sunglasses and a hangover. If his uncle wasn't one of the bigwigs in the executive suites upstairs, Brenna was certain he would have been fired long ago instead of promoted to his current position that allowed him to run rough-shod over a good team of people.

The last year had been a game of cat and mouse for her, trying to stay off his radar. Any time he focused in on her, she found herself popping antacids like they were candy. He was rude, obnoxious and arrogant, and that was when he was having a good day.

From the wrinkled appearance of his suit, looking suspiciously like the same one he had on the previous day, Brenna knew today was not going to be good.

Sinking a little lower in her seat, she wished she had some magic way to become invisible.

"Well, kids, what's shaking?" Wesley Mettler asked as he took his seat at the head of the table and looked around the room. Not giving anyone time to answer, he turned his attention to a new intern sitting close to the coffee and pointed his direction. "You, coffee."

When the young man looked around uncertainly, someone discretely pointed at the coffee pot on the table then to Wesley. Jumping up, the intern poured the coffee and quickly walked it down the long table to the boss.

Instead of saying thank you, Wesley glared at the young man over his sunglasses then sat back in his chair taking a long drink.

"Which one of you is going to make me look brilliant today?" Wesley asked, looking around the room.

Keeping her eyes glued to the legal pad in front of her, Brenna hoped Wesley wouldn't notice her. Brenna thought she was safe until she felt his gaze boring into the top of her head and fought the urge to squirm in her seat.

"Ms. Smith, what can you share with the group this morning?" Wesley asked in a snide tone. It wasn't a secret to anyone that he disliked Brenna. Maybe it was the fact she was conservative. It could have been the fact that she wasn't one of the office beauties. Some chalked it up to her intelligence and competence that constantly made him feel threatened. A handful liked to think it was the way she turned him down with a scathing rebuff the one time he propositioned her.

Brenna took a deep breath as she gathered her thoughts. "We finished researching the site retargeting project. It's definitely something we don't want to waste time considering. We need to move on this one while we can maintain an edge. I'll have a report with a proposed action plan ready by the end of the week."

"No, you won't," Wesley said, swiveling his chair back and forth, sunglasses still in place as he rested his elbows on the chair arm and steepled his soft fingers together. "I want it before you leave today."

"But, Wesley, that's not possible. It will take several days to compile the information, create the graphics, write the..." Brenna's explanation was cut short when Wesley sat forward, lowered his glasses and gave her a cold stare.

"Today, Ms. Smith. It will be on my desk before you leave today and I don't care how long it takes you and whoever you can find to help you to get it done. You've got until 11:59 p.m." Turning from Brenna, he moved on to his next victim and the meeting adjourned a few minutes later.

One of the first to leave the meeting room, Brenna hurried back to her office, ignoring the sympathetic looks of her coworkers.

Quietly shutting her door, Brenna would rather have slammed it. Her heart was still pounding and she felt a headache coming on. She knew from experience there wasn't a thing any of them could do about Wesley. The last person who complained was fired before the day was through and escorted out to her car by security.

Deciding she might as well accept the inevitable, Brenna lost herself in frantically preparing the report as the hours flew by. She doled out parts of the project to her team members and together they might get the project finished before Wesley's ridiculous deadline.

It was well past noon when a quick knock sounded on her door.

"Come in," Brenna called, looking up from her computer long enough to acknowledge her good friend Kathleen with a welcoming smile.

"Did you come bearing gifts?" Brenna asked, continuing to type as she watched Kathleen stride across her office carrying a bag from the deli down the block.

"I brought you some lunch," Kathleen said, setting the bag down before perching on the corner of Brenna's desk.

"Better not let Weasel Wesley see you doing that," Brenna said, digging a chef's salad out of the bag.

"I'm not worried about him in the least," Kathleen said, crossing her legs and swinging one foot defiantly.

Kathleen didn't need to be worried because her grandfather was one of the big wigs in the executive suites as well. He wouldn't allow Wesley to get Kathleen fired, although he did expect her to work her way up through the company and pull her own weight.

With her looks, attitude, and intellect, Brenna didn't think it would take Kathleen long to have her own office up near her grandfather's. She was tall and lithe with flowing black hair, snapping green eyes, and carried herself like royalty. She was also sharp, fearless, and Brenna's best friend.

They met the summer they both were interning with the company. The internships led to part-time jobs while they were finishing their college degrees and they both started climbing the corporate ladder. It had been a hard climb, especially in a company that still functioned with the mentality that women should be secretaries and errand-girls while men did the rest.

Working their way into management positions was quite an accomplishment for them both.

"Maybe you aren't but I am. You know what happens when he gets tired of employees. Before you can blink, you're packing up your personal belongings and out the door," Brenna said, eating her salad.

"The company knows how valuable you are, even if Wesley doesn't. They aren't going to let him chase you off like he has the rest," Kathleen said, stealing an olive out of the salad.

Brenna looked at her friend and smiled.

"Thanks for bringing me lunch. I needed a little break."

"No problem," Kathleen said, staring at Brenna's

computer screen where multiple windows were open as she worked on piecing together her report. "I heard what Wesley did this morning. Is there anything I can do to help?"

"No. My team is working on the charts and graphics while I write the technical details and formulate the battle plan. I'll probably burn a little midnight oil to get this on the weasel's desk as ordered, but I'll manage."

"You always do," Kathleen said, sliding off the desk and adjusting her slim skirt. "Just don't stay too late and for goodness sakes, make sure you put your name in that report. He always takes credit for your efforts even though everyone knows who really does the work. Call me if you need anything."

"I will, Kat. Thanks," Brenna said, waving a hand at her friend as she walked out the door, shutting it behind her.

Hours later, Brenna got up to stretch the kinks out of her neck and back, noticing the sky was no longer gray but black with approaching darkness. She waved away her team at five, telling them to go home and enjoy the evening.

Picking up the phone, Brenna called her mom and let her know she was going to be late.

"How late, honey?" asked Lettice Smith, better known as Letty. "We can wait dinner for you if you'll just be a little while."

"No, Mom. I've got a couple more hours of work to do before I'm finished, so don't wait on me. Please. I'll grab something to eat on my way home," Brenna said, staring into the watery darkness outside as she leaned against the desk.

"Drive carefully. I hate you making that long trek to and from work every day," Letty said.

"I know, Mom. See you in the morning," Brenna said, disconnecting the call.

Growing up in Silverton, Oregon, just an hour or so southeast of Portland, Brenna and her family didn't think anything about the drive whenever they needed to run into the city. It was something else entirely when you had to make the trip every day in heavy traffic.

During college and right up until about two months ago, Brenna lived in a cute little apartment with two roommates not far from her office. When the owner of the apartment building decided to sell it to a developer for a new retail center, the tenants were given a month to get out. Without time to hunt for a new apartment, Brenna moved back home temporarily.

Yeah, that's how I've always envisioned my life, she thought sarcastically: a 30-year-old living at home with her parents, in a job she barely tolerated, working for a boss she loathed in a city she often felt was sucking the lifeblood right out of her.

Someday she'd follow her dreams, but today was not that day.

Her sister Avery kept telling her to stop waiting for someday and do it now, but Brenna was too cautious, too responsible, to throw caution aside and plunge blindly into the future.

She had a nice little nest egg, a good start on her retirement, and a few close friends she enjoyed. None of that erased her longings, though, or the loneliness that sometimes threatened to overwhelm her.

When she closed her eyes, she could see a sweet cottage-style home, a man with broad shoulders and dark hair, and a gangly mutt. The smell of coffee and fresh baked pastries hung in the air, along with a hint of cedar and some other scent that drifted just out of her mind's reach.

Haunted by the same dream for years, Brenna had yet to see the house, the man or the dog. So she'd just go on dreaming and waiting.

Opening her eyes, Brenna sighed, returning to her paperwork. She was exhausted, her back was killing her from sitting at the computer all day, and she was half-starved. Pushing all that aside, she buried herself in her work.

A few hours later she neatly bound the report with a strong sense of accomplishment. Gathering up her coat and purse, Brenna turned off her office equipment and lights, shut the door and walked down the hall to Wesley's office. The door was open so she walked in and dropped the report on his desk.

Turning to leave, she saw him sprawled on the couch with an empty bottle of whiskey on the floor beside him. She shook her head and quietly walked out, knowing by his snores he had no idea she'd been in the room.

Hurrying out of the building, she asked one of the night security guards to walk her to her car. She wasn't overly paranoid, but she'd rather be safe than sorry. As they walked past two homeless men begging for change, Brenna was glad for the escort. The security guard waited until she was safely buckled into her seatbelt before returning inside.

Brenna's stomach growled as she headed south on the freeway. She planned to swing by one of her favorite sandwich shops closer to home, so she kept on driving.

Mentally exhausted, she was tired of playing the office games, tired of putting up with Wesley, and tired of having no life outside of her job.

Maybe it was time to think about making a change. Maybe she should consider Avery's advice.

Brenna was mulling over her options when she heard a loud pop and her car jerked to the right. Of course her tire would blow after she had driven past an exit. Carefully maneuvering the car onto the shoulder of the road, Brenna turned on her hazard lights and jumped out of the car into a steady fall of bone-chilling rain. Hurrying around to the passenger side, she could see her tire was not only flat, but missing a piece or two of rubber.

Perfect.

The flat tire unraveled the last thread that was holding Brenna's frustrations in check. Running back to the driver's side, Brenna slid behind the wheel and burst into tears.

Chapter Two

Brock McCrae didn't make a habit of buying strange women coffee. In fact, it was the first time he'd ever done such a thing but the cute little blond standing behind him in line piqued his interest.

For the past couple of months, he'd seen her most weekdays at the coffee shop. She always ordered a Chai latte, always smelled like fresh flowers and sunshine, always glanced at him shyly.

He'd guess her to be around five-three or so without her high heels. Brock assumed she must have an office job in the city judging by the power suits she wore and the harried air about her. Her curly golden locks were usually somewhat tamed into a clip or a bun at the back of her head. She wasn't beautiful by fashion model standards, but she was definitely someone he'd given more than a passing glance.

Her blue eyes were huge, luminous, and moist like she was absorbing everything around her. A smattering of pale freckles dusted her nose and cheeks. Lips, a soft shade of pink, seemed to rest in a natural pout, which made Brock want to kiss them in the worst way.

Not fat or thin, not tall or too short, she should seem average, but there was something about her that drew Brock's attention.

From his furtive observations while waiting in the coffee line, he knew she always seemed in a rush and appeared to be more of the quiet type.

This morning when he realized she was standing in line behind him, he wanted to do something nice for her so he bought her coffee. The grateful smile she sent his direction as she recovered from the surprise of him handing her a drink was a great trade for the price of the coffee.

Brock thought of her, and the smile that lit her face, throughout the day as he worked on finishing his current construction project.

Fresh out of high school, Brock landed a job for a construction company. His parents planned for him to become a doctor, lawyer, or something involving a high-powered career. It came as a shock to them both that he was much more interested in high-powered tools.

There was nothing he enjoyed more than building something. He thrived on the feel of the tools in his hands, the smell of cut wood, and enjoyed watching dreams on a piece of paper become a reality wrapped up in wood, steel and paint.

Summers spent working with his uncle in the small town of Silverton gave him the opportunity to learn the construction trade as well as living life at a slower, simpler pace. His uncle Andy taught him all he could and that's how Brock managed to land a job for a well-known construction firm in Portland as a gangly boy of seventeen. Brock worked his way up from peon to site manager in the years he served the construction firm, making a name for himself as someone fair and honest who did good, solid work.

When his uncle announced he wanted to retire and sell his business right before Christmas, Brock jumped at the opportunity to follow his dream of managing his own company. He took over the reins of McCrae's Construction two months ago.

Spending the past thirteen years in Portland, Brock liked the idea of moving from the big city to the small town of Silverton. His two roommates would find someone else to share their apartment when he got around to making the move.

Just last week, he spied a great fixer-upper house he thought he could work on in the evenings. Brock had an appointment tomorrow to take a look at it and see how much money and sweat it would take to get the place whipped into shape. From the street, it mostly looked like cosmetic repairs. He hoped after an interior inspection, his hunch would prove correct.

Brock made a nice side income in the past buying houses that seemed to be beyond redemption, fixing them up, and selling them for a hefty profit.

He wasn't afraid of hard work and he loved seeing the opportunity in a house, rather than looking at its current state of neglect.

Watching his crew finish up their current project just before quitting time, Brock felt a sense of accomplishment and pride. He sent the guys home, staying behind to complete the site cleanup. Loading tools in the construction trailer, he pulled it back to his office. After spending an hour catching up on paperwork, he decided he better hit the road for home.

Content and tired, he cruised north on the freeway, lost in his thoughts of the girl from the coffee shop. There wasn't much traffic out this time of night to distract him from his musings even though the rain was coming down just enough to make him glad he wasn't outside.

A car heading south suddenly veered to the right before coasting onto the shoulder. Brock watched to see if they needed help. Hazard lights flicked on before someone got out and hurried around the car. They quickly ran back to the driver's side and climbed in, but didn't pull back onto the road.

Although he really wanted to pretend he hadn't

noticed there was a problem, he knew it would bother him all night if he didn't stop. Brock took the exit, crossed over the freeway and came down the on ramp heading south. Illuminated by the last of the overhead lights highlighting the merging lane of traffic, Brock could see the back tire on the passenger side was toast.

Parking behind the car, he shut off his truck and picked up a flashlight from his back seat. Stepping out into the rain, Brock pulled his collar up around his ears and tried to ignore the chilly temperature. Walking up to the driver's side window, he tapped on the glass, startling the woman inside.

Finally, she rolled down the window just enough to hear him speak.

"Hey, I noticed you've got a flat. If you have a spare, I'd be happy to change it for you," Brock said, trying to sound cheerful as cold rain trickled down his neck and soaked into his shirt.

"Oh, that's okay. I'll call and have someone come," she said, trying to mop away the remnants of tear tracks down her cheeks. When she pulled her hand away, Brock sucked in a gulp of air.

"It's you," he said with a pleased grin at finding the woman of his thoughts sitting behind the wheel of the car. "The coffee girl."

Brenna's head snapped up and she focused her gaze on the man standing outside her car. It was the cute guy from the coffee shop. She knew that her day could not possibly get any worse.

Crying out her frustrations before calling her dad to come rescue her, she heard a tap on the glass near her head. Hoping it wasn't a serial killer, she lowered the window just enough to hear what the man was saying without actually looking his direction.

Now that she realized who he was, the guy had her full attention.

"Hi," Brenna said, wishing she hadn't spent the last five minutes crying, or the last ten hours running her hands into her hair, or the last several years avoiding an exercise routine.

Resisting the urge to pat her hair to make sure it didn't look like a wild harridan's coiffure, she instead rolled the window down a little further. She didn't think the guy was a serial killer, but a girl just couldn't be too careful.

"Hi," Brock said, continuing to grin. He didn't know why, but seeing the blond from the coffee shop had suddenly stripped away his fatigue. He caught a whiff of her fresh scent from the crack in the window. "Remember me, from the coffee shop?"

"Of course," Brenna said, offering a small smile. "It was so nice of you to buy me coffee this morning. Thank you."

"You're welcome," Brock said, hoping she'd let him change the tire sooner rather than later so he could get out of the rain and off the edge of the freeway. It wasn't the safest place to stand and carry on a conversation. "How about I change that tire for you? If you have a spare, it won't take me long."

"That's too much to ask of a stranger, especially out in the cold and rain," Brenna said, shaking her head.

"I'm already cold and wet," Brock said with an engaging smile that flashed white teeth and brought out the laugh lines at his eyes. "A little more won't make it any worse. Do you have a spare?"

"Of course," Brenna said, wondering what kind of idiot he took her for. "It's in the trunk."

"Why don't you pop the trunk? I'll change the tire, and you won't even have to get out of the car. No need for both of us to get soaked," Brock said, trying to use his most persuasive voice while laying on his charm.

"Okay," Brenna said, still not convinced this was

the smartest thing she'd ever done. He could whack her with a tire iron, stuff her in the trunk and haul her off never to be seen again.

Huffing with irritation, Brenna decided she'd spent too much time watching crime shows on television. Avery was right. She really needed to get out more.

Popping the trunk from inside the car, Brenna heard rattling sounds and felt the weight shift as the spare was lifted out. She waited a minute or two then decided it really wasn't polite to hang out in the car while he did all the work in the cold rain.

Digging through her purse, she pulled out her travel-sized can of pepper spray and opened her car door, stepping out into the rain and a big puddle.

With one foot completely soaked in freezing rain water, she shivered as she walked around the car to see her hero almost finished taking off the blown tire. He wore a funny little flashlight on his ball cap that helped him see what he was doing.

"Looks like this one is beyond saving," Brock said as he removed what was left of the old tire. He quickly slid the spare in place and tightened the nuts, lowered the jack and returned it to its rightful place. He picked up her ruined tire and threw it in her trunk before brushing his hands on his jeans and giving her a crooked smile that made her forget her wet feet, soggy clothes, and disheveled hair.

Brenna watched him work, admiring his strength and the easy way he moved, like someone confident in his own skin. Coming to the conclusion that if he was a serial killer he would probably have made his move before now, Brenna let her guard down.

"Trying to decide if I'm going to stuff you in the trunk and kidnap you?" Brock teased, obviously reading her thoughts as he walked her back around her car.

Brenna looked at him in surprise then smiled.

"Maybe."

"I promise I'm not wanted for any crimes and I've never once considered kidnapping anyone."

"That's good to know," Brenna said, releasing the breath she was holding. "In that case, can I buy you a cup of coffee as a thank you for fixing my tire?"

"Sure," Brock said, wanting to spend more time with this interesting woman. "There's a little family restaurant at the next exit. Want to go there?"

"That would be great," Brenna said. "Thank you."

It took just a few minutes to reach their destination. Brenna wasn't expecting him to take her up on her offer, but was glad that he did. Meeting him at the door, he held it open for her and they stepped inside, greeted by a cozy atmosphere and the smell of chicken in the air.

"Hello, dearies," a friendly older woman called as she bustled past the door. "Be right with you. Sit wherever you like."

Brock motioned for Brenna to go ahead, so she chose a booth not far from the door. She began to remove her coat but before she could even get one arm out of the sleeve, he helped her take it off. Draping it over the back of the booth, he removed his coat and ball cap.

Looking at his hands, he excused himself and walked off in the direction of the restroom. When he returned, Brenna sat sipping a cup of hot chocolate while a steaming cup of coffee sat waiting for him.

He slid into the booth and wrapped his hands around the toasty mug.

"Thanks for ordering me the coffee," he said, taking a sip. It was dark and black, just like he liked it. "I hope you don't mind if I order dinner. I haven't had any yet and I'm starved."

"Not at all. I haven't had a chance to eat either," Brenna said with a smile, looking through the menu in her hand. "I suppose if we are going to sit at a table together and eat, we should perhaps know each other's name."

"You think so?" Brock asked with a teasing glint in his hazel eyes. Brenna liked watching his eyes crinkle at the corners and his full lips tip up in a smile. "That takes away so much of the mystery."

"What mystery?" Brenna asked, attempting to conceal her overwhelming interest in her rescuer by returning the mug of chocolate to her lips.

Watching her mouth lift with a smile, despite her failed attempt to hide behind her mug, Brock was quite taken with the woman. He thought she looked perfectly enchanting as her big blue eyes focused on his. Giving her a once over as she sat across from him, Brock concluded she must have had quite a day from the looks of both her clothes and hair.

The coat he'd helped her remove bore water stains as well as a broad splatter of mud along the hem. Her suit was wrinkled and the sleeves were bunched like she'd continually shoved them up all day. Hair the color of autumn sunbeams, which had been neatly contained in a clip this morning, now hung in bedraggled ringlets around her face. A pencil stabbed into the mass stood at attention near the back of her head.

He'd bet money she had no idea about the pencil.

Taking another drink from his coffee cup, he offered her an engaging grin. "The mystery of figuring out 'Who is this intriguing stranger?' Is she a high-powered attorney? A doctor's wife? A wheeler dealer? Or a bank robber in disguise?"

"No," Brenna laughed, setting down the mug of chocolate. Any response she may have articulated waited as the waitress came and took their orders.

"So let's see if I can guess what you do," Brock said, leaning back in the booth and stretching out his legs to the side, while draping one arm along the back of the bench seat. "I bet you work in an office."

"Yes," Brenna thought that was an easy guess, considering her attire

"You've been there for a while."

"Yes." That was a really good guess.

"You've worked your way up to a position with some added responsibility, some type of manager."

"How did you know?" Brenna asked, sitting forward, surprised at how quickly the stranger figured out her position in the company even if he didn't know what she did.

"You wear power suits every day," Brock said, waving a hand her direction. "They don't cost as much as a down payment on a car, but they aren't the cheap suits a newbie would wear. They are tailored and empowering. Middle of the road clothing budget, mid-manager."

Brenna raised an eyebrow his direction. "How do you know so much about clothes?"

"My mom is a fashion designer. I learned more than I ever wanted to about clothes, fabrics and all that stuff," Brock said, leaning his forearms on the table and looking intently at the coffee girl. "The suits only gave away part of the answer. You have the weight of the world riding on your shoulders which tells me you aren't one of the minions who can leave the cares of the office behind when they punch out at five. You also don't have the leisure of delegating all the work to someone else."

"Hmm," Brenna said, unable to fathom how this man could know her so well from just a few simple observations. "And you know that how?"

Brock took another drink of his coffee. "You've got an ink stain on your sleeve, short nails without a manicure, and a chewed pencil in your hair further cementing my theory that you are someone who gets in and gets your hands dirty to get the job done."

Brenna grabbed for the pencil and, after locating it at the back of her bun, hurriedly stuffed it in her purse.

"You're good," she finally said, taking another sip of chocolate. "Technically, I'm a senior manager in my division. In the grand scheme of things my position equates to a mid-manager in the company."

Brock shot her a knowing smile. His dad was a muckity-muck at a big corporate office and Brock spent enough time there over the years, hiding from his mother and her fabric swatches, to be able to spot a ladder climber anywhere. Except this freckle-faced girl didn't seem the type. Although the navy suit was tailored to fit her perfectly, it somehow made him think of an ill-fitting glove. He bet it felt like one to her, too.

"What do you do at this corporate job where you are a senior manager?" Brock asked, his fingers drumming on the table. If he didn't keep them busy, he wasn't sure he could fight the insane urge to reach out and grasp the hands of the woman sitting across the table or twine them into her tempting curls.

"You mean your psychic powers have failed you?" Brenna teased, mirth filling her eyes.

Brock laughed and shrugged his shoulders.

"Research," Brenna said, fiddling with her spoon. She didn't know why she was reacting to her rescuer so oddly. The most bizarre desire to slide into the booth next to him and rest her head against his broad chest kept her fidgeting in her seat. "My team is in charge of research and development. I spend a lot of time online, trying to keep us on the cutting edge."

"Sounds interesting and tiring," Brock observed, taking in the dark circles under the coffee girl's eyes.

"What about you?" Brenna asked. Before he could answer, she pointed toward his restless fingers and gifted him with an impish grin. "Let me guess, you're a concert pianist?"

Brock chuckled and shook his head.

Brenna absorbed the sound of it as she watched the laugh lines around his eyes and mouth deepen.

"No? Maybe an artist? An accountant? A dentist?"

Brock grinned and sipped his coffee. "Not even close, coffee girl. You're going to have to do better than that."

Brenna inhaled deeply, taking in the scent of wood, outdoors and man. Looking from the top of his head, across his attractive face and down his chest, she finally noticed a bit of sawdust clinging to the front of his flannel shirt. His hands were tanned and calloused with a raw cut near the thumb of his left hand.

"You build things," she said, studying him intently. As he shifted and rolled his shoulders forward, Brenna decided she was correct in her assessment of his physique. Under that coat lurked a very fit body. A body of someone used to physical labor. He wore a thermal Henley beneath a green plaid shirt that accented the breadth of his shoulders and his overall rugged appeal. She liked the way his short brown hair stood up in tousled spikes on his head.

"Point for you," Brock said, as the waitress brought their meals. "What gave me away?"

"Sawdust."

Brock looked down and saw the incriminating evidence clinging to his shirt.

"I'm in construction," he said, slicing into his steak.

"Nice to meet you, construction man," Brenna said, taking a bite of her baked chicken.

They discussed their jobs in general terms, their families, the fact that neither of them were married or in a relationship, and thoroughly enjoyed an hour together before Brenna found it impossible to stifle a yawn that nearly cracked her jaw.

"Pardon me," Brenna said, embarrassment bringing high color to her cheeks. "It's been a long day."

"That it has," Brock said, helping her put on her coat. Before he could bend over and pick up the bill, Brenna snatched it off the table and hurried to the cash register. Brock caught her before she got there.

"Call me old-fashioned, but the guy pays," Brock said, digging out his wallet.

"If we were on a date, I might agree," Brenna said, slapping down cash on the counter and nodding at the waitress. "However, since I owe you not only for coffee this morning but also for coming to my rescue with my flat tire, and I asked you to join me for coffee, I think this should be my treat."

"It isn't necessary," Brock said, uncomfortable letting her pay. It just didn't set right with him.

"I insist," Brenna said with a smile that made heat begin to zip through Brock's blood. "Then we're even."

"Next time will be my turn," Brock said, reluctantly putting his wallet back in his pocket. He'd buy her coffee every day for a month to compensate for dinner.

Brenna turned toward the door, focused on the fact the rugged construction man thought there would be a next time. She was completely open to that suggestion.

Walking together to her car, Brock held the door while Brenna slid in and buckled her seatbelt.

"I guess this is good night, coffee girl," Brock said, leaning down so he was closer to eye level with her.

"I guess so, construction man," Brenna said, a smile lighting her eyes and softening her voice. "Thank you again for helping me out. I really appreciate it."

"Thank you for dinner," he said, not making any move to leave. "Maybe the next time we meet we'll even exchange names."

Before he could talk himself out of it, he leaned closer and pressed a quick kiss to those soft pink lips then backed away, shut her door and hurried to his truck.

Stunned by the zinging sensation left behind from his lips touching hers, Brenna wanted to sit there contemplating what had just happened. Instead, she gave herself a mental shake, started her car, and drove back to the freeway thinking for once she had a great reason to get out of bed in the morning.

She couldn't wait to see her construction man at the coffee shop tomorrow.

Chapter Three

Brenna looked around the coffee shop one more time before she took her Chai latte and left. It had been almost two weeks since she sat across the table from the construction guy at the little diner after he fixed her tire.

Twelve days of wondering if he'd fallen off the face of the earth, died in a fiery crash, or decided he didn't like girls with mascara streaked cheeks and mud splattered coats.

Every morning she looked for him at the coffee shop but he wasn't there. Maybe the kiss didn't set his lips on fire the way it did hers. Maybe her wild hair and inane conversation drove him away. Maybe women who sobbed hysterically in their cars on the side of the road just weren't his type.

Whatever it was, she missed seeing his smile and inhaling his wonderful outdoorsy scent, even if it was in passing.

Although he said he worked in construction, she had no idea where. She had described her job to him, but in broad terms, so he had no idea how to find her either. Since they teasingly decided to wait to exchange names, she had no clue how to contact him and attempted to convince herself that was for the best.

The situation at work had gone from bad to worse and without the hope of seeing the construction guy to give her ever-darkening world a little dose of sunshine, she had all she could do to get out of bed in the morning.

She sat down with her parents that night, on the eve of her birthday, and talked about her frustrations with her job.

"Quit," her dad said, not even looking up from his paper.

"I can't do that," Brenna said, staring at her father.

"Sure you can. Walk into the weasel's office, tell him you're through and leave, simple as that," Brandon Smith said. "As bad as they've treated you, or let Wesley treat you, they haven't earned the courtesy of two-week's notice."

"But Dad, what would I do? I can't just sit around here unemployed."

"Nope," her dad said, shooting her mother a look. "But I think your mom could help with that."

"Mom?"

"Hear me out before you say no, honey," Letty said. "I'm going to remodel my shop and I want you and your sister to move in with me. You could open the bistro you've always wanted to run and Avery is going to move her flower and gift shop from that dinky little store down the street up to my second floor. You could have half of the front of the store and we can have a commercial kitchen installed. I've wanted to streamline my home interior business and with that huge store of mine, I need something to fill up the rest of the space. I'll be moving a lot of the sample pieces down to a showroom in the basement which should leave plenty of room for the three of us to each run a successful business. I've already got plans on paper and approval from the powers that be to move forward with the project. What do you say to that?"

Brenna didn't know what to say. She was, in fact, speechless. In college, she worked as a barista to help cover her expenses. Along with a life-long love of baking, she'd dreamed many times of opening her own little bistro with fresh pastries, delicious coffee, and an inviting atmosphere.

Could she really take a leap of faith, along with her mom and sister to make it happen?

"Brenna, honey, say something." Letty said, looking intently at her youngest child. She hoped Brenna would agree because she had an appointment set up Saturday morning to meet with the construction company and go over details of the project.

"Mom, I... Wow!" Brenna said, rolling the idea around in her head and finding that she really, really liked it. "If I say yes, how much money do you need me to invest and how long will it take for the renovation to be finished?"

"That's my girl," Letty said with a big smile. "We can work out the financial details later. I'm meeting with the construction company Saturday and I'd really like for you and your sister to be there as well. We'll know after the meeting how long to expect, but my hope is to have this project finished by the middle of June."

"But Mom, that's just a little more than three months away. Do you think that's enough time?"

"We'll find out soon enough, won't we?"

Brenna looked at her mom then glanced at her dad who was smiling around the edge of his newspaper. Leave it to her parents to hold her dream out to her with open hands. All she had to do was accept the gift.

"I'm in. Let's do this," Brenna said as her mother let out a squeal and wrapped her in an exuberant hug.

"Wait until I tell your sister. She is going to be so excited," Letty said, kissing Brenna's cheek. "Are you going to march into work tomorrow and let Wesley the weasel have it?"

"No," Brenna said, thinking about her exit strategy. "I think I'll keep working for a while, until I can actually start getting stuff ready for the bistro. It seems like I should keep earning a pay check for as long as possible if I'm going to be investing in starting a new business. Mom, this is the best birthday present ever!"

Brenna's heart and mood were both light as she bounced out of bed the next morning. Maybe turning thirty wouldn't be so bad after all. Hurrying to get ready for work, she went downstairs to find her parents in the kitchen with her favorite breakfast of chocolate chip pancakes and crispy bacon on the table.

"Happy birthday, Brenna!" they said in unison.

"Thanks," Brenna said, giving her watch a quick glance and deciding if she skipped her morning coffee stop, she had time for breakfast. Visiting with her parents, they reminded her to be home in time for the party her sister Avery was hosting at her house that evening.

"I'll be on time," Brenna said, shrugging into her trench coat and grabbing her purse. "Thanks for the wonderful breakfast."

"Have a great day, honey," Brandon said, kissing her cheek as she hurried out the door.

"Thanks, Dad. See you both tonight."

Brenna tried not to think about the coffee shop and the lack of one charming construction man's presence there over the last couple weeks. She hoped he wasn't avoiding it just because of her.

Deciding not to let any dark thoughts mar her birthday, she instead focused on the party at her sister's house that evening.

Avery and her husband Greg were fun. Despite being sisters and not even two years apart in age, Avery and Brenna were very close to each other. When Avery met Greg and fell in love, Brenna felt abandoned for a while. She knew it was silly and Greg's persistent humor and kindness went a long way in mending Brenna's hurt feelings. Now, the three of them enjoyed spending time together when their schedules meshed, although Brenna often felt like a third wheel.

Arriving at the office right on time, Brenna maintained a positive attitude right up until Wesley walked in for the morning meeting and set his blood-shot gaze on her.

"Well, Miss Smith, why don't you tell us all why your latest and greatest project didn't properly dazzle the execs and I got reprimanded for shoddy work? Hmm?" Wesley said, leaning forward in his chair with his fingers drumming an annoying beat on the shiny surface of the conference table.

"Well, Wesley, I can only…" Brenna started to say, but was cut short before she could even complete her thought.

"You can only what? Admit your incompetence? Beg for mercy? Plead for your job? You are pathetic. Completely pathetic," Wesley waved a dismissive hand her direction and turned his wrath elsewhere.

When the meeting ended a few minutes later, Wesley motioned Brenna to stay.

"Well, Miss Smith, what do you have to say for yourself?" Wesley asked in a scornful tone as he leaned back in his chair, hands crossed behind his head.

Brenna fought down the urge to push him over and leave his shiny shoes dangling in the air. The knowledge that she wouldn't have to put up with Wesley much longer loosened her tongue.

"I'd say that if you'd stop claiming my work, then I'd be the one to get reprimanded, not you. And if you wouldn't randomly rush me before a project is ready to be completed, there wouldn't be any problems."

With a curt nod of her head, she stalked out of the room with her back ramrod straight and marched to her office where she slammed the door.

It felt really good.

Mumbling to herself, she wasn't surprised when Wesley barged into her office, banging the door against the wall.

"Don't you ever mouth off to me like that again and don't you walk away from me. Do you understand, you twit? I'm in charge. Me. I'm the boss. If you value your job at all, you will keep your mouth shut," Wesley yelled as he clenched and unclenched his soft, designer tanned hands at his sides. "If you don't want to find yourself escorted out of here by security, get busy fixing that report and make me look good."

Brenna raised an eyebrow at Wesley and matched him glare for glare. She began to rethink her notion of working for another month or two until the bistro was ready to open.

No, she wasn't going to give Wesley the satisfaction of running her off. She'd quit when she was good and ready, not a minute before, and she wasn't ready today.

Wesley took her silence for submission and stalked back out the door. It was just seconds later when Kathleen poked her head in and saw Brenna sitting at her desk looking perfectly calm.

"Are you okay?" Kathleen asked, carrying in a big bouquet of cheerful flowers and setting them on Brenna's desk.

"I'm fine, actually," Brenna said, letting out a long breath, realizing she was fine. Better than fine. It was her birthday, for once she hadn't let Wesley completely wipe his polished shoes all over her and she had a party with her family and friends to look forward to that evening.

"I heard what you said to him. Good for you," Kathleen said, plopping down in a chair with a big smile. "About time someone stood up to him."

Brenna grinned at her friend as she admired the flowers. "These are lovely."

"I'm glad you like them," Kathleen said, leaning forward in her chair. "Happy Birthday, Brenna. May today be the start of something new and wonderful."

"Have you been reading fortune cookies again?" Brenna teased, going through the stack of messages the receptionist left on her desk.

"No," Kathleen said, sitting back and crossing her long legs. "I just have a feeling good things are coming your way and it's about time."

"Well, aren't you prophetic this morning," Brenna said smiling at her friend. Since her discussion with her parents the previous evening, Brenna felt like a huge weight had been lifted off her shoulders. It was easy to see how this job was sucking up her energy and zest for life.

"Nope," Kathleen said, studying Brenna. "You're not telling me something that I really should know. Come on, spill."

"All in due time, my friend," Brenna said, not quite ready to tell Kathleen about the bistro plans. She wanted to see how long the project was going to take before she shared that information with anyone.

"You are definitely holding out on me," Kathleen said, getting a familiar look on her face that let Brenna know she would hound her until she gave her some tidbit of information to mull over.

"I met a guy," Brenna blurted out before she could reel the words back in. It would be less damaging to both her psyche and her ears to tell Kathleen about the bistro rather than the fact she had met a man. As Kathleen's scream of excitement ripped through the office, Brenna quickly ran to the door and loudly explained, "Spider. We got it."

She shut her door and shook her head at her friend as she sat back down at her desk.

"Control yourself or you'll have half the floor in

here," Brenna cautioned, leaning back in her desk chair and rocking it back and forth.

"Details, details!" Kathleen said, waving a frantic hand at Brenna.

"He gets coffee at the same shop I do off the freeway. A couple of weeks ago, he bought me a Chai latte and handed it to me with a smile. That very night, I got a flat tire on the way home and he stopped and fixed it for me. I offered to buy him a cup of coffee and we ended up at a little diner and had dinner together."

"That is so cool," Kathleen said, excitement filling her face as she looked at Brenna. "So what's his name? Where does he work?"

"I don't know," Brenna said, shuffling papers on her desk nervously.

"What do you mean you don't know? You had dinner together for goodness sake," Kathleen's voice climbed in pitch. Brenna shushed her.

"He said it removed all the mystery if you learned everything about a person all at once. He told me the next time we meet, he'd ask my name then."

"That sounds romantic," Kathleen said, her eyes looking dreamy. Kathleen could find romance in a brown paper bag given enough time and encouragement.

"It was," Brenna agreed, a soft look settling on her face as she thought of the mysterious construction man. "He walked me to my car and right before he left, he kissed me."

"What!" Kathleen screeched. Lowering her voice, she repeated herself. "Don't stop with the details now."

"He leaned in the window and kissed me so fast I wouldn't have known it happened except for the fact my lips felt like they'd been incinerated. I haven't seen him since."

"Are you not stopping to get coffee?" Kathleen asked, sitting forward with a frown on her smooth forehead.

"No. I stop every morning, but he hasn't been at the coffee shop. He was there every day just like me. He always ordered an extra large of the dark roast, straight black. He smells like cedar and musk and something else completely wonderful I can't begin to describe."

"A warm-blooded, good-looking man?" Kathleen suggested, lifting a shapely eyebrow.

"Maybe," Brenna hesitantly agreed. "I don't know if my hysterics over the flat tire, my disheveled appearance or my lack of stimulating conversation drove him away, but he is definitely gone."

"None of the above, my friend," Kathleen said, drawing dramatic inspiration from the mystery of the situation. "Maybe he was in an accident and his wounded, damaged body is waiting for you to come find him in some sterile hospital bed. Maybe he was kidnapped by drug lords trafficking their wares up to Seattle. Maybe he took a wrong exit and is still wandering around the city, lost and uncertain."

"Kat!" Brenna said a she shook her head, trying to hide her amusement with her friend behind exasperation.

"Well, anything is possible. Don't just assume it's something you did. There could be hundreds of reasons he isn't there. Does he travel on business? Does he have family out of town?"

"I don't know. He said he was in construction. His dad works in some sort of office environment and his mom is a fashion designer. He didn't mention any siblings and I don't know where he works. I'm not even sure what his truck looks like since it was dark and raining. I can tell you it was big with four doors and had some kind of logo on the side that I couldn't make out in the rain. That's all I know."

"You know more than that," Kathleen said, slapping her hand on the desk. "Let's get down to important specifics. What did the man look like?"

"He... um..." Brenna tried to think of the best way to describe the construction guy. "He isn't handsome in a conventional, magazine-cover sense, but more in a rugged kind of way. He's about five ten or so, has dark brown hair that's short and spiky. He has a great jaw and chin and the most amazing hazel eyes with those little crinkles around the edges that make it look like he smiles and laughs a lot. He has strong hands, hands that do hard labor, and there are muscles."

"Muscles?"

"Oh, yeah," Brenna said, getting lost in her dreamlike visions of her mystery man.

"How would you know Brenna Smith?" Kathleen asked with an eyebrow lifted so high it nearly met her hairline. "I thought all you did was have dinner together."

"We did, but when he took his coat off he was wearing a Henley partially unbuttoned with a flannel shirt. It wasn't hard to fill in the details. You could practically see them through the fabric."

"And why did you not tell me about this sooner?" Kathleen chided, shaking her head with disappointment.

"I didn't want to sound like I was sixteen with my first crush," Brenna said, somewhat embarrassed she had confided quite so much to her friend. No one else knew about her infatuation with the man. "Please don't say anything to anyone, Kat. I haven't even mentioned it to Avery."

Kathleen pretended to lock her lips and toss the key over her shoulder. "My lips are sealed. But we've got to figure out why he disappeared. Have you asked anyone at the coffee shop if they know him?"

"Are you crazy? That's all I need is for someone to decide I'm stalking him like some mad woman."

Kathleen laughed as she got to her feet. "Right.

Because that is just the kind of image you exude, miss girl-next-door. Have a great birthday, Brenna, and don't let Wesley get you down. If it were me, I'd leave early today and do as little as humanly possible while I'm here. Oh, and don't make plans for lunch. Some of us are taking you out at noon."

"Sounds good," Brenna said, standing up and hugging her friend. "Thanks for everything."

"You're welcome."

Picking up her stack of messages, Brenna made calls, worked on revamping Wesley's latest project and found herself escorted out of the office by a group of friends at noon for a fun lunch.

Returning to work, she had a snarky message from Wesley about taking lunch when he had warned her about her shoddy work which prompted her to put on her coat, pick up her purse, tell the receptionist she had some things to take care of and leave for the day.

Instead of going home, she went to a salon she occasionally frequented and enjoyed both a manicure and facial.

She stopped by the mall and bought herself a dress that was something she would never have purchased for herself but had always wanted and then made a trip to a restaurant supply warehouse and picked up some catalogs.

Driving home, she relished the quiet since her mom was still at the store and her dad was at work.

Running a hot bath and adding some scented crystals to the water, Brenna allowed herself the luxury of a good long soak before putting on her new dress, fussing with her hair and makeup and adding a spritz of her favorite perfume. She knew her parents would go straight to Avery's after work, so she took her time opening up mail that arrived for her, including birthday cards and a few gifts.

Glancing at the clock, Brenna put on her coat, gathered her purse and car keys, and went out the door with a smile.

Arriving at Avery and Greg's house a few minutes later, she was still grinning as she rang the bell and stood waiting for the front door to open. She could have walked right inside, but this seemed like more fun.

"Come on in. The birthday girl hasn't..." Avery said, staring at her sister in astonishment. "Brenna! You look fantastic. Come in, come in!"

Brenna laughed and shed her coat, handing it to Avery as she gave her sister an excited hug. "Wesley made me mad, so I took the afternoon off and treated myself to a few indulgences."

"You should do that more often," Avery said with an encouraging smile. Although she was a few inches taller than Brenna, the two sisters shared the same curly golden hair, big blue eyes and freckled noses. "You really do look amazing. Happy birthday, Rennie."

"Thanks, Avery, and thanks for throwing this party."

"No problem. I was more than happy to do it, as we celebrate you leaving behind your youth and joining the ranks of the aged and decrepit," Avery teased as they walked down the hall to the kitchen where Brenna could hear the voices of people she knew and loved.

"Thanks. A lot. That was really special," Brenna said, playfully slapping her sister's arm.

"You owe me more thanks than you know. Mom had it in her head to invite some 'nice young man' she met recently as a surprise and I told her no way. Lucky for you, he's out of town."

"Will she ever stop?" Brenna asked, rolling her eyes as they stepped into the kitchen.

"Not until you have a ring on your finger and a man on your arm," Avery teased, pushing Brenna toward the guests already gathered who cheered "Happy birthday!" when they noticed her walking into the room.

Brenna enjoyed the evening despite one of her old boyfriends, Will, being there. Just because he was Greg's friend should not mean he got to be included at every family gathering.

It was becoming quite clear to her that her entire family was conspiring against her to see her married. She had no problem with the idea of marriage. It was the idea of marrying someone she didn't love. Brenna dreamed of a man who could make her heart pound in her ears, her breath catch in her throat, her knees turn to jelly just by a look or a gentle touch.

The only person who came remotely close to fulfilling that dream was the construction guy and now he had disappeared.

Rather than dwell on the fact that Will was following her around like a lost puppy, she basked in the compliments over her dress, ate two pieces of her favorite raspberry filled cake, and laughed with a freedom she hadn't felt in a very long time.

Brenna decided turning thirty wasn't nearly as traumatic as she anticipated.

Preparing to leave, she gave both Avery and Greg affectionate hugs. "Thanks for making my birthday special, you two."

"Anytime," Greg said, patting her back as he and Avery walked with her out to the car.

"Will you both be at the meeting with the construction people Saturday?" Brenna asked, stopping next to her car.

"I can't make it, but Avery will be there with bells on, won't you?"

"You know it. I can't believe mom decided to do this, but it's going to be so awesome for all three of us," Avery said with obvious enthusiasm. Brenna was happy to see her sister so excited about the plans and couldn't wait to find out how long it would be until the project was finished. "Did you look over the plans she had drawn up?"

"I did and they are perfect. I don't know how Mom did it, but I can't think of anything I'd want different."

"I know. She's pretty amazing," Avery said, leaning against Greg as he slipped his arm around her shoulders.

"I think all three of you Smith women are pretty amazing, but not able to withstand freezing temperatures. So you and I are going back inside and Rennie is going home," Greg said, holding Brenna's door while she climbed in the car. He shut it and offered a jaunty wave as he tugged Avery back into the warmth of the house.

Before she drifted off to sleep, Brenna spent a few minutes letting her mind wander through her dreams. One of them was about to come true and she couldn't wait until Saturday to find out when she'd be the official owner of her own bistro. Once she had a firm date, she could start planning a spectacular end to being a doormat for that weasel Wesley.

Chapter Four

Up before five Saturday morning, Brenna decided to impress the man from the construction company her mom hired with a sampling of the pastries and sweets she would serve in her new bistro.

Butterhorns, flaky croissants filled with fluffy eggs and bits of ham, and slices of a cinnamon coffee cake filled a large platter while another tray held an assortment of fruit and cheese.

Bringing along two carafes of her specialty coffee, Brenna set a beautiful oak table in her mother's showroom with a white linen cloth, good china and silver. Avery added an artfully arranged bouquet of flowers just as the front door bell jingled.

"At least he's punctual," Avery said as she smoothed down her slacks and fussed with her blouse.

Brenna ran a hand up to her hair, hoping it was somewhat contained and tugged at her dress, making sure it hung properly before following Avery to the front of the store where their mother was hanging up the coat of one broad-shouldered man with spiky dark hair.

When he turned around, Brenna drew in a gasp of air while his eyes widened in surprise.

"Coffee girl?" Brock asked Brenna as he took a step closer to her. A lazy smile lifted his lips and his hazel eyes twinkled.

"None other, construction guy," Brenna said, stepping forward and stretching out a hand to him in welcome. When he took her hand in his own, she felt an unexpected jolt of electricity blaze through her fingers and up her arm. If she didn't break the connection soon, she thought her brain might short-circuit.

"You two know each other?" Letty asked, eying her daughter suspiciously. If she was right in her hunch, and she was rarely wrong, Brenna was quite interested in Brock McCrae of McCrae Construction.

"Sort of," Brenna said with a smile, looking down at her hand, still captured in Brock's tan, calloused fingers. She noticed the cut near his thumb had healed and no new wounds seemed evident. "We see each other in passing at the coffee shop. You know, the one near Woodburn."

"I see," Letty said, winking at Avery and nodding her head toward the back of the store.

"And he came to my rescue the night I had a flat tire," Brenna said, feeling continuing twinges of sparks in her hand even through Brock let go of her fingers.

"That was you?" Letty said, linking her arm through Brock's and escorting him to the table set with breakfast. "Thank you for rescuing our little damsel in distress."

"It was nothing," Brock said, looking over the table with interest. Letty asked him to come to a breakfast meeting to discuss plans with her two business partners. He had no idea the two partners would be cute blonds, one with whom he was already more than a little infatuated. He certainly had no idea it would include a table that would have left his fastidious mother thoroughly impressed.

"Avery, this is Brock McCrae. He took over Andy McCrae's construction business. Andy is his uncle," Letty said as Avery shook Brock's hand.

"Nice to meet you Miss Smith," Brock said, shaking Avery's hand, noticing how much she and his coffee girl looked alike.

"It's nice to meet you as well, Mr. McCrae, but I'm Mrs. Landers," Avery said offering an engaging smile.

"Is your husband Greg Landers?" Brock asked.

"Yes, he is," Avery said, surprised to hear Brock mention Greg. "Do you know him?"

"I do," Brock said with a good-humored smile. "Your husband used to give me nothing but trouble during the summers I spent here working for my uncle. We got into all kinds of ... well, we had a lot of fun, anyway. Tell him I said hello."

"I'll do that," Avery said, still smiling, absolutely charmed by Brock. "Won't you sit down? Brenna provided a breakfast feast you don't want to miss out on while it's still warm."

"I'm sure I don't," Brock said, grabbing onto the name Brenna and trying it on for size. Somehow it fit the coffee girl perfectly. She looked like a Brenna with her golden curls, freckled nose, and big blue eyes.

Once the women were seated, Brock sat on one of the large oak chairs and looked with pleasure around the table. Avery and Letty passed him platters full of delicious treats while Brenna poured him a cup of coffee.

Inhaling the rich, dark roasted scent, Brock smiled and took a drink. It was brewed to perfection.

They discussed mutual acquaintances, beautiful pieces of furniture in the shop, and the weather, leaving the business discussion for after the meal.

"Well, what did you think of your breakfast?" Letty asked as Brock helped himself to another slice of coffee cake. He'd eaten more than his fill, but everything tasted so good.

"I can honestly say I've never had anything melt in my mouth like those butterhorns. Everything is absolutely delicious," Brock said, grinning at Letty.

"I'm glad you think so because what you are going to help us do will make sure Brenna's tasty creations are available for everyone to buy," Letty said, looking at the younger of her two children with pride.

"You made all this?" Brock said, looking at Brenna with interest and admiration.

"I did," Brenna said, trying to find her voice when she was getting hopelessly lost in Brock's hazel eyes.

Brock.

What a perfect name for the ruggedly handsome man. He had wonderful manners, charmed both her mother and sister, and now looked at her like she was something of a prized novelty because she had made some of her tried and true recipes for breakfast.

"Do you cook like this often?" Brock asked, keeping his eye on Brenna as he forked another bite of coffee cake.

"Only on the weekends or when I'm not working," Brenna said, still not over the shock of their construction guy being her coffee shop hero.

"But the plan is to open up a bistro in the front of the store where you'll cook like this every day?" Brock asked with a hopeful look on his face.

"That is the plan," Brenna replied, dropping her gaze to her half-eaten croissant. She'd been so flabbergasted when the construction guy turned out to be Brock, she could hardly think straight.

"You can count me in as a frequent customer," Brock stated with a grin as he took the last bite of the coffee cake.

"If you behave yourself and get the job done in the time frame we have in mind, Brenna might let you be a taste tester as she works out her menu," Letty said with a glint of merriment in her eye.

"Let's see what you have in mind, then," Brock said, ready to get down to business. The lure of mouth-watering meals made by the adorable coffee girl was too much to resist.

They spent the next hour and a half going over details, walking around the store spaces and discussing everything from timelines to space utilization. Brock made a few suggestions the women agreed were good ideas and they signed on the dotted line, ready for Brock to begin work. He would start in Avery's second floor space, since Letty already had it empty. The basement had a few small things Letty wanted done before she moved her showroom samples down there. The final project would be the main floor and Brenna's bistro.

"Saving the best for last," Brock whispered to Brenna as they walked around the space that would be her kitchen.

Brenna blushed and ducked her head, feeling butterflies swirl in her stomach at Brock's warm breath near her ear. Everything about the man made her feel languid and befuddled. She wasn't sure if that was a good thing or a bad thing.

"I promised a friend I'd meet her in Portland at eleven so I've got to run," Avery said, kissing her mother's cheek and shaking Brock's hand. "I can see our future business spaces are in good hands with you, Brock. I look forward to working with you."

"Thank you," Brock said, raising a hand in farewell as Avery hurried out the door.

"Brenna, why don't you show Brock the space out back we were thinking about for patio seating? I have a few things I need to do before my Saturday crowd starts arriving," Letty said, disappearing into her office.

Brenna looked at Brock and saw the little lines crinkling around his eyes in amusement.

"Shall we?" he asked, pointing toward the back of the store. A large door opened up to a terraced area that was nicely landscaped to the edge of Silver Creek where it ran through the backyard.

"We thought if we could enlarge this area," Brenna said, pointing around a bricked patio. "We could offer some seating out here during the summer months."

"Wow! I had no idea. This is beautiful," Brock said, looking around the calm, green oasis. He could see people flocking in droves to experience dining on this particular patio. Remembering what Greg did for a living, he grinned. "Let me guess, this is some of Greg's handiwork."

"Right you are," Brenna said, smiling. There were many benefits to having a landscaper in the family.

"He did an amazing job," Brock said, studying not only the variety of plants, but also the way they were grouped to create the most visual impact. "The patio area shouldn't be a problem at all."

"Great," Brenna said, nervously shoving her hands into the pockets of her dress as they walked back inside. Taking seats at the oak table, Brenna offered Brock another cup of coffee.

"Anything else we need to discuss before we start work?" he asked, tapping some notes on his iPad.

"No. I think we covered everything," Brenna said. Everything except where Brock had been for the last two weeks and why he hadn't been in the coffee shop.

"Okay, then, coffee girl, I'll plan to be here as soon as we've got all the permits. I'm anxious to get started on this project," Brock said getting to his feet and walking toward the door. Before he could slip on his coat, Brenna put a hand to his arm, causing him to turn around and look at her.

"Mr. McCrae, I..." she said, feeling tingles race through her fingers at the contact with Brock.

"Please, call me Brock. Mr. McCrae is too formal for friends, don't you think?" Brock asked, placing a hand on Brenna's where it rested on his arm. Fire shot

SHANNA HATFIELD

through his hand and seared its way to his heart, but he ignored it. He was too intently focused on watching the light from the window dance through Brenna's golden curls and counting the freckles on her nose.

"Brock," Brenna said, liking the sound of the name as it rolled off her lips. She also noticed the man looked as good as he smelled this morning with his unbuttoned flannel shirt and Henley. Work boots made him appear taller than he was and she didn't think she was imagining the outline of hard muscles in his thighs visible in his well-fitting jeans. "I wanted to thank you again for coming to my rescue a couple of weeks ago. You really did save the day."

"That's just one of my talents, changing a tire in the rain at night on the freeway," Brock teased, turning so he could take both of Brenna's hands in his. "I suppose I should apologize for kissing you that night, only I can't because I'm not a bit sorry."

Brenna's head shot up and he offered her a wicked grin.

"I really enjoyed having dinner with you, Brenna, and I'd like to do it again. Maybe something that could be considered an official date, if that would be okay with you?" Brock asked, wanting more than anything for Brenna to say yes.

Brenna nodded her head in agreement. "I'd like that very much, but on one condition."

"What's that?" Brock asked, giving her a wary glance. This was where the females he knew threw out demands that would be both annoying and expensive.

"You tell me why you've avoided the coffee shop the last few weeks. It doesn't seem like you would willingly miss your morning cup of java and I hope it wasn't me that was keeping you away."

Brock looked at her in surprise. If he had a way to get in touch with Brenna he would have, but not even

48

knowing her name, he hoped to run into her at the coffee shop someday and explain what had happened. He worried that she would get the wrong idea from his absence and obviously she had.

Motioning her to a couch Letty had on display near the door, Brenna nodded and they sat down. Brock waited until she was settled then leaned forward with his elbows resting on his knees.

"I was driving to work the morning after I helped you with your flat when my mom called to let me know my grandfather was in the hospital. It didn't look good, so I turned around, packed a bag and headed to Seattle where my grandfather lives. My grandmother passed away several years ago and my dad's parents were gone before I was born," Brock explained. "Granddad was in pretty bad shape. He suffered a stroke and fell down a flight of stairs at his home. No one knew for sure how long he was there at the bottom of the stairs before the housekeeper found him. Mom and Dad and I took turns sitting with him in the hospital. Granddad was ninety-two, so it's not like he was too spry."

"I'm so sorry, Brock," Brenna said, placing her hand on his and giving it a gentle pat along with a look that encouraged him to continue his story.

"He rallied around long enough to act like he recognized us and we got to tell him goodbye before he passed away. We had his funeral last Saturday and then there were some loose ends to tie up with his estate before I came back to town. If I'd known any way of getting in touch with you, Brenna, I would have. I didn't want you to think I'm the kind of guy to flirt with a girl, steal a kiss, and disappear."

Brenna couldn't look him in the eye because that was exactly what she thought. Either that or he was terrified of crazy women with pencils stuck in their hair.

"Short of calling the coffee shop and asking them to

give the pretty little blond nicknamed coffee girl a message, I didn't know what to do. I figured I'd catch up with you eventually since we both seem to stop there most weekdays. I got back on Wednesday and ran in Thursday morning, but you weren't there. I got tied up Friday and stopped in late, knowing I missed you." Brock looked around the store. "I'm really glad your mom contacted me about this project. Now that I know your name and where to find you, Miss Brenna Smith, it won't be quite so easy to get rid of me."

"I'm glad to know where to find you as well," Brenna said with a shy grin before taking on a solemn expression. "I'm so sorry about your grandfather, Brock. If there is anything we can do…"

"No, but I appreciate the offer," Brock said, getting to his feet and extending his hand to Brenna. "I've taken enough of your time today, though. I will do my best to get your bistro open on time, coffee girl. If you feel the need, at any time, to bribe me with pastries and sweets, I wouldn't object."

Brenna laughed a smooth musical sound that resonated with Brock. He was fairly certain he'd never heard any laugh he enjoyed more.

"I'll give that some consideration," she said, grinning in a way that made her big eyes look ever larger and bluer. "Thanks for coming by today, Brock. I look forward to seeing what you can do."

"Great. Now that you know I didn't kiss and run, how about agreeing to a date with me next Friday?" Brock asked with a wink as he tugged on his coat. He was trying to maintain a calm façade while his heart was pounding. Although he had dated a lot of girls, none made his stomach clench or sweat trickle down his back like this particular girl could.

"That would be nice," Brenna said, trying to process the fact that the construction guy she'd been secretly admiring for weeks, months, was asking her out on a date.

"Okay. Think about what time would be good to pick you up and you can tell me at the coffee shop next week," Brock said as he settled his ball cap on his head and walked out the door with a friendly wave.

Brenna sagged against the doorframe and tried to collect her thoughts before cleaning up their breakfast dishes. She officially had a date with the cute construction guy.

"Honey, why didn't you tell me Brock was the hero you've been pining after?" Letty said with a knowing smile as she fluttered out of her office.

"I'm not pining after anyone and I didn't even know his name. He was just the construction guy from the coffee shop," Brenna said hotly, with just enough denial and force that she confirmed what her mother already knew. Brenna was more than a little infatuated with the man.

"I see," Letty said, wisely refraining from making further comment while she and Brenna packed up the dishes and leftovers from breakfast in Brenna's car.

Looking around the store, Brenna could see it filled with customers enjoying her culinary creations. She could smell the rich scent of freshly brewed coffee and hear the customers chatting and connecting as they started their day.

Slipping an arm around her mom's shoulders, she gave her a hug that conveyed her gratitude. "Thanks again, Mom, for making this dream come true."

"You are so welcome, honey," Letty said. "Once we've got the work dream in place I think we need to tackle the next dream."

"What one is that?" Brenna asked distractedly, still lost in her vision of the bistro filled with happy people.

"The dream where one brawny construction worker

captures your heart," Letty teased, giving Brenna a squeeze around her waist.

"Mother!"

"What? I'm right. A mother knows these things."

"You will refrain from your matchmaking attempts while Brock is working here. Agreed?"

"But Brenna…"

"Agreed," Brenna said with a firmness that was completely out of character for her and left Letty no room for argument.

"Fine. Be an old stick in the mud," Letty said, straightening an already straight painting on the wall. "Too bad he was tied up the night of your birthday party."

"What?" Brenna asked looking at her mother like she had grown a second head.

"I invited him to your birthday party. I thought it would be a casual way for us to get acquainted with him. He was just getting back into town after his grandfather's funeral. What a nice young man," Letty said, turning back toward her office. "I'm sure a good-looking boy like him with such nice manners won't have a hard time finding someone to sweep off their feet."

Brenna walked outside before her mom could see how much she wanted to be the one being swept away by Brock.

Chapter Five

Staring up at the dilapidated-looking structure before him, Brock couldn't contain his grin.

The Craftsman style house, a sweet cottage, was officially his. After doing an inspection and having a couple of his buddies who knew about solid foundations, rot and termites give it a once over, they all agreed the house was solid, just in need of some major cosmetic work.

While the roof didn't leak, it wouldn't be long before it started. All the windows needed replaced, the wiring needed updated and he planned to also have some plumbing work done.

The remodeling projects he had in mind would be simple enough to do in his evenings while working on the project for the Smith women.

Whistling to himself as he gingerly stepped across the rotting boards outside the front door of his abode, Brock let his thoughts drift to Brenna Smith. Running into her the past couple of mornings at the coffee shop, she told him she planned to keep her job in Portland until the bistro was nearing completion. He thought it was a smart move on her part to put away as much cash as she could to get her business off the ground.

Standing in what would soon be his living room Brock looked around the airy space with an impressive fireplace, hardwood floors and great view of the yard as it led out to the street.

The location of the house on a dead-end street in a quiet neighborhood was definitely a plus. Silver Creek ran across the back corner of the acre lot that was now his and Brock had visions of putting in some welcoming landscaping in that area. Definitely a fire pit. He wondered if Brenna, with all her baking talents, liked something as simple as marshmallows toasted over an open fire.

Thanks to the funds he inherited from his grandfather, he was able to put a sizeable down payment on the place. He could have paid for it outright, but wanted to reserve some cash for the remodeling work he planned to do.

With the permits approved for his plans, he would get started tomorrow making the run-down house into a home.

Wandering through the wide doorway of the living room down the hall to the kitchen, Brock knew he would never miss the dining room. He planned to remove that wall and extend the one bedroom on the ground floor into a master suite complete with a spacious bedroom and spa-like bathroom.

Beyond the living room, the ground floor included the dining room and bedroom, a laundry room, kitchen and small bathroom.

Beneath the main stairway was a storage closet and off the kitchen was a set of stairs that led down to a basement that, surprisingly, had been crudely finished. A concrete floor and sheet rocked walls were more than he expected to find since so many of the old houses still had dirt floors and unfinished walls. The big open space would be great for storage as well as a place to keep his weight equipment.

On the second floor, there were three more bedrooms and another bathroom. The house was way too big for Brock by himself, but there was something about it that spoke to him.

In a dream that continued to haunt him, he could see himself in the yard of this very house with a dog bounding around his feet. He leaned over and put his hand on the rounded belly of his pregnant wife. The feeling of contentment and love that would wash over him was almost more than he could comprehend. He would raise his eyes to see his wife's face and that was when he would wake up from the dream with a sense of loss and frustration. Just once, he wanted to see her face, even catch a glimpse of the color of her hair.

Brock had been having the dream for years, but since he bought the house, it happened more and more frequently. In his dream, the house was restored, the yard was landscaped and a feeling of loving welcome hung in the air. He could smell fresh cut grass and the scent of roses blooming from the arbor he planned to repair across the front walk. He could also smell something light and fresh, like sunshine, along with the lingering hint of rich, dark coffee.

Shaking his head to clear his thoughts, Brock would be glad to get enough of the house updated so he could move in. The hour long drive to and from Portland to his apartment each night would be better spent working on his home.

Answering the ringing of his cell phone, Brock grinned when he saw the call was from his roommate and best friend, Mike.

"Hey, man, what's up?" Brock asked, stepping through the kitchen door into the backyard. Or what was left of it. Although the grass was mostly alive, all the plants were overgrown or dying.

"Just thought I'd check and see if we're still on for tomorrow," Mike said. Brock could hear the rev of an engine and knew Mike was probably sitting in traffic, trying to get through the evening rush home.

"Absolutely," Brock said. "Are you sure you want to spend your Saturday helping me?"

"You know it, dude. I'll be there before nine. You have plans for tonight?"

"I'm going to work on the porch so no one falls through tomorrow. I'll be late but I can still grab a pizza if you want," Brock said, knowing Mike would say yes. Since neither of them was dating anyone serious and they shared an apartment with Mike's brother Levi, they sometimes hung out and watched action movies on Friday nights.

"That would be great. See you when you get here."

Brock had rounded up a group of friends and some of his construction crew who wanted to earn a little extra money on their day off to help him get a new roof on the house. Once that was done, he felt like he could concentrate on the work going on inside.

Taking some precut boards out of his truck, he spent part of the evening repairing the steps leading to the porch as well as the rotten boards on the porch running across the front of the house.

Darkness had settled when he returned his tools to his truck and left the rotten boards in a neat pile in a corner of the yard. He hoped the neighbors understood things would definitely look worse before they looked better.

There were only four other houses on his street and two of them belonged to little old ladies who deemed themselves keepers of the peace in their section of the city. He knew that for a fact because they stopped him yesterday when he came out to the house to measure the boards for the porch.

After grilling him for a good fifteen minutes, they seemed satisfied that he was not bringing "drugs and ruination" to their turf.

Yep. Living on Aspen Lane was going to be

interesting, especially with every move he made under intense scrutiny from two nosy old women.

Brock swung by a donut shop on his way to his house the next morning and picked up a couple dozen along with coffee.

Setting up a card table in the living room, he put the donuts and coffee there and called the local deli to place an order for sandwiches to be delivered at noon.

Going outside to the construction trailer he parked close to the house, he began unloading supplies they would need. Cars and trucks began arriving and his friends converged on the donuts and coffee before climbing up to the roof where they began tearing off the old shingles.

At one point Brock looked up to see his two neighbors standing in the street watching the progress. He waved at them and the short plump one waved a handkerchief his direction.

"New girlfriend?" Mike teased as he ripped up shingles next to him.

"Actually, I've got two," Brock said with a grin. "They watch my every move, talk about me to their friends, and ply me with baked goods."

"Sounds miserable," Mike said, shaking his head. "I take it you met their approval?"

"Just barely," Brock said, tossing a handful of shingles over the side of the roof into the dumpster below. "After a thorough interrogation, they decided I was not going to be dealing drugs, having wild parties, or dragging miscreants into their quiet little neighborhood."

Mike laughed. "What do you suppose they make of all this noise and disturbance?"

"I told them I was remodeling the house and it was going to be loud and noisy until I was through. They said they'd somehow suffer through it with the promise of a restored house at the end of the ordeal."

"It's probably more excitement than they've had for a long time."

Brock grinned.

"Say, are you really going to keep this house or fix it up to sell?" Mike asked, wiping sweat from his brow. Although it was March and cool, ripping off a roof was a lot of hard work.

"I think I might keep it. I need to live here in Silverton and I like the peacefulness of this place. It doesn't hurt that there is a creek in the backyard or that the house is at the end of a dead-end street."

"If you like that kind of thing, I guess it would be okay," Mike said, preferring the noise and bustle of the city. "Where's your uncle? I thought he'd be here in the middle of things."

"He took Aunt Liz on a cruise. They'll be gone for almost two weeks."

"Seriously? I'm having trouble picturing that one," Mike said. He'd spent enough time with Brock and his uncle Andy to know the older man wouldn't lightly volunteer to be stuck on a cruise ship.

"He's the one who asked her if she'd like to go. I think retirement has really agreed with him."

Mike and Brock continued talking while they ripped up shingles and soon the roof was bare. After fixing the few weak spots, they got to work putting a new roof down.

At noon, a car from the deli arrived bearing thick sandwiches, bags of chips and big chocolate chip cookies.

The guys took an hour break, joking and laughing while they let their lunch settle before climbing back on the roof to finish the job.

When the crew finished later that afternoon, Brock had a new roof on the house and was very pleased with how it looked. The cedar shakes looked good and already the improvement made the house look more like a home.

Cleaning up from the day's work, Brock drove through the peaceful town of Silverton. He slowed when he went past Letty Smith's store. She was just locking the door and waved at him as he drove by.

Although he'd been working on the store project for a couple of weeks, the only time he'd seen Brenna was at the coffee shop. The Friday they planned to go out on a date, she got stuck at work on a project and had to cancel. The following Friday his Mom had flown in unexpectedly and demanded to be entertained for the weekend. Now, another week had passed with no date. He promised himself to ask her again Monday when he stopped for coffee. The longer he waited to take her out, the more his desire to do so increased.

~◇~

"Morning, coffee girl," Brock said as he held out a Chai latte to Brenna when she walked in the coffee shop.

"Hi," she said, surprise filling her face. He could see the warmth of her smile reflected in her big blue eyes.

"Would you put me out of my misery and go out with me this Friday?" Brock asked, holding open the coffee shop door.

Although it was cool out, at least it wasn't raining. Brenna walked to her car and leaned against the door before answering. Brock took a swig of his coffee and anxiously waited for her to say something.

"If it would help ease your misery, I'd be happy to help," Brenna said, hoping he would never find out exactly how many hours she'd been obsessing about what to wear, how to fix her hair, what clever and witty things she would say when they eventually did go out. She was livid the Friday she had to cancel their date due to Wesley having a full-blown tantrum late that afternoon and insisting she stay late to work on a project that wasn't due for another two weeks.

"I wouldn't want you to go out of your way to suffer on my behalf," Brock said in a teasing tone as they stared at each other, getting lost in the possibilities of what could be. He took her hand in his and rubbed his calloused thumb over the backs of her fingers. As the blue in her eyes sparked with heat, he cleared his throat. "Do you want to meet in Silverton or somewhere else? I'd be happy to pick you up at your house."

Brock wanted to spend as much time with her as possible and he definitely wanted to be able to drive her home.

"At my house would be just fine," Brenna said, giving him the address along with a smile that transformed her face from cute to lovely. "I'm usually home about six, so why don't you come by at six-thirty?"

Brock gazed at her a moment, transfixed by her smile, then nodded his head. Finally, he squeezed her hand and opened her car door so she could climb in. When he shut the door, she rolled down the window and he leaned over to look her in the eye. "I'll pick you up Friday at your house, then. Have a great day, coffee girl."

"I will, Brock," Brenna whispered, not trusting herself to speak louder. "Thanks for the coffee, construction man."

Brock laughed and waved as he walked to his pickup. He couldn't wait for his date with the cute little coffee girl!

Chapter Six

Leaving work a little early on Friday, Brenna felt like a kid skipping class as she drove home. It had been a long and tiring day with many annoying run-ins with Wesley. The man was positively evil and Brenna wasn't convinced he was firing on all cylinders. Add in his bullying tendencies, and she found him to be absolutely despicable.

Shaking off all thoughts of the office, Brenna hurried up to her room and stood staring in her closet for a good ten minutes, trying to decide what to wear. Brock hadn't given her any hint where they were going when she saw him at the coffee shop that morning. He offered her a charming smile and told her how much he was looking forward to seeing her that evening.

Mulling over her clothing options as she took a shower, Brenna put on makeup and decided to let her curls hang down instead of pulling them into a clip or a bun. Returning to her closet, she selected a knee-length floral skirt with a soft cashmere sweater. Not too dressy, but dressy enough she wouldn't be embarrassed if they went somewhere nice.

Slipping on a pair of heels, she took a few deep breaths before looking at her watch and deciding she better get a move on or Brock would be left alone with her parents. Even at the ripe old age of thirty, her dad still acted like she was sixteen sometimes.

Shoving her phone, wallet and a tube of sheer lip

gloss into a handbag, she hurried down the stairs, only to retrace her steps and grab a cheery spring trench coat out of her closet that coordinated with the colors in her skirt.

"Here's goes nothing," she muttered to herself as she hurried down the stairs, hearing the doorbell ring.

"I've got it!" she called toward the living room, where the television was blaring with the evening news.

Opening the door, it took her a moment to gather her senses enough to speak. Brock was dressed in black slacks with a light blue shirt and a charcoal gray v-neck sweater that hugged every impressive muscle of his arms and chest. Glad she'd opted for dressed up rather than dressed down, Brenna stepped back and motioned with her hand for Brock to step inside.

"Hi," Brock said, not sure he could trust himself to form complete sentences as he looked over Brenna from the top of her curly golden head to the tips of her high heeled shoes. She looked lovely and very feminine. He'd never seen her hair down before and it hung half-way to her waist in beautiful ringlets that bounced with every move she made. Her sweater was a pretty shade of pink that matched her rosy lips, and his fingers itched to run up and down the sleeve to see if it would feel every bit as soft as it looked.

Brenna leaned closer to him and he felt the warmth of her breath tingle against his neck while her fresh scent teased his nose. He looked down at her and grinned.

"You've already met half of the dynamic duo, so be warned, my dad won't let you leave without some form of interrogation," Brenna whispered conspiratorially.

"I'll manage," Brock said with a wink as Brenna took his hand and led him into the living room of her parents' home. While the house from the street was very nice, the inside was spectacular, although Brock didn't think an interior designer would have anything less.

"Dad, I want you to meet Brock McCrae. He's

doing the remodel on the store," Brenna said, dropping her hand from Brock's as her father set down his paper and turned his attention to his daughter's date.

"Brock, nice to meet you," Brandon said, standing to his full height, which was about the same as Brock's. "Brandon Smith."

"A pleasure to meet you, sir," Brock said, giving Brenna's father a firm handshake.

"My wife tells me you're doing a fantastic job with the remodel and should be done right on schedule."

"Yes, sir. It's a great project and I, for one, have a vested interest in getting the job done sooner rather than later," Brock said, surprising both Brenna and Brandon.

"Oh, you do? What might that be?" Brandon asked, taking a step closer to Brenna, feeling his over-protective father mode kick into high gear.

"The sooner Brenna's bistro is finished, the sooner I can stop there for breakfast," Brock said with an engaging smile that made Brenna's heart flutter while melting a bit of her father's reserve.

"Can't argue with you there," Brandon said, putting a hand on Brenna's shoulder and giving it a light squeeze. "She is pretty handy in the kitchen."

"Thanks, Dad," Brenna said with a smile as she stepped away from her father and recaptured Brock's hand, pulling him toward the door. "You and Mom have a nice evening."

"We will, honey. Don't stay out too late," Brandon cautioned, then made himself clamp his lips shut before he threw out something about her curfew, being careful or driving safely. Despite his wishes otherwise, both his girls were grown women long past the age of him telling them what to do.

Brock helped Brenna on with her coat then waved at Brandon as he stood watching them from the living room. "Goodnight, sir. It was nice to meet you."

"Have fun, kids," Brandon said, turning back to his newspaper and comfy chair.

Brenna walked with Brock down the sidewalk and was impressed when he opened his pickup door for her and assisted her inside.

When they both were buckled in, she turned his direction with a big flirty grin that made her blue eyes twinkle.

"That went pretty well. I think Dad liked you."

"You're joking, right?" Brock asked, shooting her a wary glance. "Your dad looked like he wanted to eat me for dinner."

"Nope. He liked you, otherwise we'd still be standing back there while he asked you eighty-six questions about yourself that you really don't want to answer."

"Only eighty-six?" Brock teased with a sideways glance as he pulled into traffic.

"Maybe even ninety."

"I'm glad he liked me, then," Brock said, reaching across the seat and squeezing Brenna's hand. He left his hand resting on hers as they drove through town. "Speaking of like, what do you think of German food for dinner?"

Brenna knew then that Brock was taking her to Mt. Angel for a meal at a marvelous restaurant that served German food. She loved to eat there, but didn't often make the short trek off the beaten path to go.

"If you're talking about the pub in Mt. Angel, absolutely."

Brock tipped his head and grinned.

"You, Miss Brenna Smith, are a mind reader. Uncle Andy used to take me there sometimes. I seem to have developed a thing for spaetzle and sausage at a young age," Brock said with an easy smile, his eyes crinkling at the corners.

"Spaetzle and sausage, huh? My obsession goes more toward the desserts," Brenna said with a flirty look at Brock.

"So I won't have to twist your arm or expound on the virtues of German cuisine to get you to go?"

"Not unless you really want to," Brenna said, not entirely bothered by the thought of Brock close enough to twist her arm playfully.

"Good," Brock said, turning his attention back to the traffic and off his lovely passenger. She smelled so good, he wasn't sure that he'd ever again be able to stand in the sunshine on a spring day and not think of her.

Parking in an empty space not far from the restaurant, Brock ran around his pickup to open the door for Brenna and give her his hand as she slid off the seat.

She looked at him in surprise but the feeling of intense attraction that settled between them as she placed her hand in his traveled up his arm and somehow worked its way right into his heart. If he wasn't careful it would be way too easy to fall for the coffee girl.

"Shall we?" he asked, not letting go of her hand as they walked in the restaurant door. He gave his name to the hostess who escorted them to a private table.

"You must have been pretty sure I'd like German food," Brenna said with a shake of her head as she sat down at the table.

"I was hoping," Brock said, taking his seat after Brenna was in her chair. "If you'd said no, my back up plan was to feed you Italian."

"Good back up plan. I might as well tell you, I'm not a picky eater," Brenna said, smiling at the waiter as he left them menus and glasses of ice water. "I like German, Italian, Mexican, Chinese, Mongolian, Japanese, Thai, and good ol' American food."

"You are making this way too easy for me," Brock

said, studying his menu. "I can basically take you anywhere for dinner and you'll be happy."

"Basically. As long as the food is good," Brenna said, quickly deciding on what she would order. "But don't go trying to convince me grease-soaked fast-food is good."

Brock laughed. "Never. I wouldn't think of it."

After they placed their orders, they talked about the progress Brock and his crew were making at the store, the types of things Brenna planned to have on her menu and the work Brock was doing on his house.

When the waiter brought their orders, Brenna shared a few bites of her tender pork cutlet with Brock while he offered her a sample or two of his sausage.

"That's really good," Brenna said, savoring the explosions of flavors the sausage created on her tongue. "It's got a great smoky aftertaste."

"The before and during taste is pretty good, too," Brock said, taking another bite while mischief danced in his hazel eyes. "I've got a few other things I'd like to explore the before and after taste of."

"You do?" Brenna asked, keeping her focus on her plate instead of the very attractive man sitting across from her. If she looked at him too long, she was afraid she might forget everything else, like how to hold a fork or sit upright in chair.

"I do. Maybe you can help me with that later." Brock's face was impassive but the tone of his voice was husky and suggestive.

"Sure," Brenna agreed without any idea what Brock was really asking. She didn't give it a thought as she enjoyed her meal and the good company.

Brock sat savoring both his good meal and the nearness of the woman sitting at his table. Brenna was so sweet and even though he knew she was thirty there was a definite air of innocence that hung around her. He really liked that about her.

Most of the females he'd dated in the last few years had developed a hard edge and many of them appeared calculating and manipulative instead of genuine and fun.

Brenna was a breath of fresh air, Brock thought, deciding that is what she smelled like to him as well. Fresh air, spring, and sunshine.

And there, in the restaurant amid the smell of apples and roasting meat, with oompah music playing in the background while their waiter ran around in lederhosen, Brock realized he was falling hard for his lovely little coffee girl.

Brock let the reality of that revelation wash over him. He'd been in serious "like" with women before, and even fancied himself in love on a few occasions. Crushes and longings were familiar feelings. But the tender, tingly feeling that started in his chest and spiraled out to his extremities every time he thought about Brenna was completely new and foreign to him.

Love.

That certainly wasn't something he was expecting or anticipating.

Turning his gaze her direction, she glanced up at him with a sweet smile that rendered him incapable of doing anything except falling into the welcoming depths of her big blue eyes.

"What?" Brenna finally asked, looking down at her sweater self-consciously. It was taking all of her concentration to eat her meal without any disasters since being close to Brock seemed to rattle her senses. "Did I spill something?"

"No, Brenna," Brock said quietly, his voice coming out a deep rumble, rich with the sudden awareness of his feelings. "You're just so wonderfully you."

Brenna lifted her eyes to his again and a blush filled her cheeks before she ducked her head, unable to speak.

If she was more confident in her ability to understand or read men, she might have thought the look in Brock's eyes held something more than just friendly interest. The way he stared at her brought a flood of heat that began at her head and ended at her toes. If she had to stand up and walk at that very moment, she wasn't convinced her wobbly knees would hold her.

Always too busy or too timid to spend much time dating, Brenna knew she'd never felt like this around another man before. She'd certainly never had one make her feel like a twitterpated ninny, unable to talk or form complete sentences, by their mere presence.

Realizing Brock continued to watch her, she finally yanked together her thoughts long enough to mutter "thank you."

Sensing her discomfort, Brock started asking her about her mother's business, Avery's flower and gift shop, and her own plans for the bistro. Grateful for the distraction, Brenna was soon chatting away about their plans. When the waiter brought them each a piece of hot apple strudel, fragrant with spices under a steaming crust, Brenna didn't remember ordering it.

Picking up her fork, she glanced at Brock as he smiled. "Hope you don't mind I ordered for us both. Their strudel is the best I've ever had."

"No, I don't mind," Brenna said, taking a bite and enjoying the mixture of flaky crust, cinnamon and apples that filled her mouth. She realized as she ate her dessert how much she enjoyed being around Brock. Not only was he very attractive, he was also attentive, funny and kind. He made her feel special, like she was the only woman in the restaurant and that was definitely a heady feeling. If she wasn't careful, she could find herself completely distracted by the charming construction guy.

They finished their dessert but didn't linger over coffee. Brock suggested they stroll around Mt. Angel.

Since it wasn't raining and the evening hadn't yet begun to chill, Brenna readily agreed.

As they started walking down the street, Brock slid his fingers down until he captured her smaller hand in the calloused warmth of his.

Brenna glanced down at their joined hands then at Brock, offering him a delighted smile that nearly made him trip over a rise in the sidewalk.

He grinned at her and more firmly clasped her hand as they strolled along.

"So, Brenna, your mom said you're still working in the city. When do you think you'll give your notice?" Brock asked. Letty had filled him in on all the details about her despicable boss and how Brenna had stuck with the job a lot longer than anyone else would have tolerated his bad behavior.

"Probably another month or so," Brenna responded, looking in the window of a cute gift shop and admiring the display. "If our construction guy keeps things on schedule, I'll probably give my notice in three or four weeks. He's only been on the job a few weeks, but so far, things look promising."

"I'd crack the whip on that construction guy if I were you," Brock said, trying to look serious. "I heard he spends too much time watching for the boss' daughter to come in the store and not enough time getting the work done."

Brenna gave him a saucy grin and playfully smacked his arm before continuing their walk. "Shame on you for having a crush on a married woman. I'm going to have to tell Greg about that."

"Funny. Real funny, coffee girl," Brock said, shaking his head. "You know which daughter I'm talking about and it isn't the one who plays with flowers."

"Oh?" Brenna said, enjoying their teasing

conversation as they strolled along the quiet street. "What does she do?"

"She makes the most wonderful baked goods I've ever eaten, smells like springtime, and flirts shamelessly with the devastatingly handsome construction guy at the coffee shop every morning."

Brenna stopped and turned to look at Brock to see if he was serious or teasing. The grin tugging at the corners of his mouth made her lips curl up in response.

"Devastatingly handsome? I wouldn't go that far," Brenna said nonchalantly.

Brock grunted and shook his head.

"Flirts shamelessly?" Brenna asked, moving on down the sidewalk. "If I were you I'd stay away from that kind of girl."

"And just what kind of girl should I hang around?" Brock asked as he walked beside Brenna, so engrossed in their lighthearted conversation he wouldn't have noticed if the sky had suddenly opened and began pouring down buckets of rain.

Brenna shrugged her shoulders and continued walking. "That's for you to decide, I suppose."

"What if I decide I like the coffee girl with the golden curls, beautiful blue eyes and freckles on her nose?" Brock asked as they stopped to look at a fountain that ran year-round.

"It's hard to account for some people's taste," Brenna said, pulling a penny out of her bag and tossing it into the water where it landed one among hundreds.

"Is that right?" Brock said, lunging at Brenna with a laugh as he pulled her into his arms and dipped her threateningly over the cold water of the fountain.

"You wouldn't dare," Brenna said, trying to catch her breath while she clutched Brock's biceps. Brock's fingers were scorching her, even through her coat, and the feel of his muscles beneath her hands was an overpowering and entirely discombobulating experience. He could have dropped her into a lake at that point and she wouldn't have cared. The wonder of being held close to him was too exciting, too deliciously perfect, to think of anything else.

Holding her over the water, Brock looked long and deep into Brenna's eyes, liking what he saw there; trust, mirth, awe and something else. Something mysterious and intriguing. Slowly moving his lips into a smile, he turned and placed her back on her feet away from the fountain.

"You're right, I wouldn't. But it's fun to tease you." Brock let go of her reluctantly and took a step back. He felt cool air surround him where before her warmth had engulfed him. "You should probably learn right up front I like to tease."

"I'd never have guessed." Brenna said in mock dismay, trying to hide the way Brock had her flustered with his antics. She couldn't think of anywhere she'd rather be than right back in his arms. It was the single most wonderful experience she'd had in her entire thirty years.

Striving for a distraught demeanor, she placed a hand to her forehead and rolled her eyes. "What ever will I do?"

Brock laughed and offered her his arm in a gallant gesture as they strolled back in the direction they came.

"How about going to the movies with me? I promise to behave the entire time we are in the theater," Brock said, raising an eyebrow her direction as a challenge.

"The entire time?" Brenna asked, not sure she wanted him to behave for five minutes. She liked his fun and confident manner. She found it unbelievably appealing.

"Yep," Brock said as he unlocked his pickup door

and held it for her.

"Well, that doesn't sound like much fun," Brenna said, shooting him an impish grin before climbing inside the pickup.

Chuckling, Brock shook his head as he walked around the pickup to the driver's side. No doubt about it, Brenna was something special.

Arriving at the theater they soon discovered their choices were limited to an animated cartoon or a thriller so Brenna voted for the cartoon. She hated to be frightened and if they went to the scary movie, odds were high she'd have nightmares for days.

Brock managed to keep his eyes from rolling at the thought of sitting through a cartoon and paid for their tickets. Brenna insisted on buying the popcorn and drinks then they settled in to watch the show.

Mindful of his promise to behave during the movie, Brock had approximately ninety-three more minutes of sitting quietly and keeping his hands to himself. Brenna's scent settled around him much like the darkness of the theater as the movie began while they found seats in an empty top row.

Brenna held the popcorn bucket between them and nibbled on bites, paying a lot less attention to the movie than she was her date. Brock smelled so good and looked so handsome, she was surprised she was able to keep functioning normally.

If she'd tripped coming up the stairs in the theater, dropped the popcorn, or sat on someone's lap in an already occupied chair, it wouldn't have surprised her at all. She was that wrapped up in Brock.

Maybe he wasn't the most gorgeous guy she'd ever seen, but he was definitely good looking, funny, smart, and more charming than any man she'd ever encountered.

Feeling very fortunate to be sitting right where she

was with Brock, Brenna pretended to watch the movie. She kept waiting for Brock to slip his arm around her or try to slide in any one of the many moves guys tended to make under the cover of darkness.

Casting a quick glance his direction, Brenna noted he seemed absorbed in the movie. He couldn't seriously be interested in the cartoon, could he?

Holding back a sigh, Brenna took a drink from her water bottle and stuck her hand in the bucket of popcorn, bumping into Brock's. Before she could pull her hand back, Brock turned and gave her a smile that bordered on sizzling as he caressed her fingers in the buttery cardboard container.

Giving her a wink, he grabbed another handful of the salty kernels and returned his attention to the movie.

It took Brenna a moment to gather her thoughts and a handful of popcorn. This was something new. She was usually on edge dreading when her date would do something annoying or obnoxious that would force her to act indignant and irritated. Now, she was indignant and irritated that Brock was obviously not going to try anything.

Knowing she wasn't beautiful, she had the impression that Brock found her attractive. At least she assumed it was interest he'd been showing her the past few weeks of meeting at the coffee shop and flirting. She certainly hoped this date wasn't just some strange attempt to gain favor with her mother over the construction project.

Releasing a little huff, she sat back in her seat and tried to focus on the rest of the movie while reining in her thoughts.

Brock grinned as he heard Brenna sigh. Surreptitiously glancing at his watch in the dim light from the movie screen, Brock counted down until his self-imposed good behavior could end. Nineteen more minutes.

Biding his time, he watched the end of the movie with a lack of real interest in the happy-ending. As the credits began rolling, Brenna gathered up her empty water bottle and the popcorn tub. Before she could get to her feet, Brock placed a restraining hand on her arm.

"Let's wait a minute," he said, bending close to whisper in her ear.

His breath fanned across her neck and caused an involuntary shiver to slither down her spine. Unable to speak, she nodded her head, wondering what Brock was thinking.

When the last person left the theater, Brock turned to her with a wink and planted a sloppy, wet kiss on her cheek.

Laughing, Brenna wasn't surprised to see Brock look at her straight-faced. "I told you I'd behave through the movie, but it's over now."

"Are you sure?" Brenna asked. "Technically, it isn't over until they stop rolling the credits. So based on that, you didn't quite keep your promise."

"Oh, cut me some slack," Brock said, getting to his feet and pulling Brenna up beside him. He took the empty popcorn bucket from her hand and placed his other at the small of her back, directing her out of the empty theater.

For the last hour, he fought the temptation of taking Brenna in his arms and covering her with kisses. When he's asked her to stay while the theater emptied, he had planned to do more than just kiss her cheek, but when he looked at her and saw her innocent smile, he decided to keep things light between them.

With a variety of dating experience thanks to his mother constantly setting him up on dates, no matter how reluctantly he went, Brock thought he was well versed in the ways of women. He'd dated bankers, real estate agents, business executives, super models, and even had two dates with a movie star who happened to be a devoted fan of his mother's designs. None of them had ever fascinated him the way Brenna did.

Dropping their garbage in a can by the door, he helped Brenna with her coat and they walked outside.

"Gosh, it really cooled down while we were inside," Brenna said, smiling at Brock as he helped her into his truck.

"Yeah. Feels like it might rain again, too," Brock said, climbing behind the wheel and pointing his truck back toward Silverton. He didn't care if it rained, snowed or hailed. His thoughts were too consumed with the lovely girl sitting on the other side of his pickup smelling way too appealing and looking way too cute. If she wrinkled her nose up one more time when she laughed, he thought he might come completely undone.

"Such is life in this part of the state," Brenna said with a grin. "Have you ever been to Eastern Oregon? I've heard the summers out there can be long, hot, and dry."

"I've never really spent any time there," Brock said, trying to focus on what Brenna was saying instead of his overwhelming desire to kiss her pink lips. "My dad and I drove through Burns one August on our way to Boise and I think you could actually see the heat waves dancing across the pavement. It is definitely a different landscape than what we've got here."

"Although I could do without quite so much rain, I think we live in an especially lovely little corner of the world," Brenna said, looking out the window at the muted darkness.

"I'd have to agree," Brock said, briefly shifting his attention from the road to Brenna. He reached for her hand and squeezed it. Glancing at him, she offered a shy smile before returning her attention to what she could see through the window into the night.

Ready to release her fingers, Brock held on when she gently squeezed back, giving him a glimmer of hope that she was interested in him. At least a little.

Brenna was disappointed when the movie ended and all Brock had done was give her one slobbery, teasing kiss on the cheek. She'd hoped he would put his arm around her, offer some gesture of interest or show her in some way he found her appealing. Now they were driving home and if she sat any further away from him, she might as well be in the bed of the truck instead of the cab.

Once again, Brenna took stock of what she had to offer a guy and found herself lacking. She felt better when Brock squeezed her hand and gave her a smile that made warmth curl from her toes in tingly waves all the way to her head. Timidly, she returned the pressure to his fingers and enjoyed the rest of the ride home.

Her parents had long ago gone to bed but the front porch light glowed through the darkness like a warning beacon. Feeling like she was sixteen and coming in late from a date with Will, Brenna's mouth went dry and nerves threatened to get the best of her as Brock parked his pickup and turned off the lights. Sitting in the darkened cab, Brenna waited just a moment before unbuckling her seatbelt and picking up her purse. Turning to thank Brock for a nice date, she found herself staring at his chest. She wasn't sure how she'd gotten from her position next to the door to the middle of the pickup's seat.

"Brenna," Brock said in a voice that had dropped to a low rumble. "That was one of the nicest evenings I've ever had. Thank you."

Nodding her head in agreement was almost more than she could accomplish as the awareness of his thumbs tracing gentle circles across her palms rendered her speechless.

"Do you remember at the restaurant, when we were talking about before and after tastes?" Brock asked, sliding closer to Brenna as she sat wide-eyed staring at him.

Again, she nodded.

"Remember I asked you to help me with a little project?"

"Yes," Brenna whispered, finding herself just inches away from Brock. She inhaled deeply of his unique, musky scent. Hoping a deep breath would help her focus, she instead became more fuzzy-headed.

"Are you still willing to help?" Brock asked, running a thumb across her cheek and down her jaw. His eyes were intently focused on her and Brenna felt herself sucked into the charismatic force that was all Brock.

Another nod.

"Good," Brock said, putting both hands on her face. One strong, calloused finger traced down her nose, over her chin and slowly, so slowly, trailed across her lips. He stuck his finger in his mouth, like he was licking batter stolen from a batch of cookie dough. "Before taste is perfectly sweet, with a hint of popcorn."

Brenna's eyes widened as she tried to make sense of what Brock was doing. Her time for trying to think through his actions was cut short when Brock dropped his head and pressed his mouth to hers, gently, tenderly.

Sensations she'd never experienced rocketed from her lips throughout her body, making her lightheaded. Glad she was sitting down, Brenna was sure had she been standing Brock would have been helping her up off the ground. When he pulled back and grinned, she returned his smile.

"Aftertaste is sweet perfection," Brock whispered, giving Brenna a moment to push him away. Although she blushed as she realized his experiment had indeed been tasting her lips, she leaned closer to him, lashes fluttering as she closed her eyes. Groaning, Brock buried his hands in her golden curls and absorbed the rightness of being close to Brenna.

"Brock," she said against his throat, causing heat to build in him at a volatile level. "Are you finished with your experiment?"

"Yes," he rasped, trying to hang on to his control. After all, this was their first official date. A gentleman would walk her to the door, thank her for the best evening he'd ever had and take his leave. A sweet, gentle kiss was the appropriate way to end the evening.

Come to think of it, though, Brock had never been overly concerned with what was appropriate.

"Then would you mind kissing me again?" Brenna asked so quietly, Brock was sure he misheard her. Leaning back to look at her face, she offered him a smile of invitation that made him forget all about what was appropriate.

"I wouldn't mind at all, coffee girl."

Chapter Seven

Brock whistled an upbeat tune, sporting the grin he hadn't been able to wipe off his face since his date with Brenna Friday night. After her request that he kiss her again, he obliged not once or twice, but a dozen times before they steamed up the windows of his truck. The remaining speck of sense he had niggled at his conscience, making him get out and walk her to the front door.

He was completely taken with the intriguing woman and from her responses, Brock thought she might just like him a little as well. Pleased with himself for his little before and after taste game that provided the perfect opportunity to kiss her, thoughts of her eager lips made a wave of heat pool in his belly.

Forcing himself to give her one last kiss at the door and leave Friday night, Brock didn't waste any time Saturday morning going to Letty's shop. Although he didn't generally work on Saturday, he had some details he wanted to leave with Letty for her approval and used it as an excuse to stop by, hoping to run into Brenna. Although Letty kept him chatting for a few minutes and offered him some pastries Brenna made, the sweet girl who continually invaded his thoughts didn't materialize.

Letty walked him to the door with a knowing smile and a pat on his arm.

"Brenna promised a friend she'd cater a party tonight so she's in Portland today," Letty said as Brock cast one more longing glance around the store, listening for Brenna's voice.

"Am I that obvious?" Brock asked, red creeping up his neck.

"Only to a mother," Letty laughed and gave him a wave as he sauntered back to his truck.

Going to church Sunday morning, Brock hoped to see Brenna there, but her mother told him she decided to stay in Portland after helping her friend clean up following the party the night before.

Putting aside his disappointment at not seeing Brenna, Brock decided to take advantage of the sunny Sunday afternoon to do some painting on the outside of his house. If he could get it finished today, the exterior would be done.

Newly installed windows gleamed in the sunlight. Along with the new roof, the place was really starting to look like a nice home.

By the end of the week he should be able to move in. Although none of the rooms were finished like he wanted, he hoped to have the work he was doing in the downstairs bathroom completed Wednesday. A plumber was coming Thursday to make sure everything was working properly.

Once he finished the interior, Brock planned to spend the summer months working on landscaping. Greg, Brenna's brother-in-law, agreed to come help him in exchange for some carpentry work at his place.

Lost in thoughts of his house and Brenna, Brock didn't hear his neighbors approach until a throat being cleared alerted him to their presence.

"Mr. McCrae?"

Turning to greet the resident busybodies on his street, Brock kept his smile in place and wondered what the two old ladies were wanting this afternoon.

"Good afternoon fair ladies of Aspen Lane," Brock

said, doffing his ball cap and pouring on his charm. So far, these two had brought a steady supply of coffee cake, cookies and pie whenever they found him working on the house. Today, Mrs. Hearst carried a basket covered by a napkin and wafts of cinnamon were drifting his direction. "To what do I owe this pleasure?"

"We were surprised to see you out working on a Sunday," Mrs. Phillips said, glancing down her thin nose at him. It required her to tilt her head so far back she would have no doubt been at risk of drowning if it had been raining, but she seemed to have the maneuver down pat.

The worrisome widows, as Brock thought of them, were as different as two women could possibly be. Where Mrs. Hearst was short and round with a pleasant face and soft white hair looking just as a jolly grandmotherly-type should, Mrs. Phillips was bony and thin with a long face that quite often looked as though she'd taken a bite of something most unpleasant.

Both of the widows had been kind to him, although any activity at his house was still considered suspect until proven otherwise.

"It's such a beautiful afternoon I had to take advantage of the sunshine to finish my painting project. Don't you think it makes the house look more inviting?" Brock said, using a word he'd heard Mrs. Phillips bandy about on several occasions. She had previously informed him their neighborhood looked inviting, her flowers looked inviting, the way the street curved around in front of his house looked inviting, but his house did not.

Given enough time and effort, it would get there.

"Much more so, Mr. McCrae," Mrs. Hearst said with a cheery smile. "I like the color you choose for the trim."

"Thanks," Brock said, stepping back to admire the crisp white paint on the siding as it contrasted with the rich hunter green trim. "I kind of like it myself."

"Well, of course you do or you wouldn't have painted it that color," Mrs. Phillips huffed, crossing her bony arms over her scrawny chest.

Brock turned and winked at the woman, laughing inwardly as her face flushed red.

"Mr. McCrae, I don't..." Mrs. Phillips started to say, but Mrs. Hearst cut her off.

"We don't want to keep you from your work. We brought you some cinnamon bars. Thought you might need a little afternoon nourishment," Mrs. Hearst said, handing Brock the basket. He lifted the napkin and sniffed appreciatively.

"Thank you for thinking of me," he said, taking a bar from the basket and biting into it. Fresh from the oven, the treat was rich with cinnamon and butter. He closed his eyes in pleasure and sighed. "Delicious."

Both old women twittered and fussed.

"Enjoy, Mr. McCrae," Mrs. Hearst said, looping her arm around Mrs. Phillips thin one as they turned back down the street.

"I will and thanks again. And please, call me Brock!"

"You're welcome, Brock," Mrs. Hearst said, sauntering back toward her house with her friend.

Brock heard them talking as they walked.

"If I was fifty years younger, I'd do my best to turn that young man's head, Betty. Such a nice boy," Mrs. Hearst said. "And so nice looking."

"Fifty years? Shoot, Myrna, I'd give it a run if I was thirty years younger," the stodgy Mrs. Phillips said. "You suppose he's one of those boys who lift weights. Those muscles are pretty impressive. Why I bet..."

Brock grinned as he ate two more bars then set the basket inside the front door.

Wondering what the two old women looked like

fifty years ago, he renewed his whistling along with his efforts at painting and soon had the job done.

He was anxious to show Brenna his home, but wanted to wait until he had at least finished remodeling the main floor. When he brought her to see the house, he was hoping to feed her dinner and watch a movie, or something.

It was thoughts of "or something" that made heat radiate through him.

Looking around, it was easy to picture Brenna here with him, her tender presence and laughter filling the house with her own special kind of light.

At that moment, the dream he'd had so many times in the past flitted through his thoughts and he felt that unsettled, confused feeling it usually brought.

Considering what it could mean, his musings were interrupted by the arrival of his uncle Andy.

"Brock, my boy, do you ever rest?" Andy asked as he ambled down the sidewalk toward the porch.

"Sure I do but as my dear ol' uncle taught me, you've got to take advantage of cooperative weather when it's being cooperative," Brock said, giving his uncle a grin. "If you don't have anything better to do, I've got an extra brush."

"Do I look like I came over here so you could use me as free labor?" Andy asked, with a teasing gleam in his eye.

Brock eyed his uncle's paint splattered shirt and pants along with well-worn work boots. "Yep, you do."

Andy laughed and picked up a brush. "What's in it for me?"

"The satisfaction of helping your favorite nephew make his house into a home," Brock said as he climbed the ladder to finish the upper trim work.

"You need more than some paint and a few new fixtures for that, son. You need a woman," Andy said, hoping to goad Brock into talking about the woman he'd reportedly been out with Friday night. "From what I hear, you might even have found one."

"Where did you hear that?" Brock said, twisting so fast on the ladder to look at his uncle, he almost lost his balance.

Andy looked up at Brock and chuckled. By Brock's reaction, what he'd heard was true. His friends said Brock was making calf eyes at the girl all evening and held her hand as they strolled through town.

"News travels fast in a small town, you know. Heard you took some pretty little gal out to dinner and a movie and a stroll around Mt. Angel."

Brock glared at Andy. How could he possibly know all that? Irritation kept him from saying anything as he applied the paint with a little more force than was necessary.

"From what I hear, you were holding hands and looking at her like a love-sick pup," Andy said, raising a bushy gray brow Brock's direction. "Is she a local girl?"

"You mean you don't already know that? It seems you are quite well informed of everything else," Brock said, unable to swallow down all his annoyance at his uncle's teasing. "Remind me, what did I have for dinner?"

Andy stopped painting and slapped his leg as he burst out laughing. Shaking his head, he glanced at Brock, pointing the paintbrush at him. "You've got it bad, my boy. Let's hear all about this girl."

Brock sighed, knowing his uncle would only keep pestering him until his curiosity was satisfied. "Fine. Her name is Brenna Smith. Her mother is Letty Smith and she owns the home interior store that I'm remodeling..."

~◇~

The pile of restaurant supply catalogs on her lap lost Brenna's interest shortly after she opened the first one. Instead, her gaze focused on some unseen spot in the distance as she gazed out the window from the bench seat in her bedroom, her thoughts on Brock.

Although they'd only been on one date, she felt like she'd known him for a very long time. Given the right opportunities, she thought he could easily become someone very important to her. He had already claimed more than his fair share of her thoughts in the last several weeks, since the day he first bought her a coffee and gave it to her along with his utterly charming smile.

Thinking back to their date Friday night, Brenna sighed contentedly. After his little tasting game, she was worried one sweet kiss was all she was going to get. Thrilled when he lavished many more on her before walking her to the front door, he had kissed her once more, taking her hand in his and pressing his lips to the palm of her hand. It was all so exciting and romantic.

A knock on her door brought her out of her musings as her mom came in the room with a collection of fabric swatches.

"Hey, honey, I hardly got a chance to ask about Kathleen's party. Did it go well?" Letty asked as she strode across the room.

"Yes, it did. Everyone seemed to enjoy the food," Brenna said with a tired smile. She spent all day Saturday cooking then helped serve at Kathleen's party. She stayed much later than she planned to help clean up and Kat insisted she spend the night. Arriving home just an hour ago, she retreated to her room with the supply catalogs, but so far hadn't accomplished anything other than daydreaming about one handsome construction guy. "Kathleen made sure everyone knew I'm opening the bistro in a few months."

"That's great," Letty said with a big smile. "I came to bug you for your opinion. I want to put up new valances in the store windows before our grand opening. What fabric do you like?" Letty asked, holding out a pile of samples to Brenna.

Fabrics and colors had never been her thing. Avery was much better at helping their mother with those kinds of details.

"Have you asked Avery?" Brenna asked, looking through the selections, drawn to one simple pattern more than the others, but not sure what her mom and sister would like.

"Well, of course," Letty said smiling. "But I wanted your opinion, too."

"Why don't you tell me which ones the two of you like and I'll choose from those?" Brenna asked with a knowing grin. Avery and Letty had very similar tastes and over the years Brenna had learned it was faster and easier to let them narrow down the options to two or three and then make a choice.

Letty grabbed the swatches from Brenna and pulled out three. One was the simple plaid Brenna originally selected, the second was a rich damask and the third was a bright floral pattern. Brenna considered how they were blending three separate businesses under one store front - a flower shop, an interior design studio and a bistro. She thought the plaid would best serve them all neutrally and handed it to her mother.

Beaming a smile at her daughter, Letty took the swatches and kissed Brenna on the forehead.

"Excellent choice, honey. I'll order the fabric tomorrow," Letty looked at the pile of catalogs around Brenna. "Are you finding what you need for the bistro?"

"Sort of."

"Do you need some help? What aren't you finding? You don't sound very sure about it," Letty said, pushing aside a stack of catalogs containing serving pieces and dinnerware as she sat next to Brenna.

"It's fine, Mom. My thoughts are just wandering elsewhere this afternoon," Brenna said, hoping her mother wouldn't know her thoughts were only wandering far enough to land on their attractive construction guy.

"That's easy to understand. After all, he is quite handsome and that smile would distract most any female," Letty said with a teasing smile, patting Brenna on the knee as she stood. "He dropped by the store yesterday morning under the pretense of delivering some design ideas and he even came to church this morning. I'm pretty sure it was the thought of seeing you, not Reverend Mosley's sermon, that drew him in."

"Mother!" Brenna said with embarrassment turning her cheeks pink.

"He's easy on the eyes, honey, a really nice man, and he seems to be quite taken with you," Letty said, walking to the door. "I'd milk it for all it's worth if I were you."

"Mom!"

Letty fluttered her hand at Brenna as she left the bedroom. "Milk it, honey."

Despite what her mother said, Brenna had no intention of milking anything. Forcing herself to look through the catalogs, she marked pages, made notes and added up expenses. By the time the afternoon turned to evening, she felt good about her selections. Taking the catalogs with her as she went downstairs for dinner, she decided to run her choices by her mom and Avery to get their feedback before she placed the orders.

Joining her parents in the dining room, she wasn't surprised to find Greg and Avery already seated at the table. Who she was surprised to see was her old boyfriend, Will.

"Hey, I'm glad to see you Avery and Greg," Brenna said, pointedly not including Will. The guy just didn't give up. They started dating in high school and were an on-again, off-again couple, as the whim suited Will, until the end of her freshman year of college. Brenna finally got fed-up with him and told Will not to darken her doorstep again. Her declaration would have worked great, except for the fact that Will didn't take her seriously and he was a friend of Greg's.

During the course of the last several years, he would pursue her, give up and leave her alone for a while before renewing his efforts. Brenna didn't know what to do to get it through his head she was not interested in him. She was beginning to wonder if Will was just a little mentally unbalanced.

"What have you got there?" Avery asked, giving Brenna a hug that conveyed both love and support.

"Some catalogs for the serving pieces and dinnerware for the bistro. Would you mind taking a look after dinner?" Brenna asked, setting the catalogs on a side table before taking a seat across the table from Avery. Since Greg wouldn't budge from Avery's side, it left Brenna sitting next to Will. Letty shot her a sympathetic look, knowing how much Brenna disliked being around her former boyfriend. It wasn't that he was a bad guy. Just not the guy for Brenna.

"I'd be happy to," Avery said, catching Brenna's eye and giving her head a shake, indicating inviting Will to dinner had not been her idea.

As Will tried to scoot his chair closer to Brenna's, she quietly inched her chair closer to her dad's place at the end of the table. When Will leaned her direction, she jumped up from the table with an excuse of getting a pitcher of ice water.

By the time she returned, Will was shooting daggers her direction. She didn't really notice since she was throwing a few of her own at her brother-in-law.

Brandon and Greg carried the bulk of the conversation with the women throwing in comments. Will sat sullen and quiet through most of the meal.

Making quick work of the dishes after dinner, the three women retreated to the breakfast nook in the kitchen with the catalogs, avoiding Will. Greg and Will joined Brandon in the family room where they discussed sports and local happenings.

"I'm sorry, Rennie," Avery whispered as she looked at the pages Brenna marked in the catalogs. "We were just leaving the house when Will showed up and you know how hard it is to get him to go home. Greg mentioned we were coming over here and the next thing you know, he was tagging along."

"He's pathetic," Brenna said, trying not to grin. She was long ago over Will and now only felt a mild irritation that he seemed unable to let go of the notion that she would someday take him back.

"Completely," Avery said with a smile. Avery and Letty discussed Brenna's choices, offering their opinions and Brenna filled out her orders.

"This really makes the bistro seem real," Brenna said, scanning through the lengthy orders and tallying up the expense.

"Placing the orders or spending all that money?" Avery asked with a sound of amusement coloring her voice. She'd just placed her own orders to increase her stock and display areas when she moved into her new space in a few weeks.

"Both," Brenna said, making both her mother and sister laugh. They were still laughing when Greg stuck his head in the kitchen door.

"Hey, hon, we better head for home. I've got a job in Portland tomorrow so I'll have to be on the road bright and early," Greg said, coming into the room and giving Avery his hand, helping her to her feet. He pressed a light kiss to her temple and she leaned into him.

Fighting back jealousy at the closeness Avery and Greg shared, Brenna released a sigh and smiled at them. After several years of marriage, the two of them still seemed to be goofy in love. Brenna just hoped she would someday be part of a special relationship. For some reason, Brock's face came to mind and she blushed.

"Don't know what you're thinking, Rennie, but whatever it is, shame on you," Greg teased, ruffling her hair, like any good brother would be prone to do.

"Just never mind," Brenna said, dropping her voice to a whisper. "You're already in enough trouble, buster."

"I know and I'm sorry," Greg said, backing toward the door, tugging Avery along with him. "I'll find some way to make it up to you."

"You can count on it," Brenna said, giving Greg a backhanded wave that looked like she was shooing him away.

Letty followed them out to the family room where she and Brandon bid Avery, Greg and Will good-night. Will seemed to be waiting for Brenna to come out of hiding, but instead, she ran up the back stairs to her room.

She finished typing her orders in online and sat staring at her computer for a while, thinking about plans for the bistro, how happy she would be when she could quit her job in Portland, and how much she was looking forward to seeing Brock tomorrow at the coffee shop.

Maybe she'd get there early and buy his coffee for a change.

Chapter Eight

Holding her Chai latte in one hand and Brock's dark roast in the other, Brenna waited inside the coffee shop door for her construction guy to arrive.

Glancing impatiently at her watch, Brenna knew she could only wait another minute or two before she had to leave for the office. Ready to give up, she released a sigh of relief to see Brock drive in the parking lot. Pushing the coffee shop door open with her hip, she hurried across the pavement to his pickup.

Grinning, he got out and pecked her cheek, careful not to jostle the coffee she clutched in both hands.

"Morning, sunshine," Brock teased, making her smile. He felt his heart slam against his chest as he realized her smile was like sunshine to him – bright, warm, and beautiful. "What are you doing?"

"Buying your coffee. I had to set my alarm fifteen minutes early to make it out the door five minutes ahead of schedule, but for once I beat you here," Brenna said, handing him his cup of straight black coffee.

"You're funny," Brock chuckled before taking a sip of the hot coffee, trying to decipher what Brenna had said. Knowing how his mother operated, he assumed that she meant even though she got up earlier, she didn't get ready much faster. Regardless, he was glad to see her. "Thanks for the coffee and for Friday night. I had a great time."

"Me, too," Brenna said, waiting for Brock to ask

her on another date. "I really enjoyed it."

"I'm glad," Brock said, drinking his coffee and looking at her for a long moment. Finally, he leaned against his truck and pulled her against his side. Surprised, she inhaled his heady man-scent and basked in the pure delight of being near Brock with his arm around her shoulders.

"I told you about the house I bought, right?" Brock asked, taking another swig of coffee.

"Yes, you did. You said you were hoping to be able to move in soon," Brenna said, sipping her hot drink.

"Right. I'm hoping to move in this coming weekend. I'd love to take you on a date Friday night, but I'm pretty sure I'll still be packing, since I haven't even started yet. My Saturday will be shot by the time I get all my stuff moved," Brock said, looking down into Brenna's blue eyes and fighting the very strong desire to kiss her so thoroughly she'd forget about heading into the office and spend the day with him. "I don't want you to be disappointed, but I won't have time to get much packing finished before Friday and get everything done I need to do at the house."

"That's okay, I understand," Brenna said, realizing Brock worked a lot of long hours between his business and his house. "Don't worry about it."

"This will also be my last week of meeting you for morning coffee," Brock said, regret filling his voice. While he looked forward to not having the long commute twice a day to and from Portland, he was really going to miss seeing Brenna every morning. It had been about three months since she first captured his interest at the coffee shop.

"Oh," Brenna said, not thinking about Brock's move disrupting their weekday coffee routine. How was she going to force herself out of bed and to the office if she didn't have the incentive of seeing Brock every morning? "I… um…I see."

"Look, Brenna, I really want to spend more time with you so we can still plan to do something fun. Maybe we could hang out Sunday afternoon. I could meet you at church and we could go out for lunch," Brock said, hoping he could dispel the look of disappointment on Brenna's sweet face.

"I'd like that," Brenna said, looking up at him with a shy smile. Bolstering her courage, she decided to make a bold suggestion. "If you don't mind my company, maybe I could help you with your packing Friday. I could swing by your apartment after work and then come home later."

Caught off guard by her offer, Brock grinned. "Are you sure, Brenna? I don't want you to feel like you have to help, but I'd welcome your company if you really wouldn't mind."

"I'd love to help," Brenna said with a genuine interest in not only helping, but seeing where Brock lived and meeting his roommates. She'd do just about anything to spend more time with him. To say she was completely taken with the man would be an understatement. "If you want, I could pick up some take out and bring over."

"My friend Mike is ordering pizza, but thanks for the offer. Just bring yourself and whatever packing skills you have and that will be more than enough," Brock said, as he walked her to her car. He knew it was past time for her to be on the road to the office. Holding open the car door, he gave her a quick hug before she climbed inside. Once she was settled, he kissed her cheek again.

"Drive safely, coffee girl, and have a great day."

"I will, construction man. You be careful at work today. I heard those clients of yours are absolute slave drivers," Brenna teased.

"That they are," Brock said with a wink, making his

hazel eyes twinkle with amusement. "But the thought of seeing the cute daughter who's a killer baker makes me a glutton for their punishment."

Brenna laughed and waved before shutting her door and heading out of the parking lot.

Brock spent the rest of the day in a Brenna-induced haze. It was only when he nearly nailed his thumb to a joist that he decided he better focus on the job at hand instead of the lovely curly-headed coffee girl.

At the end of the day Thursday, Brock was satisfied with the amount of work that had been completed at Letty's store. He was also pleased with all he accomplished that week at his home. The guest bath downstairs was finished and the kitchen was now in a useable state. He wanted to paint and resurface the cabinets and install new counters, but for now everything was at least functional. The plumber made a few adjustments in the kitchen, declared the rest of the plumbing in good working order and went over Brock's plans for the new master suite.

Excited about moving into the house, Brock pulled into the coffee shop parking lot Friday morning, surprised to see Brenna leaning against her car waiting for him.

"Did you set your alarm for an hour early this morning?" he teased as he walked up to her and kissed her cheek. The look of adoration and admiration she sent him made Brock's fingers tremble so much he almost dropped the cup of coffee she handed him.

"Nope. Only twenty minutes," she said with an impish grin. "And if you sweet-talk me a little, I might have a treat for you."

Brock placed his cup of coffee on the top of her car, wrapped his arms around her and placed his lips close to her ear. "How much talking will I have to do, coffee girl?"

"That's enough," she whispered, trying to suppress the shiver of excitement that ran through her at Brock's touch. His breath on her neck made her tingle from her head to her toes and stirred the embers already sparking to life in her stomach dangerously close to a full-blown flame.

If she wanted to drive to the office and arrive in one piece, she couldn't let him get her too distracted. Spending all day wrapped up in his arms seemed like a perfectly wonderful place to be, especially when his unique scent filled her senses.

Unfortunately, she had a job to get to and things that had to be done that day. Stepping out of his embrace, Brenna opened her car door and retrieved a basket covered with a cloth napkin, handing it to Brock.

"What's this?" he asked, inhaling a berry scent as he lifted the napkin and spied muffins.

"Raspberry muffins with streusel topping. I hope you like them. If you feel so inclined, you can share them with your crew," Brenna said, tipping her head and studying Brock. "If you guys wouldn't mind giving me some feedback, I'd appreciate it. I might want to put these on the bistro menu."

"We'll be sure to let you know what we think. At least I will," Brock said, forcing himself to fold the napkin back over the still warm muffins. His crew would be lucky if he left more than crumbs for them to pick over. "Thank you for making these."

"You're welcome," Brenna said, looking at her watch and opening her car door. "I better get going, but I'm looking forward to seeing you this evening. Does five-thirty still work for you?"

"Yep," Brock said, picking his coffee off the top of her car and trying to juggle it along with the basket of muffins. He finally gave up his attempts to free a hand to hug Brenna and kissed her cheek instead. "I know I gave you directions, but if you get lost, just call my cell."

"I will. Have a great day, construction man."

"You, too, coffee girl."

Brenna blew him a kiss and he nearly dumped his coffee down his side trying to catch it. She was giggling as she pulled out of the parking lot, shaking her head.

Spending the day trying to avoid Wesley, Brenna was successful until about four-thirty that afternoon. Feeling a set of eyes watching her, she looked up to find Wesley standing in her doorway glaring at her.

"Ms. Smith. I asked you to have the Smytzer report on my desk by four this afternoon," Wesley said curtly, walking to her desk. "Where is it?"

"I… it…" Brenna was, as usual, perplexed by Wesley's insane demands. He never mentioned he wanted a report of any kind on his desk today. She hadn't even been working on a Smytzer project. Taking a deep breath, she tried to keep her emotions in check as she looked up at her loathsome boss. "I'm sorry, Wesley, but I'm not working on the Smytzer project. If you requested a report it wasn't from me."

"Don't try to get out of doing your work, Smith. I asked you yesterday for that report and you're not leaving until I get it," Wesley said, slapping his hand down on her desk with such a loud clap, it made her jump in her seat. "Now get busy!"

"But Wesley," Brenna started to explain again why she couldn't produce a report about something of which she had no knowledge, but only managed to splutter at Wesley's retreating back. Rolling her eyes, she dumped two antacid tablets out of the large bottle she kept in her desk and swallowed them before picking up the phone and calling Kathleen.

"Hey, Kat, do you know anything about a Smytzer project?" Brenna asked when her friend answered her phone.

"I think Thiebolt and Jenks are working on it. Why?" Kathleen asked.

"Wesley just took me to task for not having it done and I don't have a clue what he's talking about. He told me I can't leave until it's on his desk," Brenna said, relieved at the confirmation Wesley was mistaken about his request, not her.

"He's losing it, Brenna. Completely losing it," Kathleen said. "Meet me at the elevator and we'll go track it down together. Don't you have a hot date with the hottie construction guy tonight?"

"Not a date, exactly, but I am meeting him after work tonight," Brenna said, not wanting to be late because of her crazy boss. "Thanks, Kat. I'll see you in a few."

It took Brenna and Kathleen until a quarter past five to track down the report. While Kathleen smoothed over ruffled feathers, Brenna took the report to Wesley's office where he sat pouring himself a glass of whiskey.

"About time you got that in here. What's wrong with you?" Wesley snapped, snatching the report from her hand. "You are just the stupidest little twit. If it were up to me, you'd be standing in the unemployment line, blondie. I've never met such an incompetent idiot and yet you somehow managed to worm your way up to a management position. Get out of my sight!"

Brenna tried not to take his cruel words or tone personally, but it was hard not to when they were meant that way. Indignation spurred her back to her office where she gathered up her things, turned off her computer and locked the door. Hurrying to catch the elevator, she managed to smile at her coworkers, wish Kathleen a pleasant weekend and get to her car before a few tears trickled down her cheeks.

Giving herself a pep talk, she brushed them aside, took a deep breath and programmed Brock's address into her GPS system. She was going to be late, but she hoped he understood.

Following his directions, as well as the orders barked at her from the GPS system, she finally arrived at his apartment building. Going inside, she took the elevator up to his floor and found the correct apartment. Just as she was about to ring the bell, the door opened and she was nearly run over by two burly guys carrying boxes.

"Whoa, babe, didn't see you out here," the taller of the two said, dropping his box and placing a steadying hand on Brenna's arm before he knocked her over backward.

He was dark-headed with an easy grin and deep green eyes. Brenna assumed he had probably broken more than a few hearts. When he shook her hand, she couldn't help smiling back at his infectious grin.

"You must be Brock's coffee girl. I'm Mike, his oldest, best and sometimes only friend."

Brenna laughed.

"It's nice to meet you, Mike. I'm Brenna."

"This is Levi, my brother and sometimes accomplice in crime," Mike said, nodding toward the other man who also set down his box and shook Brenna's hand. Brenna noticed the brothers shared a striking resemblance to each other, although Levi was just a little shorter than Mike and seemed to be the more reserved of the two.

"Nice to meet you both," Brenna said. Looking at the boxes, she nodded toward the door. "Are you already moving stuff out?"

"Nah," Mike said, pushing open the apartment door and motioning Brenna inside. "Brock had some stuff he wanted to get rid of so Levi's going to drop it by the youth center where he works. Go on in and make yourself at home. Brock ran to the store to get more bubble wrap, but he'll be back in a minute."

"Oh, I can wait here in the hall," Brenna said, not wanting to intrude without Brock there.

"Go on in. We live here, too, so I say it's fine. There's pop and drinks in the fridge, just help yourself," Mike said, stepping back into the hall and picking up the box. "We'll be right back."

"Okay," Brenna said, hanging her coat and purse on a coat rack by the door then stepping into what appeared to be all-male domain.

While she half-expected a mess and weird smells, the apartment had a faint aroma of something fresh and outdoorsy, like a candle or wall plug in. The living room was neat and clean with a mix of hunting lodge, hand-me downs, and garage sale finds for furnishings. Some, like her mother, might call it a decorating nightmare but Brenna thought it was unmistakably unique.

Walking around the room, Brenna noticed a few very nice pieces of antique furniture that didn't quite fit in with the other eclectic pieces. She was running her hand over the smooth top of a cherry-wood end table when she felt arms wrap around her from behind, effectively stealing her breath.

"Hey, coffee girl, I thought you might be driving around this cold, dark city lost, alone, and frightened. I was about ready to send out a search party," Brock teased, placing a wet kiss on her neck. "Sorry I wasn't here when you came. I needed more packing supplies and ran down to the office supply store."

Brenna relaxed against him and turned around in his arms. "I had a little problem at work I had to take care of before I could leave and got off a little later than planned." Thinking about work made her neck muscles tense.

"Hey, is everything okay?" Brock asked, sensing her tension as he leaned down and looked into her big blue eyes that didn't glisten with their usual spark of fun and enjoyment. He could read annoyance and hurt there instead.

Forcing herself to relax her shoulders, Brenna smiled. "Everything's fine, but thanks," Brenna said, leaning closer to Brock and kissing his chin. "Shall we get busy with your packing?"

"Sure," Brock said, squeezing her hand as he stepped away from her and motioned to a pile of bubble wrap he left just inside the door. "I've got enough padding to wrap everything in here at least twice and then cover Mike and Levi, too."

"Now that might be fun to watch," Brenna said, giggling as she walked to the bags of bubble wrap and opened one. Discarding her high heels near the coat rack, she started wrapping whatever Brock handed her and then helped him place things in boxes. She tried to keep the contents of the boxes organized but the guys were more interested in just getting everything packed. Levi wrapped while Mike shoved items into boxes and by the time the pizza arrived, a noticeable dent had been made in the packing.

Sitting around the living room eating pizza, the four of them laughed and teased. Brenna felt comfortable around Mike and Levi, which was odd for her. She was usually reserved with strangers, especially men, but she liked the brothers immediately. They were fun and friendly and if Brock thought they were good guys, she assumed they must be. Finishing up the pizza, Brock and Brenna took boxes to his bedroom to pack while Mike and Levi worked on gathering Brock's things in the kitchen.

Brenna admired photos of Brock's family as she carefully wrapped them and placed them in a box. She asked him questions about his grandparents and parents. Her favorite photo was of Brock with his uncle Andy, both of them covered in sawdust, holding chainsaws like warrior's swords.

"This is a great photo," Brenna said with a laugh. "You two look like you had quite a day."

"We did," Brock said, standing next to Brenna and looking over her shoulder at the photo. "Uncle Andy and I always had a lot of fun. I'm looking forward to living a little closer to him, too. I'm hoping when he and auntie return from their latest round of travel, he'll still want to get his hands dirty with my construction business once in a while."

"I think it's pretty special you and your uncle are close," Brenna said, finishing up with the photographs and moving on to a shelf full of odds and ends. A few high school wrestling trophies caught her eye. It didn't surprise Brenna that Brock was a wrestler. He had the solid build to be good at it.

Interesting pieces of wood, like a knot of pine, along with a few odd looking rocks drew her attention. "What are these, Brock?"

Finishing wrapping a lamp, Brock set it aside and walked over to Brenna, taking a reddish-toned rock from her hand. "It's petrified wood. See the grain here in the pattern?"

Brenna bent a little closer to get a better look, following where Brock's finger pointed. The piece Brock placed back in her hand was really heavy and hard. "How does wood petrify?"

Picking up another piece from a shelf, Brock balanced it from one hand to the other. "Trees fall and are covered in sediment. This cuts off the oxygen and slows the decay. Groundwater containing silica seeps through the wood either replacing all the organic matter or just replacing the cell contents and spaces leaving the original structure - or tree - intact. Eventually the silica crystallizes into quartz, preserving the wood."

SHANNA HATFIELD

"Oh," Brenna said, processing the information. The piece she held was a different color from the purple-hued rock on Brock's hand. "What about the colors?"

"The minerals in the silica water create the colors. You can get shades of yellow, red, black, blue, purple, brown, white and even pink," Brock said, wrapping the piece in his hand in bubble wrap before placing it at the bottom of a sturdy box. "Leave those bigger pieces for me. They're pretty heavy."

"No argument here," Brenna said, wrapping up the piece she held and adding it to the box.

They packed for a few more minutes in silence while Brock studied Brenna. Her shoulders still looked tense and a frown kept pulling the corners of her smile down.

"What's wrong, coffee girl? You can talk to me," Brock said, placing a pile of books into an antique trunk.

"I'm fine, Brock," Brenna said, realizing she wasn't doing a very good job of hiding her anger with Wesley. Why did that obnoxious man have to disrupt everything, even when he wasn't around?

Thinking about her lingering annoyance, Brenna knew it was because she let him have too much power over her, let his opinion and his words matter to her more than they should. She really needed to learn to just let things go instead of mulling them over and over in her mind.

Although she was enjoying her time with Brock, Wesley's tirade kept invading her thoughts, interrupting her happiness.

"You're not fine," Brock said, taking the antique toy car she was wrapping out of her hand and setting it back on the shelf. Turning her toward the bed, he tugged on her hand until she sat down beside him. "If your shoulders get any tighter, they'll be permanently attached to your ears."

Brenna gave him a look of caution.

"Come on, tell me what's wrong. Did Mike or Levi say something to upset you?" Brock asked, rubbing her shoulders with a gentle hand that, unbeknownst to him, was searing her skin through her blouse. She abandoned her suit jacket shortly after she discarded her shoes. He liked the feel of the silky material beneath his hand and imagined it would feel like Brenna's skin, all soft, smooth and warm.

"No, nothing like that. They've both been great," Brenna said, lifting her big blue eyes to Brock's twinkling hazel ones. "I had a little problem with Wesley this afternoon and I guess I let it get to me more than I should."

Brock felt his own shoulders stiffen. Although he and Brenna hadn't been dating for long, he knew she disliked her boss and was unhappy with her job. From what Brenna hadn't said, he got the idea that Wesley often hurt her feelings and made things pretty miserable at the office. "What happened?"

Releasing a sigh, Brenna stared at the hands clenched in her lap. "He got a little upset when a report wasn't on his desk when he thought it should be and confronted me about it. The problem was that I wasn't the one he asked for the report and didn't know anything about it. By the time Kat and I tracked it down, it was after five. When I took it in to him, he said some rather unpleasant things that I should have ignored."

"What did he say, Brenna?" Brock asked, trying to control his urge to hunt Wesley down and punch him in the nose. He sounded like an awful person to have as a boss.

"Just that I'm a... it's not important, Brock. Really. I'm fine. I'll have all weekend to get over it," Brenna said, trying to force a cheery tone into her voice. "Let's get back to your packing."

103

"Not quite yet," Brock said, taking her hands in his and studying her face. He could see that something had really bothered her. "Go on. What did he say?"

"Brock, I'd rather not..." Brenna said, but decided Brock was probably going to keep asking until he got an answer. She knew he was persistent but also wanted to help if he could. "He said if it was up to him I'd be standing in the unemployment line. He called me blondie, the stupidest little twit, and an incompetent idiot who managed to worm my way up to a management position. Then he ordered me out of his office."

A look of thunder settled on Brock's face and he bit his tongue to refrain from telling Brenna what he thought of her boss. Taking a couple of deep breaths, he pulled Brenna into his arms and gave her a comforting hug.

"I'm sorry, Brenna. No one has the right to speak to you that way, especially when none of it is true. You're smart and witty and clever and they ought to be grateful you've stuck with their company as long as you have considering who you have for a boss," Brock said, kissing her cheek. "Why don't you just call them Monday and tell them you're finished. Your friend Kathleen would pack up your office and you'd never have to see Wesley again."

As tempting as that idea was, and Brenna had thought about it herself prior to Brock's suggestion, she wanted to leave on her own terms in her own time. Although she didn't plan on being there much longer, she had a few projects she wanted to finish for her own sense of accomplishment.

"No. I'm not going to let him get the best of me. When I'm ready to leave I'll leave, but I'm not going to let him push me out or make a coward out of me," Brenna said, straightening both her spine and her resolve.

"You're something else, you know that?" Brock said, gently tracing his thumb along her cheeks. "Remind me not to come visit you at your office or I might give your boss a piece of my mind."

"Okay," Brenna whispered, leaning into Brock's tender touch. One minute they were hugging and the next they were lost in a kiss that chased all thoughts from her head except for the wonderful man holding her in his arms. Brock guided her down on the bed and leaned over her, continuing to kiss her with such heat and intensity she thought her tights might actually melt off her legs in a puddle of nylon and lycra on the bedroom floor.

Running his hand across her ribs in tempting circles, they were both surprised when a throat cleared at the door.

"I can see you two are making a lot of progress," Mike teased leaning against the door frame. "Too bad it isn't with the packing. I told Levi we should have split you up."

Brenna blushed a fiery shade of red while Brock cast an annoyed look over his shoulder at his friend. Fortunately, his broad back protected Brenna from having to face Mike.

"We'll be done in here in a minute," Brock ground out, trying to catch his bearings, still intently focused on Brenna and her alluring, soft presence on his bed.

"I just bet you will be," Mike said with a wicked grin as he wandered back down the hall. Brenna heard him say, "You owe me five bucks, bro. Lip-locked doesn't even begin to describe it."

Brenna blushed even more furiously and pushed Brock away as she sat up. "Maybe I better go."

"No," Brock said, wrapping his arms around her and kissing her again. "Although I think we better get off this bed and back to packing. If we stay here like this much longer, I can't be held accountable for anything that happens."

Brenna raised an eyebrow at him and grinned, then returned to wrapping items and packing them in boxes.

By ten-thirty, they were finished with the packing, but tired, and Brenna still needed to drive home. Brock offered to let her stay, saying she could have his room and he would sleep on the couch. The thought of sleeping in the bed Brock normally occupied made Brenna's knees feel wobbly and her heart beat pick up tempo.

"I appreciate your thoughtfulness, but I'm going home," Brenna said, stuffing her feet back into her shoes and slipping her arms into first her suit jacket and then the coat that Brock held for her. Grabbing her purse, she shook Levi's hand followed by Mike's. "It was so nice to meet you both. Thank you for the pizza."

"It was nice to meet you, Brenna. Drive safely and drop by anytime," Mike said as Brock opened the door and walked her down the hall. He escorted her to her car and held the door as she climbed inside. Fighting down the urge to kiss her a few dozen more times, Brock instead gave her one long intense parting kiss.

"Thanks for your help packing, coffee girl," Brock said, twisting a golden curl around his finger, relishing the feel of the silken strand. "Keep your chin up about work and just tell me if I need to go pound some sense into your boss."

Brenna gave him a look that let him know no pounding would be necessary. "If you call me when you're ready to unload boxes tomorrow, I'll come over and help you."

"Are you sure? I thought you already had plans for tomorrow," Brock said as he put off saying goodbye.

"I have to watch the store for Mom for a few hours, but that isn't until noon. If you want it, my morning is all yours," Brenna said, placing a hand on Brock's cheek. He gave new meaning to five o'clock shadow as the stubbly growth on his face pricked against her smooth fingers. She liked the sensation more than she probably should.

"Oh, I definitely want it. I'll call you in the morning," Brock said, swooping down for one last kiss. "Drive carefully, coffee girl."

"I will, construction man. See you tomorrow," Brenna said, blowing Brock a kiss as she started the car and drove away.

Brock stood watching her taillights until they disappeared around a corner, wondering how he was going to be able to keep a handle on his feelings for Brenna when he lived just a few blocks from her. It had been challenging enough with them living and working an hour away from each other.

Going back in the apartment building, Brock took the stairs, hoping to give himself enough time to cool down the heat that Brenna stirred in him so that he could face Mike and Levi's teasing without doing either of them bodily harm.

~◇~

Brenna was making a large platter of breakfast burritos filled with cheese, eggs and sausage the next morning when Brock called to let her know he was pulling up at his house.

"Are you sure you have time to come over?" Brock asked, sounding distracted. Brenna could hear voices in the background and knew Brock's help had arrived as well.

"Do you still want me to? I've got some snacks I can bring over along with coffee," Brenna said, wrapping the last of the burritos and setting two carafes of coffee into a box.

"Yes, I still want you to come over," Brock said with a teasing tone in his voice. "As soon as possible. The guys wouldn't let me stop for coffee and I'm suffering major withdrawals."

"What were they thinking?" Brenna said, pretending to be astonished. Drawing on any dramatic abilities she had, she couldn't stop a smile from creeping into her voice, "I'll be right there. Try to hang on until I arrive with the java."

"I'll try, but hurry, coffee girl. Hurry fast."

Brenna laughed as she hung up the phone and finished packing a box of napkins, insulated cups and paper plates. Grabbing her car keys and purse, she hustled out the door and over to Brock's.

She knew where to find the house he bought, but hadn't made the time to even drive by and check it out. As she turned down the street, a moving truck, along with two pickups were parked in front of the house at the end of the cul-de-sac, drawing the attention of the neighbors, particularly the widows Hearst and Phillips, who were already marching toward Brock's truck.

"What's all this kerfuffle about?" Brenna heard Mrs. Phillips ask Brock. Getting the box of breakfast supplies out of the back seat of her car, she watched Brock loosen a tie-down strap on the back of his pickup, holding in a kitchen table and chairs.

"Good morning, lovely ladies," Brock said, turning to look at the widows with a smile. "Are you here to help move in boxes?"

"Good gravy, you idi…" Mrs. Phillips spluttered, interrupted by Mrs. Hearst.

"No, dear boy. We just wanted to see if you were in fact moving in today," Mrs. Hearst said with her customary smile. "It certainly looks like you are and you've got plenty of help. Speaking of help, there's

Brenna. Oh, hello, dear!"

Brenna set the box on the trunk of her car and waved at the elderly lady. "Good morning, Mrs. Hearst. How are you today?"

"Fit as a fiddle, Brenna. I didn't realize you knew our Brock."

Brenna walked over to where the widows stood near Brock. When she was close enough he could touch her, he leaned down and kissed her cheek causing her to blush, Mrs. Hearst to twitter, and Mrs. Phillips to frown.

"I see you do know Brock. Quite well, perhaps?" Mrs. Phillips said, looking down her nose at Brenna.

"Not as well as she will tomorrow," Brock teased, squeezing Brenna's hand. He looked over at her car and spied the carafes of coffee. "You beautiful angel, you brought coffee."

"And food," Brenna said, trying to ignore the heat that flamed into her cheeks at his teasing compliment.

"Well, go on, you two, and don't mind us old ladies. We'll check back later and see how things are progressing," Mrs. Hearst said, patting Brenna on the arm, offering an encouraging smile.

"Thanks, Mrs. Hearst, Mrs. Phillips," Brock said, turning his attention from the worrisome widows to the lovely woman next to him. Dropping his arm around her shoulders, he walked with her to the car where he picked up the box in one arm and escorted her up to the steps of the porch. He placed the breakfast goodies on a card table, nudging aside a box of stale donuts one of the guys grabbed from a convenience store.

"Something smells wonderful, Brenna. And the food smells pretty good, too," Brock said with a wink, fishing out the insulated cups. Brenna handed him a carafe and he poured himself a cup of coffee, inhaling the rich scent, along with a hefty whiff of Brenna's perfume. Smiling, he watched her get out platters of food, paper plates and napkins.

"You didn't have to bring food, you know," Brock said, grateful that she had. The donuts weren't appealing at all, especially with hot, fresh food made by Brenna's capable hands.

"I know, but I wanted to," Brenna said, handing him a plate with two breakfast burritos, slices of fruit and a piece of still warm banana bread. "You'll need your strength for moving all this stuff in, won't you?"

"Absolutely," Brock said, turning to look at the rest of the guys who were ambling up the walk. "I guess it's too late to hide this in the house and force the donuts on the rest of them."

"That's no way to treat your slave labor," Mike said, reaching for a plate and grinning at Brenna. "Thanks for taking care of us, Brenna. Someone got in such a hurry this morning, he forgot about important stuff like food and coffee."

"Well, I can see why he'd get in a hurry to get here," a short, but very good-looking man said, taking Brenna's hand in his and kissing her fingers. "You, lovely lady, are a jewel among women."

"Keep your hands and your lips to yourself, man," Brock said, stepping between him and Brenna. Not one who was ever given to fits of jealousy, it gnawed at Brock with a previously unknown ferocity.

"Oh, pipe down, dude," Levi said, taking a cup of coffee from Brenna and tipping his head at her in greeting. "Someone just got up on the wrong side of the bed this morning."

When Brenna smiled at him, he grinned and pointed at the other guys assembled on the porch. He introduced Jett, the hand kisser, Ned, Juan and Tony, all friends who'd known each other for years.

Sitting down on the porch steps, the guys made short work of the food, emptied the carafes of coffee and thanked Brenna multiple times for supplying breakfast. Then they got up, put their muscle and backs into the business of unloading and made moving Brock's belongings into the house look like something fun instead of sweat-inducing effort.

Not wanting to unpack much until he had more of the house remodeled, Brock directed most of the boxes, except those labeled kitchen or bathroom, to a large upstairs bedroom. He planned to sleep upstairs in one of the rooms that didn't need any work beyond a coat of paint, so the guys lugged his king size bed up the stairs. A loveseat and a few antique pieces were left in the living room, and the table and chairs were hauled back to the kitchen.

Brenna took on the task of wiping out drawers and cabinets. Down on her hands and knees with her head stuck in the depths of a cupboard near the stove, Brock wandered into the kitchen looking for her and got an eyeful of her cute posterior. Rather than announce his presence he watched her for a moment or two. It probably would have been three or four but Mike called to him and Brock hollered back that he'd be right there.

Cringing when Brenna smacked her head on the cupboard in surprise, he gave her a devilish grin when she glared over her shoulder at him. Squatting down next to her, he took her chin in his hand and gave her a quick kiss.

"When I told you I was suffering from withdrawals this morning, I didn't exactly mean the coffee," he said pressing a lingering kiss to her lips before disappearing down the hallway.

Brenna sat slightly dazed, absorbing what he said. If she had been able to think clearly, she might have accused him of being an outrageous flirt.

Going back to her job of scrubbing, something she assumed the guys would not think to do, she glanced around the large kitchen, imagining it with new counters and freshly painted cupboards. In her mind, cheery yellow curtains would float in the breeze at the window above the sink and the smell of something cinnamon baking in the oven would fill the space with a welcoming fragrance. Turning she could almost see herself in the kitchen, giving Brock a good morning kiss.

A tingling sensation started at her toes and worked its way to her head. It was the same strange feeling she got whenever she had her dream of the perfect house with the perfect man. Before she could grab on to the vision of her dream, it flew away. Deciding to think about it later, she finished cleaning the kitchen and began unpacking boxes with a few plates, cups and kitchen utensils. If Brock did anything more than very basic cooking, he was going to be sorely lacking in kitchen tools.

When she finished what she could in the kitchen, she went to the guest bathroom to see if she needed to clean in there, but it was spotless. It was evident that Brock had done some remodeling recently, including a fresh coat of paint, a new toilet and tub. Running her hand along what appeared to be a brand-new sink and counter top, she smiled, impressed with Brock's handiwork.

"Hey, Brenna, you want a quick tour of the house?" Brock asked, popping his head around the door. "I know you said you have to be at your mom's store at noon and it's almost eleven. I assume you'll have to run home and change before you go since I apparently worked you too hard."

Brenna glanced down at her dusty jeans and T-shirt with a dark smear across the front.

"You're a tyrant, for sure," Brenna said, giving Brock's arm a squeeze. She felt electricity jolt through her fingers and spiral down into her stomach at the touch. Brawny muscle filled her hand and her quick intake of breath filled her nose with Brock's unique scent. Trying to mentally steady herself, she let go of his arm and took a step back. "I'd love a tour."

Brock didn't immediately respond or move. He was too caught up in the way curls had escaped Brenna's ponytail to bob around her face. She had a smudge of dirt on one cheek and her big blue eyes were twinkling with mischief and something he couldn't quite identify.

He'd never seen her dressed so casually before and appreciated the opportunity to check her out in jeans. It had definitely been worth the wait. When she touched his arm, her fingers not only seared his flesh, he felt like his bones began melting as well.

Taking a step back into the hall, he took her hand and turned her toward the back stairs.

"Let's start upstairs and work our way down," he said, leading her up the narrow steps to the second floor. He pointed out the bedrooms, bathroom, stairs to the attic, and the room he was going to remodel for an office with a great view of the backyard and creek. Coming down the main front stairs, he showed her the area at the back of the house he planned to turn into a master suite and discussed his ideas for revamping the kitchen.

Giving the backyard a quick perusal, Brenna knew she needed to leave, although she'd much rather stay with Brock.

"It's a wonderful house, Brock. I know you'll make it into a lovely home," Brenna said as they walked around the side of the house.

Rounding the corner of the front yard, she noticed the guys were hauling in the last pieces of furniture. Brock inherited several pieces from his grandfather and placed them in storage until he was ready to move. A quick stop by the storage unit this morning cleaned it out and gave him some nice basic furnishings.

"It was nice to meet you all," Brenna said with a wave as Brock gathered up her box of breakfast supplies, now devoid of food and coffee, and walked her toward her car.

A chorus of "thanks" and "great to meet you" followed her retreating back.

"Are we still on for lunch tomorrow?" Brock asked, setting the box in the back seat while Brenna opened her door.

"Sure. I'd really like that," Brenna said with a sweet smile. "I'm glad you'll be living closer now."

"Me, too, coffee girl," Brock said, gently wiping away a smudge of dirt on her cheek. "Thanks for coming this morning and bringing breakfast."

"Anytime," Brenna said, thinking she should get in her car before she became any more distracted by Brock and forgot about going to her mom's store.

Brock put his arms around her and gave her a kiss that let anyone watching, which would have been Mike, Levi and the crew of helpers as well as the worrisome widows, know exactly how much he liked Brenna.

"Thanks again for coming this morning, Brenna," he said in a husky voice, his lips just a breath from hers.

"You're welcome," she whispered, giving him a tight hug before getting in her car, starting it and blowing Brock a kiss. "See you tomorrow."

He watched her drive down the street before heading back in the house. Brock was almost to the porch steps before he noticed his friends standing on the porch, giving him goofy grins, raised eyebrows and kissy faces.

"Animals," he growled, walking through them into the house.

Laughing, they filed along behind him, offering a variety of teasing comments that did nothing to help lighten Brock's mood. He probably shouldn't have done such a good job of kissing her a minute ago, knowing they more than likely had an audience, but he just couldn't seem to help himself.

"For the record, dude, she's one of those," Mike said, stopping Brock with a hand to his shoulder.

"One what?" Brock asked, turning to look at his best friend, confused.

"She's one of those girls that make you think about buying houses, growing up and settling down. She's sweet and fun and a great cook. It's the rare girl like her who makes marriage seem like it would be a great adventure rather than a lifetime of suffering," Mike said, looking at Brock with a serious expression on his face, which didn't happen often. "She earned our stamp of approval."

"Good to know," Brock said, taking in what Mike said. Although he hadn't thought of her in exactly those terms, those were precisely the thoughts she made him have. She made him want a home, a wife, kids and a picket fence. Maybe not a minivan, but definitely a dog.

Brock felt his blood stir as he thought about how much she made him want - especially her.

Chapter Nine

"Brenna, there's someone here to see you," the receptionist said softly from the door.

Glancing up from her computer, Brenna looked at the receptionist with confusion. Nan always buzzed her when she had appointments. She never came whispering to her door that she had a visitor. She knew she didn't have any appointments scheduled because she was frantically trying to finish up a report before Wesley demanded it on his desk.

"I don't have any appointments today, Nan. Are you sure the guest is here to see me?" Brenna asked, turning back toward the computer.

"I'm sure, Brenna. He said he didn't have an appointment, but I'd definitely make time to see him. His name is Brock and he's pretty cute," Nan said with a grin, stepping closer to Brenna's desk.

"Oh," Brenna said, swinging her chair around and staring at Nan. Brock was here? He'd come to see her? He never mentioned dropping by when she talked to him last night. Or when he texted her this morning. Shoving down the little thrill of his surprise visit, she put a hand to her hair to remove any errant pencils, tucked a few stray curls back into place and straightened her suit jacket when she stood. "Please show him in."

"Right away," Nan said with a nod of her head, trying unsuccessfully to hide her smile.

With just enough time to pop a breath mint in her

mouth, Brenna watched Brock walk into her office and bring a boost of sunshine with him to her day.

"What are you doing here?" she asked, walking around the edge of the desk to give him a hug. He returned the embrace, kissing her lightly on the lips, which made Brenna flustered. She sat down on the edge of her desk while Brock took one of two chairs in front of it.

"We had to come to Portland to pick up a load of supplies for this store we're remodeling. Bunch of slave driving maniacs, they are, so I had Tom drop me off here," Brock said with a charming smile that addled Brenna's ability to think. "Would you mind terribly if I took you out to dinner and then rode home with you?"

"I'd like that," Brenna said quietly, getting lost in Brock's smile and the twinkling mischief in his eyes. It had been a month since he'd moved into his house and they'd been on many dates since then. She spent a lot of time at his house helping with his remodeling projects, which mostly involved her holding things and handing him tools or wielding a paintbrush. She enjoyed every minute of it because it was all spent with Brock.

Infatuated with him at first, she was certain now what she felt for him was something deeper, something more abiding. He consumed way too many of her thoughts during the day and filled her dreams at night. In a few more weeks, when she gave her notice here at work, she would be able to see him even more as he finished the remodel project on their store.

Although Brock and his crew were trying to keep things on a tight schedule, he had mentioned more than once that one of the inspectors kept giving them a hard time and forcing them to redo things that should have been fine. Now, their completion date was looking like it would be pushed back a few weeks.

Brenna honestly didn't mind because it boiled down

to more time with Brock nearby.

"Great. What time can you leave?" Brock asked, glancing at his watch. It was only four and he assumed Brenna would probably work until five.

"I... um..." Brenna wanted more than anything to grab her purse and run out the door with Brock, but that little part of her that could still be practical in his presence told her she better finish the report she was working on before she left. "I'm just finishing up a big project. Can you hang out for an hour? I should be ready to leave at five."

"Sure, no problem," Brock said, leaning back in the chair and crossing an ankle over his knee in a move that made Brenna smile at its growing familiarity.

When Brock appeared to settle into the chair and make himself comfortable, Brenna's smile faded.

"You're not planning to hang out here for an hour, are you?" Brenna asked studying him with increasing concern. She couldn't possibly get anything done with him sitting across the desk from her. He had already obliterated her concentration. Having him sit a few feet from her looking so charming and smelling so good would be a distraction she couldn't possibly overcome.

"If I'm not wanted, I can go elsewhere," Brock said with feigned indignation, getting to his feet. "Sorry to have bothered you."

Brock only took two steps toward the door when he felt Brenna's hand on his arm.

"Brock, I'm sorry. Don't leave, it's just... I..." She looked up at him with moist eyes and he grinned down at her.

"I'm just teasing you, coffee girl," Brock said, tweaking her freckled nose. "I know you'll get your work done faster without me hovering around your desk. I'll go stroll around the block and be back just before five. Okay?"

"Thanks," Brenna said with a sigh of relief. "That would be great."

"See you in an hour, then," Brock said, squeezing her shoulder gently as he placed a quick kiss to her lips.

Brenna watched him walk out the door then returned to her desk where she forced herself to focus on finishing the report. Her fingers were flying across the keys as she typed the closing statement when she felt the hairs on the back of her neck prickle.

"I'll have the report finished in about five minutes, Wesley," she said, without looking up. Even though she hadn't made eye contact with him, the scent of booze and overwhelming aftershave filled her office, letting her know he was in fact standing near her desk.

"How did you know... Never mind," Wesley said, sneering at her from narrowed eyes. "Just be sure that report is on my desk before you leave tonight, you twit. I shouldn't have to come ask you for it. If you were deserving of your position in this company, I wouldn't have to be constantly after you to do your job. You are such a loser."

Shooting him a cool glare, Brenna returned to her typing. "I'd finish a lot faster if you'd quit coming in here and harassing me. I wonder if Mr. Harchett would like to know how you treat his employees. Do you think he'd appreciate the bad reputation you've created in this department? I bet he would..."

Whatever else Brenna planned to say was cut off when she felt herself jerked out of her chair. Wesley grabbed her by both arms with a strength she would have thought beyond his ability to possess and gave her a shake that rattled her teeth as it knocked the pins from her hair.

A yelp of surprise escaped her lips.

Leaning near her ear he hissed, "If I were you, I'd keep my mouth shut. There are ways to hurt you beyond seeing you unemployed, Ms. Smith. I could take what you won't give freely, if you get my meaning. I don't think you want that do you? Now be a good little twit and get back to work."

Wesley started to shove her away, but a warm hand at her back steadied her. She turned her startled gaze to see Brock, his face contorted with anger. A muscle worked in his clenched jaw and rage radiated from him.

"You have no right to speak to the lady like that. Back off and leave her alone before she advises both your boss and an attorney about your threats," Brock said tightly. Although he and Wesley were about the same height, Brock seemed to tower over the other man.

Wesley shrank away from Brock, like the coward that he was, casting another sneer at Brenna.

"Who is this, Brenna?" Wesley said, taking a step back from Brock, who was now flexing his hands into fists at his sides.

"No one you need to know," Brock said, taking a menacing step toward Wesley. "I meant what I said. Leave her alone."

Without another word, Wesley left Brenna's office, slamming the door behind him. Brenna sank on weak knees to her office chair and sucked in a deep breath. She wasn't sure what had happened in the last five minutes, but she thought Wesley had threatened her while Brock came to her rescue.

Looking at Brock, his muscles tensed for battle and the cords in his neck strained, she could feel anger pouring from him.

"Let me guess, that was Wesley," Brock said, turning to look at her, his hazel eyes dark and cold. He struggled to rein in his temper. Seeing Brenna so rattled and upset did little to alleviate his concern.

"Yes," Brenna said, her voice barely more than a whisper. If things had been bad with Wesley before, he'd make her life misery now. She might as well box up her belongings and quit because he'd have her fired before the week was out.

Brock squatted down next to Brenna and rubbed her icy fingers between his hands. She looked like she was in shock, pale and limp in the chair. Her hair tumbled around her shoulders and her eyes held a frightened gleam.

"Are you okay? Did he hurt you?" Brock asked, trying to calm down. He really wanted to use Wesley as a punching bag or at least shake the man the way he had apparently shaken Brenna.

When Brock returned to her office, he caught the rumble of voices and waited outside the door. Hearing what sounded like a muffled scream, he opened the door to see Wesley say something to Brenna that drained every bit of color from her face and made her shake like a leaf. Her hair was tumbling around her shoulders and she looked terrified.

It was clear that Brenna's boss was a weak, cowardly bully. Brock had no use for people like that, especially when they were hurting someone he cared about. Someone he loved.

Wesley was darn lucky Brock was raised to be a gentleman otherwise he'd be crying on the floor with a busted nose and a few broken ribs. If he caught him near Brenna again, Brock knew he'd forget all about his upbringing or the repercussions of punching a man in his own office.

"I'm fine," Brenna finally said, pushing her hair away from her face, realizing it had fallen down. Trying to gather her wits, she turned back to her computer and started typing.

"What are you doing?" Brock asked with disbelief. "After what he just did, you're going to sit there and finish your report?"

Brenna typed the last word, hit save and print, then got to her feet.

"A lot of people worked hard on this project and I don't want to let them down. Although Wesley is a… a pig, I don't want the rest of the team to suffer," Brenna said, trying to justify why she should care about any of it.

Tomorrow she would bring in her letter of resignation, see if she could make an appointment with Mr. Harchett, and say her goodbyes to the people she'd enjoyed having as coworkers.

Gathering up the report, she slapped it in a binder, picked up her purse and trench coat, turned off the lights and motioned Brock into the hall while she locked the door behind them. For all her calm movements, her hands were trembling and her legs still felt weak.

"Will you come with me, please?" she asked, turning eyes full of pleading to Brock. She didn't think Wesley would try anything, but it gave her a measure of security to know Brock had her back.

"Do you want me to take it in for you?" Brock asked with a frown as he walked with her down the hall to Wesley's office.

"I'll take it in, but if you wouldn't mind standing in the door and looking like you could rip his arms off at any moment, that would be good," Brenna said quietly, a little of her humor returning.

"Be happy to." Brock didn't have to work very hard at looking furious or intimidating as Brenna stopped outside Wesley's door and knocked.

When he barked "what?" she opened the door and walked inside. He was already partway through a bottle of whiskey and his eyes were glazed as she set the report on his desk.

"There's the report," she said and turned to leave.

Wesley staggered to his feet and snaked a hand out

toward her when he noticed Brock in the doorway, looking formidable. Sinking back down in his chair with fear on his face, he turned to stare out the window.

Brenna walked out, took Brock's hand, and left the building without saying a word. In the parking garage, she handed Brock her keys and asked him to drive.

So much for the romantic evening he had planned.

Knowing he needed to retrieve a truck load of supplies in the city, he asked one of his guys to come along. After they picked up the order, he had Tom drop him off at Brenna's office with all sorts of romantic notions about how the evening would progress.

One of his favorite Italian restaurants wasn't too far from her office. Brock envisioned a quiet dinner at a cozy corner table. Italian food was the food of love, or so his mother had told him over and over again. From past dating experience, he had to agree with her. There was just something about the rich food, spicy smells and cozy atmosphere that stirred a little romance.

After dinner and maybe a stroll, he would have taken the rest of the evening to eventually get Brenna home.

Instead, he was mad, she was traumatized, and romance was the farthest thing from her mind.

He still drove to the Italian restaurant and hoped they could salvage what was left of the evening. Brock and Brenna both were quiet, lost in their own thoughts, as they ate the delicious food set before them.

Finally, Brock took Brenna's hand in his and kissed her palm.

"Are you sure you're okay?" Brock asked quietly, studying Brenna's face as he gently rubbed the back of her hand with his thumb. She played with her food, kept her eyes downcast, and her shoulders were riding dangerously close to her ears as she sat through dinner tense and upset.

At her nod, he released a deep breath and let his own shoulders relax a little. He watched her stiff posture relax as well. Instead of leaving well enough alone, Brock felt the need to advise Brenna on how to better handle herself.

"Brenna, you've got to stand up for yourself. You can't let people walk all over you like that. Don't let them treat you like a doormat. Show them you're tough. Get some teeth and use them," Brock said. When she only looked at him, he continued expounding on what she needed to do in regard to handling people like Wesley. "There will always be Wesleys. Even when you leave the company, you'll still run into his type. You've got to learn to stop them or you'll always have problems like this."

Now that the shock of Wesley's threats had past, Brenna was mad. And every word Brock said only added fuel to the fire of her anger. How dare Wesley treat her like that? How dare he threaten her? How dare Brock assume she was a spineless weakling? Who gave him the right to lecture her on what she needed to do? She needed support from him, not a step-by-step guide to taking on a bully.

Before the waitress could ask if they'd like dessert, Brenna jumped to her feet. Grabbing cash from her wallet to more than cover the bill, she thanked the waitress as she handed it to her, and told her they were leaving.

Brock spluttered and choked on his soda as Brenna paid the waitress and started toward the door.

Grabbing her forgotten coat, he followed her out of the restaurant, knowing he'd never seen Brenna mad before. He'd seen her miffed, insulted, and annoyed, but mad was something new. Apparently his little coffee girl had a temper.

Searching through her purse, Brenna finally huffed

in frustration and held her hand out to him.

"Keys," she said tersely, wiggling her fingers in his face. Realizing she wanted her car keys, Brock was not convinced giving them to her was the smartest move at the moment. He thought she was too worked up to drive with any thought to safety.

"I'm not sure you should drive, Brenna," Brock said, keeping the keys firmly in his hand after he fished them from his jeans pocket.

"Keys," she said again, angry fire flashing from her blue eyes, taking Brock by surprise.

Brock's own eyes widened at the fury he saw in Brenna's as he reluctantly handed over the keys. Saying a prayer for their safety, he held her door and hoped she wouldn't leave him standing in the parking lot. Running around the car, he barely shut the door when she peeled out into traffic. Grappling for his seat belt, he made sure it was securely fastened. There was more than one moment when Brock closed his eyes and hoped for the best as Brenna swerved between cars, exceeding the speed limit as they drove through the evening traffic in Portland.

Muttering under her breath as they merged onto the freeway, Brenna sped through cars without speaking to Brock, turning up some lively jazz music on the radio. The farther they headed south, the more the traffic thinned and Brock let out a sigh of relief.

He'd ridden with Brenna any number of times and she was normally a good, safe driver. If this had been his first experience riding with her, he might have refused to ever sit in the passenger seat again. Seeing Brenna seething with anger was not something he as particularly enjoying. She seemed to be okay, other than quiet, until he started telling her how to handle Wesley. That couldn't have set her off, could it?

Brenna passed a big extended cab pickup. Brock

noted the driver staring at Brenna's little car. It wasn't long until the truck sped up and passed her pulling, right in front of her and slowing down.

Waiting for a break in traffic, Brenna again passed the truck only to have him pull in front of her then slow down.

Brock watched as her shoulders tensed even more as she passed the pickup for a third time. The driver swerved toward Brenna, trying to intimidate her. She glared over her shoulder at the man as she passed him.

"If being passed by a woman makes you feel threatened, you better check the expiration date on your man-card," she said, continuing to speed down the road.

Despite her anger and his fear of her driving, Brock roared with laughter.

"That's a good one, Brenna. Really good. I'll have to remember to tell Mike you said that. He thinks you're all sweetness and no sass, but I think I just got a glimpse of the real Brenna."

She glared at him a moment then her anger began to seep away and finally she offered him a shy smile. Slowing down to normal speed, she continued driving toward home, but her hands no longer gripped the steering wheel with whitened knuckles.

"I'm sorry. I guess I should have warned you I have a bit of a temper," Brenna said with a sheepish look, now that her anger was cooling.

"If I hadn't experienced it first-hand, I don't think I'd have believed you," Brock said with honesty. Brenna looked exactly like someone who would never have a temper fit. With her big blue eyes and golden curls and unassuming personality, it was easy to see why people took her for granted. Obviously, she did have the ability to draw the line somewhere. He just wasn't sure what had pushed her over it at the restaurant.

"I know. Everyone thinks I'm a big pushover.

Brenna the doormat," she said, sounding deflated.

"What happened earlier?" Brock asked, taking Brenna's hand in his and gently rubbing her palm.

She took an exit that left them sitting in the parking lot of a fast food restaurant. She didn't want to try to drive and have a conversation with Brock about Wesley or her temper.

Glad that she decided to stop the car to talk, Brock unbuckled his seat belt and turned toward Brenna. He was a take charge, squash all problems before they start kind of guy. That's why he couldn't understand why Brenna let Wesley bully her like she did. Bullies would back down when confronted.

"Let's start with what made you so mad at dinner. Which, by the way, I was planning to buy," Brock said, holding both her hands in his. His hope was that she wouldn't get mad at him again if he was caressing her hands. "I had plans to ply you with cannoli until you were begging for mercy."

"You made me mad," Brenna said, not even registering Brock's teasing as she blurted out the truth.

"Me?" Brock asked, surprised by her response. "What did I do to make you mad?"

"You were bossing me around, telling me what to do, how I should handle Wesley, how I need to be someone other than myself," Brenna said, feeling the little embers of her anger rekindle as she recalled what Brock said. "I don't need you to tell me how to fight my battles. I don't need you to point out all my character flaws. What I needed from you was a little understanding and encouragement."

"That wasn't what I meant," Brock said, watching sparks ignite in Brenna's eyes. "I hate seeing people bully you and take advantage of you. I was just pointing out ways to stop that kind of behavior."

"In your pointing out my faults, it kind of hurt my

feelings. And made me mad," Brenna said, staring at the dark hairs on the backs of Brock's hands as they rubbed gentle circles on her own. It was hard to hold on to her irritation when he was doing that. It made heat of a whole different variety fill her stomach.

"Yeah, I got that part just fine," Brock said with a trace of humor in his voice. "Help me understand what made you so angry."

"I felt like you were saying 'poor stupid little Brenna can't take care of herself. Someone smarter and stronger has to do it for her. Too bad she can't just figure it out and handle her problems without help.' What I heard you say made it sound like I was too dumb to figure out what to do. You also made it sound like you expected me to follow the orders you were barking at me. That's what made me angry."

Brock stared at Brenna, trying to digest what she was saying. Brenna obviously had some issues with confrontation that she needed to work on. Although he offered his opinion on how to keep from getting into a similar situation, Brock never intended to make her feel stupid or that he was giving orders he expected her to obey. With a natural tendency toward problem-solving, it was easy for Brock to see what needed done and do it. He'd have to remember to offer a more circumspect response the next time.

"Brenna, you're strong and smart and beautiful. You deserve better than to be treated the way Wesley treats you. I just wanted you to realize you don't have to put up with it," Brock said, starting to feel frustrated with himself, with Brenna, but mostly with Wesley. "I was only trying to help. I was a little upset when I walked in to find Wesley manhandling you as well as threatening you. He's lucky I held on to my temper as well as I did. If we hadn't been at your office, he'd still be trying to figure out which way was up or down."

"Violence begets violence, you know," Brenna said with the barest hint of a smile. She sat quietly for a moment, considering what happened during the last few hours. "I'm sorry, Brock. I just don't like to be bossed around. I have to put up with it at work, but I won't put up with it elsewhere. I understand if that changes things between us."

"Actually it does change things," Brock said giving Brenna a solemn look. When she raised teary eyes to his, he felt the corners of his lips lift in a smile and his eyes twinkled. "I'll do my best not to stir up that wicked temper again."

"Brock," she whispered, leaning toward him.

He took her face in his hands and kissed her tenderly, stroking his thumbs across her cheeks to wipe away the few tears that escaped her closed eyes.

"Now, about Wesley," Brock said, leaning back, still holding her face in his hands. "What are you going to do?"

Brenna released a sigh and sat back. She fiddled with a button on her jacket and looked out the windshield.

"I'm going to write my letter of resignation tonight, give a copy to Wesley, his boss, Kat's grandfather and Mr. Harchett tomorrow and see if I can get an appointment with Mr. Harchett to tell him what Wesley has done. I might have been leaving anyway, but the company needs to know how he behaves. I plan to clean out my office tomorrow, because I don't exactly feel safe being around Wesley now," Brenna said. She looked out the window while she talked, organizing the details in her mind of all the things she'd have to do tomorrow to clean out her office and leave the projects she was working on in good hands. "And just so you know, I was already mad at him and myself by the time we sat down for dinner. Your comments sort of pushed me over the edge."

"Not fair trying to cast all the blame at my door for driving you into your temper fit," Brock said with a teasing grin. When Brenna shot him a glare, he continued to smile. "Why were you mad at yourself?"

"For not slapping him silly or stomping on his foot with my heel or screaming for security. I'm a complete and total wuss, and having you point it out didn't help matters."

"You're not a wuss, Brenna, just too sweet for your own good sometimes," Brock said, then added with a mischievous grin, "but never too sweet for mine."

"Is that so?"

"That is so, coffee girl," Brock said, kissing her cheek. "Now, since we're already parked here in front of this fine food establishment, what do you say we run inside and get some ice cream? Someone ran me out of the restaurant before I got my dessert."

"I'm sorry," Brenna said, getting out of the car. "If I buy you a double scoop, will that help redeem the situation?"

"Maybe," Brock said, putting his arm around her shoulders as they walked toward the door. "Except I'm buying."

~◇~

By the time Brenna left the office the next day, Wesley had been escorted from the building by security with a full investigation launched into what he'd done for the past many months. Kathleen high-fived Brenna as they watched him fight against the security guards at the elevator, calling out more threats. Not even his uncle was going to be able to save his job this time.

"Are you sure you won't consider staying now that Wesley is gone?" Kat asked as the elevator doors closed on a screaming Wesley.

"No. I'm sticking with my letter of resignation. I'll finish out the two weeks, but then I've got to get things set up for my bistro. I just hope Wesley doesn't try anything before I leave," Brenna said, looking thoughtful as she and Kat walked back to her office.

"I don't think he'd dare with the threat of lawsuits hanging over his head. Granddad says he'll be lucky if he doesn't face some jail time for all the things he's done. There seems to be some evidence pointing to him pilfering company funds in addition to all the other strikes against him," Kat said, sitting on the corner of Brenna's desk and swinging her leg back and forth.

"I hate to see anyone suffer, but he certainly deserves whatever he gets," Brenna said with a hint of venom. Just seeing Wesley this morning made her stomach churn with nerves and fear but she followed through with her plans. Mr. Harchett was quite interested in what Brenna shared and called in several members of the board to listen to her statement. When she mentioned she had a witness who could verify what Wesley had done to her the previous evening, they seemed to snap to attention in a hurry.

"Did Brock really threaten to clean his clock?" Kat asked. Although she'd only met Brock twice, she had assured Brenna he was a keeper.

"He was so mad, I thought he might explode," Brenna said, remembering that Brock had looked pretty intimidating, with muscles bulging and anger flaring.

"More points to Brock for not losing his cool. If I were a man, Wesley would still be crawling around under your desk trying to find the rest of his teeth," Kat said, forming a fist and punching it into the air like a prize fighter.

Brenna laughed. "Who needs a man around when you've got moves like that?"

"We both do and you know it," Kat said, taking Brenna by the arm and walking her to her car.

Thinking about Kat and her fun-loving nature, Brenna was smiling the next morning as she parked at Brock's house and started down the walk. Since today was Saturday, she was joining a few of his friends to help Brock work on his kitchen remodel project.

While the guys installed new counter tops, she was going to paint the cupboard doors. Brock removed them from the cupboards and stripped off the old finish. He wanted to paint them white, seal them, and add new fixtures.

The cupboards themselves were in good shape so Brock sanded them down and painted them. He'd also painted the walls a buttery shade of yellow after dragging Brenna to look at paint samples and asking her to pick out the color she liked best.

Knocking at the door before sticking her head inside, she could hear voices coming from the kitchen. She knew Mike's pickup was parked outside and thought the other pickup belonged to Jett.

In addition to coffee, she also made pastry pockets filled with ham, eggs and cheese, and brought a plate of cookies for snacking on later.

Walking into the kitchen carrying her box of coffee and food, Brock and his friends stopped what they were doing, stood at attention, and each held out a small card for Brenna's inspection.

When she looked at Brock in confusion, the guys broke out laughing.

"What's so funny?" she asked, setting the box on the table and turning to look at the card Brock handed her. One of the guys had been busy with a computer graphic program creating personalized cards with bold lettering.

"This Man Card belongs to Brock McCrae, certifying membership into the Manly Man Club. Expiration Date: whenever Brenna says."

Glaring at Brock, she shook her head. "Nice, guys. Very nice."

Brock kissed her cheek and whispered in her ear. "They thought what you said to the driver was pretty funny, too."

She blushed and smacked at his shoulder while Mike and Levi took the coffee and food out of the box.

"You truly are an angel, Brenna, despite what Brock says about you," Mike said, kissing her cheek and jumping away before Brock could slug him. "Thank you for feeding us."

"You're welcome," Brenna said, a little flustered over their attention, not to mention the man-cards. Turning to Brock, she gave him a mock salute. "Point me to the paint, taskmaster, and I'll get started on the cupboard doors."

"I put them outside. It isn't supposed to rain today and I thought that way you wouldn't have to worry about making a mess or inhaling paint fumes," Brock said, opening the kitchen door and walking her down the back steps to the yard. She took note of the cupboard doors resting across sawhorse tables, making it easy to access them.

Brock shook the paint can before opening it and giving it a good stir. Handing her a brush, he lavished her with one of his charming smiles that made her knees wobble and her thoughts muddle. Seeing a spark flame in her blue eyes, he wrapped her in his arms, kissed her neck and whispered in her ear. "I hope you don't mind the teasing. Mike and Levi thought your comment was hilarious and Levi made the cards when he found out you'd be here today."

"It is a little funny," Brenna said, trying not to smile, but the twinkle of amusement in her eyes gave her away.

"More than a little, my feisty coffee girl," Brock said. He looked back at the house to see five faces staring back at him from the windows so he hauled Brenna around the corner to the side yard and kissed her with an intensity that made her drop the paint brush and wind her arms around his neck.

He groaned and pulled her closer, inhaling her wonderful scent while losing himself in the kiss. Knowing he had to stop before one, if not all, of the guys came looking for them, he gave her one more tempting kiss, then let her go.

She quirked an eyebrow at him and grinned as he picked up the paint brush and handed it to her. When she turned toward the cupboard doors, he popped her on the bottom before she came back into view of the kitchen windows.

Whirling around, she shook the brush at him. "You better behave yourself, construction man, or you'll be sorry."

"I'll be good," Brock said, throwing his hands in the air in surrender. "Just don't unleash that temper on me."

Brenna grinned and as Brock walked past her he said in a voice so low she had to strain to hear, "At least not right now."

Giving a wave to the faces pressed against the kitchen windows, she turned back to her painting and got lost in the project for the next several hours. She stopped once to use the bathroom and get a bottle of water from the fridge. The guys were partially done with the counters and were laughing at a joke Jett was telling. When they noticed her listening, the conversation dropped off in a hurry.

"Hey, Brenna, taking a break?" Levi asked from where he was holding onto one end of a large piece of granite while Mike and Brock worked it into place.

"Yes. I was thirsty," she said, holding up the bottle of water. "Don't stop your joke on my account, Jett. Please continue."

"Oh, well, I was... it wasn't that funny anyway," Jett said, blushing a little under Brenna's intense glare.

"Sure it was, man," Ned said from the other end of the granite Levi was holding. "You were just getting to the part where she..."

"Told off the guys and stormed out of the restaurant," Mike added, giving Ned a look that told him to be quiet and not argue about the substituted ending to the joke.

"I'm pretty sure that isn't how the joke ends. Are you boys afraid I won't find it funny?" Brenna asked, enjoying her ability to make the guys squirm much more than she should. She felt like a school teacher catching a group of naughty little boys about to play hooky. "Or are you scared I'll figure out you're really a bunch of knuckle-dragging cavedwellers under all that charming exterior?"

"Neither," Brock said, giving her a wink. "Now quit harassing my crew so they can get back to work."

"Yes, sir," Brenna said, grinning as she went back out the door.

"You are in such trouble, dude," Mike said, watching Brock watch Brenna as she returned to her painting outside.

"Trouble?" Brock asked, tightening the screws holding the countertop to the cabinet base. "With Brenna? She's just teasing."

"We know that," Mike said, doing some teasing of his own. "But you've got the look that says you've finally fallen in love and that, my friend, definitely means trouble. The next thing you know, we'll be planting daisies and sending out engagement party invitations."

Brock glared at him and went back to tightening the screws. His friends knew him too well and, darn it, they might just be enlisted to plant daisies and who knew what else before everything was all said and done.

Chapter Ten

Enjoying a second cup of coffee, Brock looked around his newly finished kitchen in admiration. Choosing a light tan color for the countertops with flecks of darker brown and green, the stone looked good against the backdrop of the gleaming white cupboards and soft yellow walls.

His new appliances had arrived, also in white, and Brenna added simple yellow gingham valances above the windows to finish off the update. Mini-blinds offered privacy, should Brock feel the need to close them, but since the kitchen faced the backyard, he wasn't worried about it.

Last night Brock completed his installation of new light fixtures that glowed with a soft white light completing the airy, welcoming look of the kitchen. The room caught the morning sun and from the table where he sat with coffee and paper, he could look out at a beautiful view. He could hardly wait to have Greg landscape the yard, but that was project that would wait a few weeks.

Thinking about how glad he was he purchased the house, Brock heard an odd thumping noise outside. Getting up from the table, he looked out the window but didn't see anything.

Returning to his chair, he opened the newspaper and read through part of the sports section before hearing the noise again.

Opening the kitchen door, he stood on the back porch and looked around, trying to locate the cause of the noise. He glanced out at the creek and thought he saw movement near the bank so he ran down the steps and across the yard.

A bedraggled mutt sat on the bank of the creek with his head stuck in a plastic gallon jar.

Whining, the dog would use one paw then the other trying to push the jar off his head. When it didn't budge, he would shake his head viciously, rest a moment and start over again. The jar thumped loudly as the dog's head bumped the sides during a particularly violent shake.

"Hey, dog," Brock said softly, walking up to the pathetic looking animal. "I won't hurt you. Let me help you get that thing off. Just be a good dog and hold still."

While he was talking, Brock placed a light hand on the dog's back. It jumped at first and started to bolt, but as Brock talked to it and kept his hand moving gently along its back, the dog stilled.

"Okay, dog, I'm going to see if I can pull this off and you promise not to bite me. Is that a deal?" Brock said, working carefully to pry the jar off the dog's head. There was probably a good story about how the dog got his head stuck in the jar. Brock decided by the protruding ribs and starved appearance, the animal was most likely digging through someone's garbage trying to lick whatever remnants of food from the jar he could find. Applying one final, firm tug, the jar came off with a loud pop and the dog took off running.

Brock watched the dog follow the creek around a bend and sighed. He hated to see an animal mistreated and that one looked like he'd been on his own for too long. It appeared to be a half-grown puppy with floppy ears, too-big feet and long tail. Mottled brown and covered in filth, he wondered what the dog would look like clean.

Always wanting his own dog, Brock wished the animal would come back. Growing up, his parents could never be bothered with pets. They finally allowed him to have a hamster until Hank escaped from his cage and found refuge in his mother's lingerie drawer. He didn't know if the poor thing died of fright from his mother's screams when she opened the drawer or if she beat it to death, but that was the first and last pet he'd owned.

Living in an apartment and busy with work, he knew he didn't have time for a pet. Now that he was a homeowner on a quiet street with a creek and trees coming right up to his back yard, he thought about getting a dog. By next week, he'd have a new fence across his front yard and it wouldn't take much to bring it around the sides, enclosing the property for a pet or kids.

As he put the jar in his garbage can, he thought again of his dream of having a house with a wife and a dog. The dream came to him so frequently he sometimes saw it in the day when he was working, not just at night when he closed his eyes. What he really wanted was to be able to see the face of the woman in his dream. Whenever he thought it was about to be revealed, he'd wake up and visions of Brenna would fill his head.

Thoughts of Brenna made him grin. He hoped to see her at the store today. Last Friday was her final day at the office and she mentioned she'd be spending more time helping Avery and Letty rearrange their spaces while they waited for him to finish construction on hers.

Avery's flower and gift shop section as well as Letty's portion of the store were finally done. The project was taking much longer than it should due to a very picky electrical inspector. He found fault with everything they did and made them redo things that were done correctly the first time just because he could. If

Brock didn't know better, it seemed like the man had a personal vendetta against him, but he'd never met him before.

Maybe he'd pay a visit to Greg and see if he could shed some light on the subject since the inspector had mentioned being a good friend of his.

Waiting a moment to see if the dog would return, Brock went back inside, finished his coffee along with the sports section then left for Letty's store. He arrived before his crew and soon was absorbed in his work. At seven-thirty, when the rest of his guys arrived, Brock was already knee deep in that day's project. The guys laughed and joked as they worked throughout the morning and when they stopped for lunch, they were in good spirits.

Brenna came by bearing a platter full of hearty sandwiches and Brock took time to sit down and visit with her while he ate. She left a plate of cookies for his crew on a table in the corner along with a cooler of soda and water bottles. She went upstairs to visit with Avery while the guys returned to the business of creating her bistro space.

Back into the rhythm of his work after the lunch break, Brock looked up at the jingling bell on the door announcing a customer. Instead of someone interested in shopping, Brock held back a sigh as the inspector sauntered through the doors.

"Perfect, just perfect," Brock muttered to himself as he walked over to the inspector. Putting on a friendly smile, he greeted the man. "Afternoon, Will. Anything we can help you with?"

"Not today. I'm here to see Brenna," Will said, looking around the store. When he found out Brenna was dating the construction guy, it made him see red. Will knew if he gave her enough time and space, she'd come to her senses and take him back, but he was getting tired of waiting. Now that she seemed to be quite taken with the brawny and charming Brock McCrae, Will was desperate to win her back.

Knowing it was wrong, he continued to hold up the project by making ridiculous demands, hoping Letty, Avery and Brenna would think it was Brock's shoddy work causing the problems. So far, they didn't seem to be casting the blame for the delays at the construction guy and were instead looking at him.

"She's with Avery," Brock said, pointing up the stairs, not liking the possessive way Will said Brenna's name. If Will knew to find her at the store it meant he was more than a casual acquaintance. Brock felt jealousy twist his gut and he struggled to keep it in check. Was Brenna dating someone else? Was she playing some kind of game with him?

Without saying a word, Will climbed the stairs. He was only gone a minute when Brock heard the thud of fast footfalls and glanced up to see Brenna running down the stairs, Will right behind her. Not stopping to say goodbye, she hustled out the door slamming it in Will's face. Will wrenched it open and followed after Brenna.

Knowing he couldn't fight Brenna's battles for her, Brock decided to leave her alone. He lasted almost a minute before he hurried outside. Looking up the street, his gaze narrowed when he saw Will holding Brenna in his arms, kissing her fully on the mouth. Shocked, he stood rooted to the spot, overwhelmed with feelings of betrayal and anger. Trying to talk himself out of confronting the lovers, he watched as Brenna jerked away and swiped her hand across her mouth in disgust. Despite what he thought, Brenna was obviously not enjoying Will's attentions.

In a few quick strides, Brock pushed Will away from Brenna with a threatening look.

"I suggest you not do that again," Brock said,

easing Brenna behind him while glaring at the inspector. If things had been delayed before, Brock knew this confrontation wasn't going to help his cause any.

"Get out of my way," Will said, trying to reach around Brock to grab Brenna's arm.

Brock could feel her hands on his belt as she moved with him, keeping out of Will's reach.

"I don't think that's a good idea," Brock said, stepping to the side as he again blocked Will from Brenna. "What's your problem, man?"

"My problem is that you seem to be chasing after my girl," Will said, still trying to reach Brenna.

"Your girl?" Brock said, stunned by his statement as he shielded Brenna from Will.

"Yes, my girl," Will said, glaring at Brock with loathing in his eyes. "She's been mine since she was sixteen."

"You're sure about that? You sure that's what Brenna wants?" Brock asked, feeling intense jealousy as a gnawing sense of worry began to eat away at him. He took a step closer to Will, muscles tense and fists clenched.

"She belongs to me," Will said, avoiding a direct answer to the question, poking Brock in the chest.

"No, she's mine," Brock said, sounding every bit as possessive and childish as Will when he poked him back.

"She is right here and perfectly capable of speaking for herself," Brenna said, shoving between the two men who were acting more like preschoolers. Listening to them discuss who she belonged to had made her boiling mad. She wasn't a possession they could lay claim to or fight over. "I don't belong to either of you, for your information, you idiots. You two are just… oh!"

Brenna stormed off down the street toward her car. Getting in, she drove off before either man could say anything.

"You stay away from her," Brock said in warning, as Will watched Brenna leave.

"Yeah, whatever," Will said, walking toward his car.

Clenching his jaw until his teeth ached, Brock finally sighed and went back to work. At least he had a better idea of what the inspector didn't like about him. They were both in love with the same girl.

~◇~

"They did what?" Avery asked when Brenna phoned her a while later to see if Brock had calmed down.

If she hadn't been so angry with Will in the first place, then annoyed by both men talking about her like she was a pack of baseball cards they were going to fight over, she would have reassured Brock she was not interested in Will.

Giving herself some time to cool down once she arrived home, Brenna realized she didn't dispute what Will claimed. She worried that would only encourage him to continue hounding her while making Brock question her interest in their relationship.

"They stood on the sidewalk and argued about which one I belonged to," Brenna said with a disgusted sigh. "Both of them acted like complete idiots."

"I'd say," Avery said, unable to hide the hint of humor in her voice. "I hope you set them both straight."

"I made it known I didn't belong to either of them and left in a bit of a snit, which I realize now was not the best way to handle things. Can you please ask Greg to quit talking to Will about me? I know they're friends, but this is ridiculous. The only way he would have known I'd be at the store today was if Greg told him,"

Brenna said, trying not to lump her brother-in-law in with all the men who were on her hit list today, but it was hard not to.

"I'll remind him, again," Avery said. Greg and Will weren't as close as they had once been. Will had been acting bizarre for a while and neither Avery nor Greg enjoyed being around him. Greg maintained the friendship more out of a sense of duty than anything else but maybe it was time to gently let it go. Will often seemed obsessed with Brenna and Avery now wondered if that obsession was reaching an unhealthy level. The fact of the matter was that Will seemed much more interested in Brenna since she started dating Brock than he ever was when she had been dating him, which was years ago.

"I'd appreciate it. In the meantime, if you see Brock could you tell him I'm not interested in Will? The only thing about that dork that interests me is him staying out of my life," Brenna said, slamming things around the kitchen as she made dinner for her family.

"I'll find him before he leaves. I could ask him to join us for dinner, if you want, since you're cooking for all of us," Avery said, knowing Brenna could find her way to Brock's heart through her cooking, although at this point, she didn't think it would take much effort on her sister's part.

"Sure, if he wants to come, that's fine. I'll make plenty," Brenna said, warming to the idea of Brock coming for dinner. "Thanks, Avery. See you in a little while."

Avery gathered her things to leave the store a few minutes after five and found Brock working away in what would be Brenna's bistro kitchen. By the tense line of his shoulders and the muscle working in his jaw, she assumed he was probably still upset from the little escapade with Will and Brenna.

"Hey, Brock, have you got a minute?" Avery asked over the sound of his drill.

Cutting the power, Brock turned to her with a smile that didn't come close to reaching his eyes. "Hi, Avery. What can I do for you?"

"Brenna called and wanted me to extend an invitation to you for dinner tonight. Greg and I are going over as well. She's been cooking all afternoon, so it should be good," Avery said with an encouraging smile.

"Thanks, but I think I better pass," Brock said, staring down at his dusty boots. As mad as Brenna was earlier, and as poorly as he'd handled the situation, Brock thought he should probably give her a little time and space.

"If you're wondering about what Will said, I wouldn't let it get to you. He's not exactly rational when it comes to Brenna and it seems to be getting worse," Avery said, placing a hand on Brock's arm. His gaze returned to her face. "Rennie said she's sorry she didn't make it clear today to you both that she's not interested in Will. For whatever reason, she seems pretty taken with this construction guy she met a few months ago."

"She is, huh?" Brock said, feeling his tense muscles loosen and his humor return. "You're not kidding me are you?"

"I, sir, would not kid about such serious matters as the state of my sister's heart," Avery said, holding a hand to her own heart. "Seriously, though, she's crazy about you. Come to dinner. If nothing else, you might as well enjoy a good meal and some entertaining company."

"You talked me into it," Brock said, waving at Avery as she walked to the door.

He finished up a few things, stored the tools and cleaned up the work area. He met Letty at the door as she locked it and walked with her to her car.

"I hear you've been invited for dinner," Letty said with a glint in her eye. Her desire for matchmaking between Brock and Brenna was strong, although it hadn't taken much effort on her part since the two of them seemed drawn to each other without any of her help. "Are you joining us?"

"Yes, ma'am," Brock said, holding open her car door. "Do I have time to run home and change?"

"You bet," Letty said, smiling up at Brock as she sat in the car. "We'll eat at six."

Brock hurried to his pickup, rushed home and in the back door, then jumped in the shower. He shaved in record time, put on clean clothes and slapped on after shave. Running his fingers through his sun-kissed hair, he decided to let it be tousled and grabbed his keys, cell phone and wallet before hustling back out the door. He pulled up at the Smith house with five minutes to spare.

Ringing the bell, he offered a friendly greeting when Brandon opened it and invited him inside.

"How are you, sir?" Brock asked, shaking the hand that was offered to him.

"I'm well, Brock. How have you been?" Brandon asked, motioning Brock into the family room where the evening news was on the television. "Brenna said you're whipping that house of yours into shape."

"I'm trying," Brock said, sitting down on the couch while Brandon eased into his recliner. Although he inherited some nice furniture from his grandfather, Brock decided the next thing he needed to buy was a big, comfy recliner. "Thanks to some good help, I've got the kitchen done. My next project is the master suite. Brenna is pretty handy with a paint brush so she's helped me paint most of the other rooms."

"She's a good worker, unless you make her mad. Then you better just stay out of her way," Brandon said with a teasing grin. He'd heard about the man-card incident as well as Brenna losing her cool with the guys today.

"She does seem to have a bit of a temper," Brock said carefully. A smart man knew better than to say anything that could later be used against him, especially by a girl's dad.

"A bit? Obviously she held back from unleashing it in full force if you only think she's got a bit of a temper. Why that girl can..." Brandon was interrupted by Avery stepping into the room to announce dinner was ready.

Brock followed Brandon to the dining room where Brenna shot him a shy smile as she placed a basket of hot rolls on the table.

During the meal, which was a succulent pork roast with creamy polenta, sautéed apples, roasted squash, fresh home-made rolls and a delicious lemon meringue pie for dessert, the conversation ranged from progress on the store to the experiments Greg was conducting with some new varieties of plants.

Brock marveled at how comfortable he felt with these people and how easy the conversation flowed between them. He could see himself sitting around this table for many meals in the years to come, especially when he felt Brenna's hand squeeze his beneath the table.

She looked up at him from beneath her long lashes and his heart tripped in his chest.

Helping carry the dishes back to the kitchen after the meal, Greg and Brock offered to clean up while the women looked through a box of Brenna's bistro serving pieces that arrived that day.

"I hear Will gave you some trouble today," Greg said as he handed Brock plates to load in the dishwasher.

"More so Brenna, I guess," Brock said, not sure he wanted to discuss this with Greg, knowing his friendship with Will.

"She's not interested in him, just so you know. She hasn't been for a long, long time. Will seems to be having a hard time admitting defeat and moving on," Greg said as they finished loading the dishwasher and wiped down the counters. "Don't let him bother you."

"Thanks, I'll try not to," Brock said, glad to hear that Brenna really wasn't dating Will on the side.

"Will hasn't been acting quite himself for a while," Greg said, as he dried his hands. "He's just about worn out his welcome at our house. I know he certainly has here."

"Do you know if Will would compromise his professional standards in an effort to get back at me?" Brock asked, deciding to see if Greg had any idea how far Will would push things.

"What do you mean?" Greg asked, leaning against the counter.

"He's the electrical inspector on our project and I've never had an inspector be so particular. He made our electrician redo part of Avery's project three times when, by all industry standards, it should have passed inspection the first time. That's why we're running behind with the project. He keeps slowing us down," Brock said. He knew Greg would be able to tell if Will was capable of sabotaging the project.

"Interesting," Greg said, mulling over what Brock said. A year ago, he would have said no, Will would never do anything like that. But after seeing him and listening to him the past few months, he wouldn't be surprised if he was trying to hold back the project and make it look like Brock was incompetent. "I'll keep my eyes and ears open. Can you request a different inspector?"

"I can," Brock said, thinking tomorrow he would give one of his friends a call and see if he could get a different inspector assigned to their job.

"That might be best," Greg said then slapped Brock on the back. "Shall we go make over Brenna's new dishes like Mom and Avery? According to the women, they are 'gorgeous.' Although I'm not sure that is a term I'd apply to something that will hold messy sandwiches and plates of muffins."

Brock laughed and followed Greg to the dining room where serving pieces covered the table and the Smith women discussed the virtues of each dish.

When he walked in the room, Brenna caught his eye and gave him a look that said she was glad he was there. After a few more minutes of admiring the dishes, Greg and Avery went home and Letty disappeared saying she had things to do, leaving Brock and Brenna alone.

"Care to go for a walk?" Brock asked, trying to keep his hands to himself when he really wanted to pull Brenna into his arms and apologize for behaving childishly that afternoon.

"I'd love to," Brenna said, preceding him out the front door and down to the sidewalk. They started to amble along when Brock reached down and captured Brenna's hand in his.

Turning her big baby blue eyes on him, he brought her hand to his lips and kissed her palm with tenderness.

"I'm sorry, coffee girl," Brock said with sincerity. Brenna raised an eyebrow at him, but he continued. "I behaved badly today and I'm sorry. You aren't a possession and I had no right to speak of you as such."

"Apology accepted," Brenna said, using her free hand to reach over and squeeze Brock's bicep. The feel of those strong muscles beneath her fingers made her stomach flutter, but she didn't relinquish her hold. "I'm sorry I failed to make it perfectly clear to you both that I'm not interested in Will. I hope you know I didn't want him to kiss me."

"I know, Brenna. Greg said he'd talk to Will, but if

he gives you any trouble, let me know," Brock said in a tone that still carried a protective edge.

"I'll think about it," Brenna said with a sigh. She studied Brock surreptitiously as they walked along, enjoying the beautiful spring evening. Thinking about how she would feel if she caught him in the arms of an old girlfriend, with their lips together, she realized she would have been blistering mad at both him and the woman.

Leaning her cheek against his arm, he smiled down at her, flashing his white teeth and crinkling the corners of his eyes. She loved that smile. She loved the way he made her feel. She loved being with him and acknowledged she was completely and irrevocably in love with Brock.

When had that happened? She didn't know that she could put a finger on the exact moment, but somewhere between drooling after him at the coffee shop and him taking her out for German food, Brenna had fallen in love.

Brock was everything she'd ever hoped for in a man. He was funny and smart as well as handsome. As hard as he worked, he'd be a good provider and his gentle strength hinted that he'd be good with children. He could be a little domineering and over protective, but she thought his charm and tenderness compensated for those faults.

Thinking of the dream that had long haunted her, Brenna was beginning to wonder if the man in it was Brock. Although she couldn't see the man's face, the back, wide shoulders, even the color of his hair all made her think of Brock.

"What's that look for?" Brock asked, letting go of her hand so he could place an arm around her shoulders and pull her closer to him as they walked.

"What look?"

"The look that has you all dewy-eyed and made your face so soft," Brock said in a husky voice, stopping in front of a huge tree and caressing her cheek with his thumb. "A look like that is a strong temptation, hard for a man to ignore."

"Oh, I..." Brenna searched for some explanation but before she could find one, Brock was kissing her. Not a chaste standing on the sidewalk just blocks from her parents house kind of kiss, but one meant to dissolve her into a pliant mass. When the second car honked as they drove by, Brenna grasped onto her remaining shred of common sense and pulled away. "Brock, I think we better head back to Mom and Dad's."

"I think you're probably right," Brock said, his voice low and raspy with emotion. If Brenna looked any more alluring, he wasn't sure he could continue to keep his desire for her under control.

Her hair was down and hanging in lovely curls along her back and she wore a silky blouse with a soft floral print skirt. She looked so utterly feminine and smelled so good, it was hard for him to focus on putting one foot in front of the other to retrace their steps.

"Do you have plans Friday night?" Brock asked as they stood at the end of the walk at her mom and dad's house.

"Well, I was really hoping this cute construction guy would ask me on a date, but if he doesn't get around to it, I guess my evening will be open," Brenna said with a teasing smile.

"In that case, I'll take my leave," Brock said darkly, taking a step away from Brenna. "I wouldn't want to mess up your plans."

"You just get back here, buster," Brenna said, lunging at Brock and managing to get in a few tickles before he easily pinned her arms across her torso and held her with her back to his chest. Brock was laughing as she struggled half-heartedly against him until she suddenly went limp.

Sweeping her into his arms, his laughing tone changed to one of worry, as her arms dangled down and her head flopped against his shoulder. "Brenna? Baby, are you okay?"

He hurried up the steps and was just about to ring the bell to bring Letty to the door when Brenna went from limp to having her hands on his face, pulling him down for a kiss. Brock nearly dropped her in surprise.

"Got you," she whispered with her lips just a breath of space from Brock's.

"You scared me half to death and almost got dropped on your cute little backside is what you got, miss smarty pants," Brock said with a disapproving glare, although he pulled her closer instead of setting her down. "I could have a heart condition, you know. You may have given me a coronary. That was so not nice."

"I'm sorry," Brenna said, not feeling very remorseful as she twined her fingers behind Brock's neck and played with his hair while he held her tight against his chest. "I didn't mean to scare you and I promise I won't do that particular thing again."

"I'm not sure I liked the way you said that. It sounds like you'll be plotting further evil, just not an exact repeat," Brock said, a wary look on his face. Brenna was so much fun, he just never knew what to expect from her, even if she sometimes frightened him. He really did think she'd passed out a minute ago.

"Would I do that?" Brenna asked, batting her lashes at him and flashing her big baby blue eyes.

"You certainly would, you little imp," Brock said, setting her down on the porch. "Now, about that date Friday. If your super busy calendar isn't overflowing, can you pencil me in?"

"I'll see what I can do. If I'm ready at six, does that

work for you?" Brenna asked, still looking at him flirtatiously.

"That would be great," Brock said, kissing her cheek and turning her toward the door. He popped her bottom and grinned when she gazed at him over her shoulder.

"Maybe I can get you to call me baby again," Brenna said softly with a look of promise before running in the house.

Brock shook his head as he got in his pickup and headed home.

One thing was for certain, life with Brenna in it would never, ever be boring.

Chapter Eleven

At five minutes to six, Brock pulled up outside the Smith residence and did a quick check in the rearview mirror to make sure he looked presentable. He was in a rush after work to get cleaned up and was trying to if he used mouthwash or combed his hair. Thoughts of Brenna had him so befuddled, it was a wonder he could remember how to tie his shoes.

A glance in the mirror confirmed his hair was combed and the mint he popped in his mouth assured fresh breath. Getting out of his recently washed pickup, he whistled his way to the front door and rang the bell.

Brenna answered and took his breath away. She wore a dress in a pale shade of pink that made her skin look like porcelain and her eyes twice as huge. Her hair hung down her back and she carried a sweater on her arm. As she smiled at him and took a step closer her scent, the smell of spring and sunshine, flooded his senses.

"Hi, Brenna. You look lovely," he said, kissing her cheek and placing a warm hand on her arm. "Are you ready to go?"

"Yep," Brenna said, picking up her purse from the bench just inside the front door and calling to her parents. "I'm leaving. You two enjoy your evening."

Brock heard an answering call of "have a great time" as he ushered Brenna out the door and down the steps to his pickup.

"Wow, shiny clean truck. Lookin' good, construction man," Brenna said as he held the door and helped her in. He was really going to have to install running boards one of these days, but for now he'd rather have the pleasure of helping Brenna in and out of the pickup.

"Glad my efforts were noticed," Brock said as he ran around to the driver's side and climbed behind the wheel.

"Absolutely," Brenna said, nodding her head. She gave him a jaunty grin and stretched across the cab to place a hand on his cheek. "All your efforts were noticed and appreciated."

Brock turned to her with heat filling his hazel eyes and Brenna watched them turn more gold than green or blue. Leaning back in her seat, she fussed with the skirt of her dress and dug in her purse for some imaginary item until she could calm her fluttering stomach.

Although she was teasing Brock, the minute she opened the door to see him standing there with a charming smile all for her, she felt her knees weaken while her pulse seemed to pick up speed with every beat. He wore a polo shirt and newer jeans with hiking boots. His hair glistened with highlights from his time spent in the sun while that same time spent outdoors had turned his face and arms an appealing shade of bronze. Muscles were clearly defined beneath the light fabric of his blue shirt and his unique manly scent invaded her nose.

Glad he was driving, Brenna wasn't sure she could have gotten a mile down the road without wrecking the car as distracted as she was by Brock. Not sure how it was possible, she was convinced he got better looking every time she saw him.

As they drove out of Silverton and headed toward Salem, Brenna wondered what Brock had planned for the evening. He was dressed casually, so she hoped hiking hadn't been on the agenda because even though the heels she wore were low, they weren't meant for long walks.

"So, what exotic locale are you whisking me off to this evening?" Brenna asked, trying not to stare at the muscles in Brock's arms as he held the steering wheel.

"I'll have you know I'm not that kind of boy, coffee girl. Who said anything about an erotic locale? Have you been browsing in the naughty book section of the bookstore?" Brock said with a wicked grin.

"Exotic! Exotic, you idiot," Brenna said in exasperation, smacking her forehead with her hand.

"Pardon me. I guess I misunderstood," Brock teased as he captured Brenna's hand in his and brought it to his lips.

"You most certainly did," Brenna huffed, jerking her hand back from him. She let him wonder just for a minute if she was really upset before she gave him a saucy grin and put her hand back in his.

"What's on the agenda for the evening? Or is it a big secret?"

"A surprise," Brock said, keeping his eye on the road.

"What kind of surprise?"

"If I told you that, it wouldn't be a surprise and would defeat the entire purpose of the evening," Brock said, sending her a devilish grin. "No more questions."

"Well, fine, then. Just be that way," Brenna said, turning up the radio as they drove west.

Unable to stay quiet, Brenna asked Brock about his family, he told her about the dog with the jar on his head, and they discussed events coming up in the town. Brock asked if she wanted to come by the house the next day to see the progress he was making on the new master suite and she asked him if he and the guys would like to do some taste testing the following week.

Watching with interest as Brock pulled up at a restaurant, Brenna looked at him and smiled. It was a diner known for its 1950s food and atmosphere.

"No way," she said, as Brock found a parking space and turned off the truck.

"Way," he said as he ran around and helped her out. "Have you eaten here before?"

"No, but I've heard about it. This is great, Brock," Brenna said, squeezing his hand as they walked inside.

Finding an empty booth, they placed orders for burgers, breaded fries and super-thick milkshakes.

They both commented on the fun atmosphere and good food. They sat and watched a few couples dancing to fifties music before paying their bill and leaving.

"Thank you so much. That was just awesome," Brenna said as Brock helped her into the truck.

"You're welcome. If you aren't ready to call it a night, I've got another surprise," Brock said before running around to the driver's side and sliding behind the wheel.

"Then by all means, please continue with the adventure," Brenna said, waving her hand regally making Brock laugh.

Driving further west out of Salem, Brenna was surprised to see they were headed toward the small town of Dallas.

"Are we going where I think we're going?" Brenna asked with a big grin, sure she had figured out their next destination.

"Where do you think I'm taking you?" Brock asked, trying to keep from smiling.

"Somewhere that involves parked cars, buckets of popcorn and a big movie screen," Brenna said, her anticipation growing when she could see by Brock's face that she guessed correctly.

"Ding, ding, ding. Give the lady a prize," Brock

said, pointing at her with a big smile. "How'd you guess?"

"Well, a fifties diner for dinner and we're headed toward Dallas. Unless they've had a major population boom and added a lot of interesting things to see I haven't heard about, the only reason I could surmise we'd be going there is for a drive-in movie. Isn't that what you do on a fifties date?"

"So it is," Brock said, still grinning as they turned off the road and joined the line of cars waiting to get into the drive in. "Have you been to the drive-in before?"

"Dad took us a few times when we were younger and I went once when I was in high school to the one near Newberg," Brenna said, looking around at the other cars. It was a double feature and Brenna felt like clapping her hands in excitement. "I'm so glad you thought of this Brock."

"Me, too," Brock said, unable to take his gaze from Brenna. Her cheeks glowed pink, her big eyes sparkled like twin sapphires and she was absolutely radiant. He could care less about the movie, but he liked the idea of being locked in the pickup with his arm around her for a few hours under the cover of darkness. Trying to remember the lecture he'd given himself about behaving like a gentleman, he knew it was going to be a long evening of maintaining control and keeping his wits about him.

Pulling into a space with a great view of the screen, Brock told Brenna to sit tight and disappeared in the direction of the concession stand. The movie previews were starting to play when he returned with a big bucket of buttery popcorn, a large Dr. Pepper and a bottle of water.

"Are you ready for this?" he asked, as she sat still buckled in her seat on the far side of his truck.

"Absolutely," Brenna said with her eyes on the

screen.

"I don't think you are," Brock said, shaking his head. Ignoring Brenna's look of confusion, Brock released her seat belt, stuck one hand beneath her legs and the other behind her back and drew her across the seat to sit next to him.

"Now you're ready," Brock said, putting his arm around her and kissing her temple.

Nestled against Brock's side, Brenna suddenly lost interest in the movie as she inhaled his wonderful scent and got lost in the golden depths of his eyes.

"Brenna?" Brock asked softly, not allowing himself the pleasure of falling into her magnetic gaze.

"Hmm?"

"Are you going to watch the movie?"

"Yeah."

"Then you're going to have to look at the screen, sweetheart," Brock said, gently turning her face from his toward the front of the pickup.

Brenna blushed and laid her head on Brock's shoulder, releasing a sigh. He rubbed her arm and kissed the top of her head before they both turned their attention to the movie.

As the last credits for the second movie rolled across the screen, Brenna was feeling contented and lighthearted. If she was a cat, she would definitely have purred.

"What did you think, coffee girl?" Brock asked and Brenna looked up at him with half-lidded eyes making his blood shoot through him in hot bursts.

"I think we need to do this again sometime. It was wonderful, Brock. Thank you," she said, placing a soft hand on his chest and leaning forward to give him a kiss on his chin. Brock tipped his head down at the last second and captured her lips in a kiss that was deep, intense and thorough.

Brenna brought her other hand up and placed it behind his neck while he ran his hands up and down her back, branding her skin through her dress.

Tightening his arms around her, Brock was frustrated with the gear shift in their way, and started to scoot to the other side of the pickup when he realized he was about to get carried away. Pulling Brenna's hands from around his neck, he kissed the backs of each one before setting her away from him and running a hand over his face.

"Baby, if you keep kissing me like that, I can't promise to get you home tonight. I think we better hit the road," Brock said, straightening up in his seat and buckling his seat belt.

Brenna blinked at him as reality sank back in and he could see her embarrassment, even in the darkness. Without saying a word, she slid back to her side of the pickup, fastened her seat belt and folded her hands primly in her lap.

They were quiet most of the way home with tension hanging thick between them. Brock wished Brenna would say something, anything, but was afraid to shatter the silence. When he glanced over at her, she had her eyes closed and appeared to be asleep. Her head was turned toward him and rested against the back of the seat. Her slightly parted lips were an invitation Brock found hard to resist so he turned his attention back to the road.

When he stopped the truck in front of her house, he sighed before unfastening his seat belt.

"Brenna, we're home," Brock said quietly as he squeezed her hand. He hated to wake her up but knew he had to. What he really wanted was to take her home with him, but that was a thought he derailed before it gathered any more steam. "Hey, coffee girl, rise and shine."

Watching her eyes flutter open and focus on him,

Brenna gave him a sleepy smile that turned his already hot insides molten.

"Hey. Sorry, I didn't mean to fall asleep," Brenna said as she sat up and released the seat belt.

"No problem, although I did miss your non-stop chatter in my ear on the way home," Brock teased, trying to keep the moment light.

"Chatter, huh? I'll remember that for future reference," Brenna said, gathering her sweater and purse before leaning across the seat toward Brock. "Thank you for another amazing evening, Brock. I really enjoyed it."

"I'm glad. I did, too," he said, taking her face in his hands and giving her one last kiss that was meant to be brief and chaste although it quickly turned into something more. When they broke apart they were both breathless. Before he changed his mind, Brock jumped out of the truck and ran around to open her door and help her down. Walking her to the front door, he kissed her cheek and gave her a tight hug. "Thank you, Brenna, for going with me."

"Anytime, Brock," Brenna said, opening the door. She blew him a kiss and whispered, "Thanks for the sweet dreams."

Brock caught her kiss in his hand and pressed it to his cheek, making her giggle as she shut the door. He was still grinning as he drove off toward his dark, empty house.

Chapter Twelve

"Look, there he is," Brock said, pointing to the stray dog he helped out of his head jar. He and Brenna sat on the back porch drinking coffee the next morning when Brock noticed the dog watching them from the edge of the back yard.

"Oh, Brock, he looks so pathetic. Can we feed him?" Brenna asked, slowly sitting forward in her chair, trying to get a better look at the dog.

"I've got some lunch meat we can put out, but I'm not sure he'll let us get close to him," Brock said, easing out of his chair and going into the house. He came back with a package of sliced ham and made a trail from the porch out toward the dog.

When he got about three feet away from the canine, it backed up and hunkered down by the creek bank, trying to hide. Brock returned to the kitchen, getting the dog a bowl of water and filling another with milk. He quietly set them at the base of the porch steps.

Taking Brenna's hand, they went inside the house, and watched from the kitchen window.

It only took a few minutes before the dog inched his way to the meat and devoured the pieces close to him. Following the trail, he ate it all and discovered the bowl of milk, which he lapped at greedily. He slurped from the water bowl then looked around for more food.

"The poor thing," Brenna whispered, clenching Brock's hand. When she looked up at him with tears in her eyes, he felt his heart melting. He was already prepared to champion the dog, but seeing tears glisten in Brenna's bright blue eyes made him want to slay dragons for her.

"I'll run to the store and get some dog food," Brock said, kissing her temple. "You want to keep an eye on our dirty little friend?"

"Sure," Brenna said, barely aware Brock had left her side as she gazed at the scrawny mutt.

The dog flopped down by the empty bowls and looked around warily before settling his chin on his front paws.

Ransacking Brock's cupboards, Brenna found a pouch of tuna fish and opened it. Standing at the screen door, Brenna started talking softly to the dog. He lifted an ear but didn't raise his head. She took that as a good sign and continued carrying on a quiet dialogue as she carefully opened the screen door and slid outside onto one of the wicker chairs Brock placed on the back porch.

When the dog lifted his head and looked at her, Brenna was afraid he would run, but he settled back down when she continued talking, not making any move to get closer to him. With slow, easy movements, she pulled the tuna from behind her and fished out a few chunks, gently tossing it toward the dog. He jumped at the movement, then sniffed to find the pieces.

Looking at her with big, hungry eyes, he took a step toward her with his head down and tail tucked between his legs.

Smiling, Brenna kept talking as she tossed out a few more chunks of the tuna, placing it closer to her. The dog took a tentative step forward and lapped up the fish. They played this game until Brenna dropped the last chunks near her feet and the dog stood staring at her with fear in his eyes.

Hunkering down he stretched as far as he could and

snagged the tuna then jumped down the steps, resuming his place by the water bowl. She heard Brock's truck return and went back in the house, washing the tuna from her fingers as Brock came in with a huge bag of dog food on one shoulder and two grocery bags in his hand.

"What all did you buy?" Brenna asked with a laugh as she took the bags from him.

"Just a few things for the mutt," Brock said, taking the dog food outside to the porch. Opening the bag, he filled the bowl that had held the milk and set it back by the empty water dish before stepping onto the porch next to Brenna.

"I fed him some tuna," she said quietly, watching to see what the dog would do next. "He came all the way up here to get the last bite. I don't think he's mean, just hungry."

"I agree," Brock said, holding her hand as the dog nosed the bowl of food and began crunching his way through it. "But we should still be careful."

They talked quietly while the dog ate, wondering where he came from and how hard it would be to tame him. When the mutt finished eating every last crumb in the bowl, he flopped down with a sigh and appeared to go to sleep in the warm morning sunshine.

"I guess you'll have to take that as a thank you," Brenna said with a grin as the dog grunted in his sleep. His belly looked bloated with food as he stretched on his side.

"Someone needs to teach him some manners," Brock teased, pulling Brenna to her feet. "Let's leave him in peace to get some beauty rest while I show you what I accomplished this week."

Brock moved the dog food inside the kitchen door to keep the mutt from getting into it and then showed Brenna the progress he was making on the master suite.

While they stood in the room, envisioning what the finished product would look like, Brenna found herself wishing it would be her that shared the house, that room, with Brock.

"You've made a lot of progress in the last week," Brenna said, admiring the sheet-rocked walls and the newly installed windows.

"Uncle Andy's been coming over most evenings to help," Brock said, watching Brenna as she walked around the room. He needed to finish this room quickly because any time he was in it, he envisioned Brenna sharing it with him. "Not only does he work circles around me, he provides a lot of entertaining conversation."

Brenna smiled. "If he's anything like his nephew, I'm sure there's never a dull moment."

"You know it," Brock said, walking to Brenna and placing a gentle hand on her shoulder.

"It's going to be wonderful, construction man, but I wouldn't expect any less from you," Brenna said, offering Brock a look that made his already pounding heart go into double time. Leading her back toward the kitchen, he had to get out of the bedroom before his wayward thoughts got the best of him.

"Thanks, coffee girl," Brock said, kissing her cheek as they wandered out to the front yard where Brenna helped him tame the flower beds.

Down on their hands and knees, pulling weeds and planting some shrubs, they soon got in a fight tossing pieces of bark at each other. When Brock came at Brenna with a handful of weeds, threatening to dump them down her shirt, she ducked her head and shrieked.

A blur of mottled fur came around the corner of the house with teeth bared, and forced itself between Brock and Brenna. Snarling, the dog glowered at Brock until he dropped the weeds and took a step back.

"So much for not biting the hand that feeds you, mutt," Brock said, surprised by the dog's protection of Brenna. "Don't make any sudden moves, Brenna, until we see what he's going to do."

Dropping down to his belly, the dog whined when he felt the threat of danger to Brenna was past. Rolling to his side, he exposed his neck in a submissive move. Brock carefully took a step toward the dog, talking softly to him. He gently placed a hand on the dog's back and waited for the dog to snap or bite. When he didn't, Brock started stroking the dog's back, continuing to talk to him.

"Hey, Mutt, are you ready to be friends, now?" Brock asked, working his way slowly toward the dog's head. "We won't hurt you, boy, but we'd like to help you."

Brenna sat observing Brock's gentle touch with the dog and knew here was a man who would be an excellent father with his patient, easy manner. If she hadn't been in love with him before, seeing the way he nurtured the stray dog would have pushed her over the edge.

Deciding the animal could only welcome one human at a time, Brenna stayed back as Brock worked to win over the dog. When he started scratching the mutt behind his ears, then on his belly, Brenna knew Brock had made a best friend for life. The dog looked at Brock like he was a hero as his tongue lolled out the side of his mouth.

"So, you think I'm a friend and not a foe?" Brock asked the dog as he continued rubbing and scratching him. The dog appeared to be in a state of pure bliss by the goofy expression on his face. Turning to Brenna, Brock grinned and held out a hand. "I think it's safe for you to come pet him if you want to."

"You bet I do," Brenna said, kneeling by the dog

and offering him encouraging words while she rubbed his ears and head. The dog sighed and was perfectly still while they touched him.

"Brock?" Brenna said, turning her head away from the dog.

"Yeah?"

"He really needs a bath."

"I noticed that, coffee girl, but what do you suggest?"

"I'm not sure. I suppose we need to wait a few days until he can trust us before we get too carried away," Brenna said, trying to breathe through her mouth to avoid the dog's stench.

"That's probably a good idea," Brock said, getting to his feet and pulling Brenna up with him. The dog opened one eye and watched them before returning to his nap.

Later that afternoon, Brenna was in the backyard with a hose watering some of the flowers she'd helped Brock plant the previous weekend. The dog seemed to love the water, chasing the stream as Brenna sprayed it, jumping through the droplets.

"Brock, do you have a something we could use as a washtub?" Brenna called toward the back door. Brock stuck his head outside and saw the dog's antics.

"Be right there," he said going to his garage and returning with a big aluminum tub he mostly used as a container to hold ice and drinks when he and the guys held a party.

Filling it part way with hot water and squirting in some soap, he carried it out to the backyard and had Brenna spray in some cool water. When he was satisfied it was just the right temperature, they tried to coax the dog into the tub.

He ran around them barking and yipping but wouldn't get into it.

"See if he'll chase a stick," Brenna suggested. "If so, you could throw it in the water."

"We can try," Brock said, finding a stick on the creek bank and throwing it for the dog to chase. The mutt quickly retrieved it and brought it back to Brock, wagging his entire rear-end at the game.

Brock threw it a few more times around the backyard, each time getting it closer to the wash tub where Brenna waited. When he threw it in, the dog leaped into the air to catch it just as Brenna stood up to get out of the way. The force of his momentum carried him into the tub with such a huge splash, Brenna was drenched in soapy water, looking like a soggy kitten.

Laughing uproariously, Brock rushed to the tub to keep the dog in and started scrubbing the canine while Brenna pushed dripping curls out of her face.

Her pout turned into a bubble of laughter and soon she was laughing as hard as Brock while they bathed the dog. They were both soaked to the skin by the time they were done, but a much cleaner dog stood looking up at them with a doggy grin.

"Mutt, you don't look half bad without several coats of grime," Brock observed as they looked at the dog. He was still a mutt mix but his coat was mostly white with flecks of tan and brown. One front paw was a reddish brown along with his tail and part of one ear. He barked and gave himself a good shake, further wetting down Brock and Brenna before they could towel him dry.

"Enough, I can't take anymore," Brenna said with a laugh as she got to her feet. "I think I smell worse than the dog now and I know I'm wetter than he is. I'm going home."

"Where's your sense of adventure?" Brock teased, handing her a couple of old towels to dry off with and another to place on the seat of her car.

"It's a little soggy at the moment," Brenna said with a grin as she walked out front and carefully slid into her car. "I'll call you later, construction man. Thanks for another fun day."

"Anytime, coffee girl," Brock said, shutting her door then leaning in the open window to give her a kiss. "Thanks for coming over and helping me tame the wild beast."

Brenna laughed as she drove off and Brock, along with the dog, watched her car until it turned the corner at the end of the street. He noticed the worrisome widows looking his direction and waved with a big smile before returning to clean up the mess in the backyard.

It looked like he finally had himself a dog.

~◇~

After placing ads in the newspaper for a found dog, putting flyers around town and posting a photo of the dog online, Brock decided whoever once owned the mutt no longer wanted him. He took him to the vet for his shots, bought him a name tag and collar, and built the dog a house that was painted the same shade of white with green trim as the house.

Watching Brenna rub her hand lovingly over the dog's head one afternoon, Brock felt a sharp pang of jealousy. He wasn't completely convinced Brenna didn't come to visit the dog instead of him these days, although she did still feed him. Right now he could smell the delicious scent of pastries that would soon come out of the oven as it drifted through the open kitchen window.

When she leaned down and whispered something to Mutt, the dog looked at Brock and gave his happy bark, wagging his tail.

"He said he thinks we should play a game of tag," Brenna said, looking at Brock with a mischievous smile.

"Mutt thinks together we can take you on."

"Is that right? The two of you against me? That doesn't seem quite fair," Brock said, leaning back in his chair and taking a drink of his rich, dark coffee. "Maybe I should go fetch the worrisome widows to help you out, even the odds."

Brenna laughed. "You are so conceited, construction man. You're going down."

"You and whose army is going to take me?" Brock asked, getting up from his chair and pulling Brenna to her feet.

"The army of Mutt," Brenna said, slapping her leg to call the dog and jumping off the porch. She and the dog raced around to the front yard, with Brock hot on their heels. Brenna ran and dodged, squealed and twisted, with Mutt running circles around both the humans, barking and wagging his tail at the fun.

When Brock finally caught Brenna, he wrapped his arms around her and pulled her close. "Gotcha, coffee girl," he said as her chest heaved against his, setting his blood on fire.

"Yes, you do," she said on a whisper, her eyes focusing on his mouth.

Explosions of heat and longing burst between them when his lips touched hers. Brenna drew in a sharp gasp as she realized with perfect clarity the vision in her dreams was this moment in time.

Her dream had always included a beautiful cottage style home in the background as a man with broad shoulders and dark hair held her while a gangly mutt ran around their feet. The smell of coffee and fresh baked pastries hung in the air, along with a hint of cedar and some other scent, Brock's scent. She knew beyond any doubt the man in her dreams had been Brock all along.

"Brock, it's you," she said cryptically, kissing him with a growing fervor in front of the dog, the worrisome widows, and anyone who cared to look down the street.

"Of course, it's me," Brock said against her lips. "Who else did you expect?"

Brenna smiled and sighed in contentment, resting her head on his shoulder.

Raising her eyes to his, she looked at him with such heat, such love, Brock found it hard to catch his breath.

"I love you," Brenna said, throwing her arms around his neck and hugging him close.

Pushing her back so he could look into her face, Brock wasn't sure he heard her correctly. He needed to hear the words again to be sure.

"Would you mind repeating that?" he asked quietly, hoping she would.

Surprised she had let the words escape her lips, Brenna looked at Brock, considering his request. She could see in his face he merely wanted confirmation that she meant what she said.

Standing on tiptoe, she pulled his head down so his ear was close to her lips and whispered, "I love you, Brock McCrae."

"I love you, Brenna, my lovely coffee girl," Brock said, grasping her waist in his big hands and swinging her around and around in the yard, making her giggle.

The worrisome widows stood at the end of Mrs. Phillips walk to see what all the commotion was about. Looking at the young couple, they merely shook their heads. Mrs. Hearst was grinning broadly while Mrs. Phillips worked to contain her smile.

Seeing them outside, Brock waved one hand at them, before sweeping Brenna into his arms and carrying her inside the house.

"That will surely give them something to gossip about for at least a week," Brenna said as Brock set her down in the living room.

"Maybe two," Brock said, nuzzling her neck as his

hands toyed with her hair. He was swooping in for another kiss when Brenna popped her eyes open wide and ran through the house to the kitchen. Brock followed and arrived just in time to see her pull the pan of pastries from the oven.

"Saved, just in the nick of time," she said with a grin, setting the pastries on a hot pad on the counter. "You'll have to learn not to distract me when I'm cooking or things can burn in a hurry."

"It's a chance I'm willing to take," Brock said, as he tugged her closer for another sizzling kiss. With her declaration of love, who cared about a few burned berry tarts?

Chapter Thirteen

"Boss, she's here," one of Brock's construction crew said as they watched for Brenna to come in the shop with their morning sustenance. If they had no more delays, the bistro should be ready to open in just a few weeks, right on time.

While McCrae's Construction labored on the bistro, Brenna worked to perfect her recipes and often brought samples for the crew. She told them they were providing her a great service by being taste-testers. They thought she was an angel with the ability to turn ordinary ingredients into extraordinary wonders of palatable bliss.

Brock smiled thinking how every last one of his rough and tumble crew would do anything for his lovely little coffee girl.

The workers stopped what they were doing and watched to see what treat Brenna would share with them this morning. Brock was as eager as any of them to eat her creations but he always waited until the other guys had their fill before taking his share.

Brenna's eyes lit with pleasure as she saw Brock and the look she gave him sent heat spiraling from his head right down to his boot-clad feet.

He had no idea when he took this job that he'd end up falling in love with the girl who wanted to open a bistro. Of course, he also had no idea that it was the same girl who had captivated him from the coffee shop. Brock normally stopped at another shop but he recalled with clarity the particular day he had missed the exit for his normal stop and took the next one. The moment he walked in the door, he noticed Brenna in the crowd, waiting impatiently in line, yet still seeming sweet and fun. It took him all of one day to decide to switch coffee shops and by the end of the week he knew his coffee girl always ordered a Chai latte.

His coffee girl.

He liked the sound of that. As soon as they finished with this project, Brock planned to have a little conversation with Brenna's dad and request his permission to marry his youngest daughter. Old fashioned as it might seem, Brock wanted to do things right and that was step one in his plan in making Brenna his wife, if she agreed to have him.

Lost in his thoughts, he was surprised when he felt her arms slide around his waist and her scent float through his senses.

"Thinking deep thoughts this morning, I see," Brenna teased, turning her blue eyes to his hazel ones with a sassy smile.

"Absolutely. If you leave me alone until noon, I'm pretty sure I'll have a cure for the common cold and figured out world peace," Brock joked, giving Brenna a hug and kissing the crown of her head.

"I'll leave you to your thinking, then," Brenna said pretending to pull away, but Brock held her close.

"In case I haven't told you, the guys can hardly wait for you to arrive with your samples every morning. It's going to be a hard, hard thing for them to want to work anywhere else after being spoiled by the three Smith ladies, particularly you," Brock said, grinning at Brenna. He leaned down closer to her ear and whispered. "But me, you can spoil all you want."

"You're spoiled enough, you arrogant man," Brenna said, smacking playfully at Brock's chest. "Now, tell me again how you can't live without me and I'll get out of your hair for the day."

"Oh, lovely coffee girl divine, you alone doth make the sun so shine, and beat upon this lowly heart of mine, my lovely coffee girl," Brock recited, going down on one knee with a hand held to his heart and the other stretched out to Brenna. The look on his face was one of devilment and his eyes twinkled with mischief.

Brock's crew clapped and whistled while Brenna blushed at least six shades of red. Burying her face in her hands, Brock got to his feet and enfolded her in a hug. Using a finger to nudge up her chin, he grinned broadly at her red face.

"You get the idea, coffee girl?" Brock asked, tucking an errant curl behind her ear.

"I think I do," Brenna said on a happy sigh. "I didn't realize you were such a talented poet. Are you sure you haven't studied Shakespeare?"

"Nope," Brock said, not going to admit that his mother made him take two years of drama class in high school. "It must be the inspiration."

Still flustered, Brenna waved goodbye to the men, gathered up the dirty dishes and let Brock carry the box out for her. He kissed her soundly before she got in the car then waved as she drove down the street. It was going to be hard to concentrate on work today. Just like every other day since he'd met Brenna.

~◇~

"Is it true Brock was spouting an impromptu love poem to you at the store this morning?" Avery asked when Brenna picked up the phone.

"Possibly," Brenna said, still surprised by Brock's theatrics.

"That is just about the most romantic thing, ever,"

Avery said. "You're not going to let him get away are you?"

"Not if I can help it," Brenna said with a smile. She hoped once the bistro was open that Brock would make some declaration of his intentions. Being the old-fashioned guy that he was, she assumed he wouldn't say anything until the job was finished.

"If you need to tie him up, I know where Greg keeps some rope," Avery said, making Brenna laugh.

"I'll keep that in mind," Brenna said, putting the finishing touches on the lunch she was taking to the guys at the site. "I'll be there with lunch in a few minutes. Do you need anything?"

"I have the oddest craving for salted caramel chocolate squares, the ones they sell down at Mrs. Rooney's shop."

"It's no trouble to run by and grab you a few," Brenna said, wondering when Avery developed such a sweet tooth. Last week she devoured an entire package of miniature Mounds bars and only let Brenna steal a couple.

"I'd really appreciate it if you're sure it isn't any trouble."

"Consider it done," Brenna said, hanging up the phone. She loaded the lunch supplies in her car, picked up the candy for Avery, and arrived at the shop at noon. Eager hands met her at the door, ready to take the lunch offerings. After giving Brock a big smile and a quick kiss, she ran up the stairs to Avery's store, handing her the candy.

"You are a lifesaver," Avery said, taking out a piece of the candy and biting into it like it was the most delicious thing she'd ever tasted.

"Anytime. At least until I open the bistro and spend all my time here," Brenna said with a grin. Wandering around Avery's store she noticed some changes her sister recently made. "I love how you've set up your displays, they look so pretty. Is business going okay?"

"It's going really well. I've had more customers here in the past month than I had in three months at my old location," Avery said, taking another piece of chocolate from the bag. "I'm glad Mom agreed to hire a couple of people part-time that we can share. That way we can have some extra hands to float between the three businesses as needed."

"I think it's going to work out really well," Brenna said, so excited about finally opening the bistro. They planned to have a big grand opening celebration with an open house in three weeks. Brock said if all the work passed the inspections, Brenna should be able to start bringing in the supplies and testing out the equipment next week.

The last of the finish work was being completed and then after the final walk-through, they should be good to go. Thank goodness Will had been pulled as their inspector or they would no doubt still be weeks behind with the project. It was hard to imagine he would deliberately try to make Brock look bad while holding up the project, but she wouldn't put anything past him.

As though thinking about him caused him to materialize, Brenna glanced up from one of Avery's candle displays to see Will walk in.

Not wanting to see him or be forced into another awkward conversation with the jerk, she ducked behind a cabinet holding a display of linens and carefully maneuvered her way behind the counter where Avery sat munching on her chocolates.

"What are you doing?" Avery asked, looking down at Brenna as she crawled to the back storage area.

"Hiding," Brenna whispered, pointing toward the door.

"Oh," Avery said noticing Will. She managed to

keep from rolling her eyes as Will walked up to the counter.

"Hi, Avery, have you seen Brenna? I looked around for her downstairs and her car was parked outside," Will said, frantically looking around the store. "That construction guy said she was up here."

"Sorry, you just missed her. Brenna had some errands to run and I'm not sure what she had planned after that. I think she mentioned walking down to the bank, or maybe it was the post office."

"Okay, thanks," Will said, leaving in a hurry with hopes of catching up to Brenna.

When the sound of his footsteps thudding down the stairs died away, Brenna walked out of the back storage room and sighed. "I didn't mean for you to lie for me. I just didn't want to have to deal with him today. Is he ever going to get the message?"

"Probably not. Don't you have any enemies you could introduce him to?" Avery asked with a saucy smile.

"The only one who comes to mind is Wesley the weasel and I don't see either of them appreciating that introduction," Brenna said, leaning against the counter and snitching a piece of candy.

Avery grinned at Brenna's comment, snatching back her bag of candy.

"Thanks for covering for me. I'd say I owe you one, but I did bring you candy," Brenna said with a smile as Avery bit into her third piece. "I hope Greg didn't want you to share."

"Nope. These are all mine," Avery said with a grin. "Thanks for bringing them."

"Anytime," Brenna said, walking to the door. "I'm going to work in Mom's office this afternoon so if you need a break just buzz me."

"Will do," Avery said as Brenna returned

downstairs. Brock was finishing the last of his sandwich when Brenna sat down beside him. "What do you think?"

"I like the flavors and textures, although I think overall the sandwich you made last Thursday has been the best so far," Brock said, wiping his mouth on a napkin and taking a long drink of the iced tea Brenna brought with the sandwiches. "I'd say this one should definitely stay on the menu, though, along with the chicken wraps you made Tuesday."

"Good to know. What did the others say?" Brenna asked, picking up the few remnants of lunch and putting them in the small fridge in her mom's office. Brock leaned against the wall watching her as he ate a rich, fudgy brownie.

"It's hard to distinguish words with the grunts of approval and sighs of contentment. Although Mark said the brownies you baked today were the best he's ever had. I'd have to agree," Brock said with a grin. "If you keep feeding us like you have been, we'll be too fat and complacent to finish the job."

Brenna walked to Brock and placed a hand on his hard stomach, feeling the muscles through his t-shirt. "I don't think you have to worry about that."

Capturing her hand, Brock kissed her fingers, giving her a heated look that made tingles start at her toes and work their way up to her head. They were going out to dinner after work and Brenna knew that look was a promise that he would deliver on later.

"Thanks for lunch, coffee girl," Brock said, kissing her fingers again before going back to his crew.

Sinking down at her mom's desk, Brenna picked up a file and fanned her face, giving herself a moment to regain her composure. After months of being exposed to Brock's charm and molten glances, she should have become immune to them by now, but the opposite seemed to be true. The more she was around him, the harder he was to resist.

Pulling invoices from a file she brought with her, Brenna started calling vendors to verify orders for food products and to track down the commercial oven she ordered two months earlier. It was slated for delivery last week and although she'd already paid for it, the oven had yet to arrive.

After a series of frustrating phone calls, she finally tracked down the company that supposedly made the delivery Friday afternoon. Since she knew for a fact it had not been delivered, she continued trying to explain to the man on the other end of the phone line that there was a mistake. Several minutes into the conversation with him giving her the runaround, Brenna finally had enough.

"Look, mister, I paid for that oven. It hasn't been delivered and if one of your drivers said it has been, then he's pulling one over on you. I suggest you figure out right away where my oven is and get it here by tomorrow afternoon or I'll inform your supervisor of your inability to properly manage your staff or your deliveries. You've got until tomorrow afternoon at three to have my oven here or you better have a really good reason why. Thank you and good day."

"She's got teeth and she knows how to bite," Brock said from the door where he leaned against the frame. "I'm both shocked and proud, coffee girl. I didn't think you had it in you."

Brenna looked up at Brock and huffed, slightly embarrassed to be caught telling off the delivery company. A wave of guilt at having been curt was making her feel bad, but her temper was already boiling. "Don't you start with me."

"Ah, the teeth are still snapping," Brock said, sitting down in one of the office chairs across from Brenna.

"Who messed with my girl and stirred up that wicked temper?"

"Those idiots at the delivery company. They claim my oven was delivered Friday and I know it wasn't. When I asked them to find it, he kept telling me I was wrong and asking if I could understand what he was saying. The condescending jerk. What he was really saying was he thought he had a simpering, dumb woman on the phone and could blow her off and not do his job. I've spent the last hour tracking down my oven and, by golly, if it isn't here tomorrow, someone's head is going to roll," Brenna said, stomping her foot beneath the desk for emphasis.

"You tell 'em, Lefty. You want Bugsy and me as backup?" Brock teased as Brenna glared at him across the desk. A slow smile finally spread across her face and her anger melted away.

When she let out a laugh, Brock knew he'd accomplished his mission. He could hear Brenna's raised voice clear over in her kitchen and wondered what had her all worked up. He stood outside the door and listened to her politely ask, then firmly demand the delivery of her oven. Considering how far she'd come in the last month in being able to speak up for herself, Brock felt very proud of Brenna.

"You're not nearly as funny as you believe you are," Brenna said, getting up from the desk and walking around it to stand in front of Brock's chair. He pulled her down on his lap and gave her a lingering kiss which is where Letty found them when she came back from running errands.

"So, is this how you get so much work down around this place? Kissing my daughter in my office?" Letty teased as she plopped her shoulder bag down on the desk.

"No, ma'am," Brock said, red creeping up his neck

to be caught kissing Brenna in her mother's office. They might as well have been in high school caught necking in detention. "I'll just get back to work now, Letty."

"Go, go," Letty said, pointing at the door with an exaggerated frown. Watching him hurry back toward the kitchen, Letty turned to Brenna and grinned. "I really like that boy, Rennie. He's a keeper."

"You shouldn't tease him like that, Mom. He thinks you're serious," Brenna said, sitting in the chair Brock vacated. "In case I haven't mentioned it, thank you again for making all this possible."

"You're welcome, honey," Letty said, kissing Brenna on the forehead before taking the seat behind her desk. "Just so you know, Will is sitting outside by your car, like he's waiting for you. You may want to walk home, steal your sister's car, or resign yourself to hanging out here the rest of the day."

"He's seriously stalking me?" Brenna asked, completely annoyed. "Will came in earlier and I hid in Avery's back room. She told him I was walking around doing some errands. I thought he'd give up and go away. Doesn't he have a job he needs to go to? How can he just loiter outside the store all afternoon?"

"Want me to call the police?" Letty asked, only half-teasing. Will had never acted quite normal around Brenna. When they were in high school, Letty chalked it up to him being a gangly teen. Now that they were well into their adult years and Brenna had long ago told Will she wasn't interested, his behavior was bordering on obsessive. Maybe she'd ask Brandon to speak with Will's dad, since they worked together.

"That won't be necessary, but I guess I'm probably stuck here for a while," Brenna said with a sigh, looking around Letty's neat office.

"In that case, would you mind going downstairs with me and helping me rearrange some displays?" Letty asked getting up from the desk and looping her arm through Brenna's as she pulled her out of the chair.

Without time to run away or decline, Brenna groaned. Moving furniture was one of her least favorite things to do, but she followed her mom downstairs.

An hour later, Will was still sitting by Brenna's car and she had things she needed to do, like get ready for her date with Brock. Deciding to walk home, she snuck out the back of the store and crept along the creek for a few blocks before climbing over the fence of the newspaper office. Sneaking around the corner of the building, she walked cautiously along the sidewalk, until she could turn down a side street and head for home.

When she made it inside the house, she leaned against the door and breathed a sigh of relief.

Going to her room, she spent another hour working on her menu design, finished her final product order and decided what she would wear for her date with Brock. He said to keep it casual because they were going to a barbecue at a friend's place.

Taking a shower and letting her long curls air dry, she put on a pair of new jeans and rolled up the cuffs then added a bright blue cotton blouse and a pair of ballet flats. She applied mascara, a light coat of lip gloss, and a spritz of perfume before fluffing out her hair. Grabbing a sweater in case the evening turned chilly, she stuffed her phone, wallet, lip gloss, keys, and breath mints into a small brown leather handbag and ran downstairs just as Brock rang the bell.

"Hey, coffee girl, you look playfully awesome," Brock said, stepping inside and giving her a quick kiss.

"You don't look so bad yourself," Brenna said taking one of his calloused hands in hers, pulling him further into the house. "You didn't say if the barbecue was potluck or not so I made some cookies to take. Is that okay?"

"Better than okay," Brock said, wrapping his arms around Brenna from behind and walking in step with her to the kitchen. They both were laughing as they sauntered into the room and Brenna picked up a foil-wrapped platter, handing it to Brock.

"Do I get to taste-test these?" Brock asked, trying to slip his fingers inside the foil.

"No. You'll have to wait until dinner," Brenna said, slapping his hand. She turned around and made her way back to the front door.

"You're a tyrant with your baked goods, you know. Instead of the soup Nazi, we'll call you the pastry dictator," Brock said with a look of utter dismay as they walked to his pickup. "Maybe we better find you a spiked helmet to wear tonight."

Brenna was giggling so hard she couldn't climb into the pickup. Brock finally handed her the tray of cookies, picked her up and set her inside, shaking his head at her laughter. He attempted to subdue his grin as he climbed behind the wheel.

"You're a certifiable nut, Miss Brenna Smith," Brock said, as he started down the street.

"That may be, but you know you love me anyway," Brenna said, batting her eyes at him, making him smile and his heart melt at the look on her face.

"Yes, I do," Brock said. He wouldn't have believed it possible to fall more in love with the silly woman sitting across his pickup each and every day, but he did.

"So where are we going?" Brenna asked as they headed north on the freeway.

"To Mike and Levi's. They're barbecuing on the balcony. It drives their vegetarian neighbors upstairs insane," Brock said with a devilish smile. "Mike has a crush on one of them and is hoping the smell of charred meat will cause her to come bang on his door."

"I'm sure you never did such a thing when you

lived there," Brenna said, trying to look unimpressed by Mike's elaborate scheming.

"Absolutely not, Miss Smith. I'd never be a naughty boy like that. It might get me in trouble," Brock said, keeping a straight face although it was hard for him to hide his smile. "And the only trouble I want in is with you."

"Why would you want in trouble with me?" Brenna asked, knowing he'd been on the receiving end of her bad temper a few times and seemed to have survived the experience, barely.

"So you'll feel the need to make up with me after you calm down."

"You are such a tease, Brock. A complete tease," Brenna said, shaking her finger at him.

"Yes, I am, but you love me anyway," Brock said, his voice growing husky. "And I'd never tease about making up with you. That is a serious matter that requires my full effort and attention."

The conversation on the rest of their drive was filled with easy banter. They were almost into the city when Brenna's phone rang. Looking at the caller id, she quickly answered.

"Hey, Kat, how are you?"

Brock listened to the one-sided conversation. When it sounded like Brenna's friend Kathleen asked if she could see her, Brock interrupted.

"Ask if she wants to come to the barbecue. Mike and Levi won't care," Brock said, hoping Kat would come. He knew Brenna missed her friends from the office and it would be fun for her to have someone she knew well at dinner.

"Do you want to join us for dinner?"

When Brenna rattled off the address, Brock smiled and winked at her, knowing Kat accepted the invitation.

"That's great Kat can join us. I hope the rest of the

guys don't frighten her off," Brock said as they took an exit and wound their way toward his old apartment.

"Kat isn't easily frightened," Brenna said, with a grin. In fact, she thought Brock should be more concerned about Kat scaring the guys. She was one very attractive, very confident young woman and for a lot of guys, that was somewhat intimidating.

Going up to the apartment, Brock held the platter of cookies in one hand with Brenna's fingers captured in his other. When they got to the door, a sign stuck outside with duct tape invited anyone to come in, so they did without knocking.

Pop music played in the background and Brenna smiled to see Jett and Ned arguing over who brought the best salsa, albeit from a jar, for the corn chips. A few other guests sat around the room visiting and she could see Mike on the tiny balcony flipping burgers on a super small grill.

Brock placed the cookies on the kitchen counter and tugged Brenna out to the balcony.

"Hey, man, what's up?" Mike said as he grinned in welcome at his latest guests. He was thrilled to see Brock looking so happy and he genuinely liked Brenna.

"Not much, bro. How's it going?" Brock said, slapping Mike on the back.

"Hello, beautiful angel," Mike said, giving Brenna a one-armed hug. "Are you keeping this guy in line?"

"I try, but it is a thankless, never-ending job," Brenna said, trying to sound overwhelmed by the enormity of the task.

Mike laughed as Brenna squeezed Brock's hand and gave him a flirty smile.

"Brock didn't tell me we were coming here or I would have made some food to bring along," Brenna said, hiding a laugh at Mike's crestfallen look. "I did bring some cookies."

"Man, what are you trying to do to me?" Mike asked Brock as he flipped a few more burgers. "If you'd told her she was coming here, who knows what kind of wonders she would have made to eat."

"I don't want you guys to get used to her good cooking. It will spoil you," Brock said, dropping his arm around Brenna and pulling her close to his side.

"Like I'm sure you've been spoiled the past few months," Mike said, sending a cool glare at his friend. "It's not nice to hold out on us."

"Maybe you and Levi can come for dinner some evening. I could cook at Brock's," Brenna offered, trying to smooth any ruffled feathers. "You both are welcome to drop by the bistro anytime once it's open."

"So when is the big day planned?" Mike asked, interested in knowing when the public would have access to Brenna's culinary talents.

"Two weeks," Brenna said, then gently poked an elbow into Brock's side. "If the construction guy gets done in time. Seriously, it's hard to find good help these days."

Mike laughed again and pointed his spatula toward Brock. "She's got you there, buddy."

"Before I forget," Brock said, changing the subject, "I had Brenna invite one of her friends tonight. I didn't think you'd mind."

"The more the merrier," Mike said, stacking burgers on a plate. Turning to Brenna he grinned. "Can she cook like you?"

"Nope. She can barely make toast or boil water," Brenna said with a sad shake of her head, thinking of Kat's disastrous attempts at cooking. "I've tried to teach her but she isn't a very willing student."

"Is she like you? Have a sweet personality?" Mike asked, hoping there was something redeeming about the girl.

SHANNA HATFIELD

"Not a bit," Brenna said. She tried not to squirm when Brock tickled her sides, knowing she was about to lead Mike into a trap.

"Is she shy?"

"I don't think that is a word anyone would use to describe her," Brenna said, her eyes twinkling with mischief.

"What does she look like?" Mike asked as they left the patio and walked back inside to the kitchen.

"You know the girl that does the morning news show?" Brenna asked, managing to keep a smirk off her face.

"The leggy blond that looks like she should be a model for Victoria's Secret?" Mike asked with enthusiasm as he set the platter of burgers on the counter.

"Yeah, that's the one. She doesn't look a thing like her either," Brenna said, with an impish grin that made Brock throw back his head with laughter.

"Brenna, you are so going to get yours," Mike said, sending her a warning glare. "That was not nice. Not nice at all."

"But it was funny," Brock said, slapping Mike on the shoulder as Levi came in the front door carrying bags of ice and hamburger buns.

"Sorry. I got off work late and the traffic was awful then I got stuck behind two old ladies at the store who were arguing over who was more romantic, Cary Grant or Clark Gable," Levi said, dumping his load on the counter.

Silence followed Levi to the kitchen as everyone stopped to look at the tall dark-haired beauty who walked in the door and confidently strode toward Brenna.

"Definitely Cary Grant," Kat said as she walked up behind them and smiled at Brenna. "Hands down, he wins. Smoldering good looks, smooth voice, and just the right amount of humor."

"Kat!" Brenna cried, throwing her arms around her friend and giving her a huge hug. "I've missed you so much."

"I missed you, too, Brenna," Kat said, stepping back from Brenna, but keeping hold of her hands. "Look at you. Being in love definitely agrees with you."

Brenna blushed, but pulled Kat closer to Brock and his friends. Jett dropped the chip he was eating when he spied Kat, dribbling salsa down his shirt while Ned was still coughing trying to dislodge the olive he swallowed when she came in the door. Mike was standing open-mouthed while Levi was absolutely transfixed.

"Hey, guys, this is my friend, Kathleen. She and I worked together at Harchett Enterprises. Kat this is Mike and Levi, hosts of the party this evening, and our friends Jett and Ned."

Mike recovered first, welcoming Kat to his home. Jett and Ned spluttered something and escaped to the living room until they could regain the ability to speak while Levi stood staring at her. He finally took Kat's hand in his and smiled.

"Cary Grant it is, then," Levi said, kissing the back of Kat's hand in a show of gallantry Mike and Brock would have said was impossible for him to pull off. "Welcome to our humble abode."

"Thanks for having me," Kat said, staring back at Levi with a look of interest Brenna hadn't seen before.

Levi, just a year younger than Mike and the same age as Brock, didn't seem like the type of guy Kat would normally date. He worked with troubled youths and took odd jobs to make extra money since his position was not one that paid well monetarily although he said the feeling he got helping "his kids" more than made up for it.

Tall and handsome, in a rugged sense, Levi was the more serious, quiet one of the two brothers, which made Brenna even more surprised by Kat's interest in him.

As the party wound down and guests began to leave, Brock started to offer to drive Kat home, since she'd taken a cab to the party. Levi jumped in to volunteer and she accepted, giving Brenna a quick hug as she headed out the door.

"I can't thank you enough for inviting me to this party, Brenna. We'll definitely have to talk later," Kat said, giving Brenna one more quick hug as she followed Levi down the hall.

"You've besotted my brother with a beautiful wench," Mike said, as Brock and Brenna helped him clean up the kitchen.

"I wouldn't let Kat hear you call her a wench," Brenna advised Mike as they wiped down the counters and put away the remaining food. "You wouldn't like the reaction."

"Good to know," Mike said, grinning at Brenna and Brock. He was still in shock over Levi's reaction to the beautiful and charming Kathleen. "Can you believe him?"

"I've never seen him act quite so interested in a woman before," Brock agreed.

"Interested? Are you, blind, dude? He was practically drooling at her feet," Mike said, shaking his head at Brock. "It's all your fault for dragging this little matchmaker into our midst."

"Hey! I didn't plan on setting either of them up," Brenna said in her own defense. "It just happened. Maybe it was meant to be. Maybe ten years from now when Uncle Mike is bouncing a beautiful dark-haired niece on his lonely bachelor's knee, he'll remember who introduced the two love birds."

"Isn't it time for you to take this sassy little miss

home?" Mike asked Brock while putting a hand on Brenna's head and ruffling her curls. "The later it gets, the lippier she becomes."

Brenna playfully slugged Mike in the ribs and he grabbed his side, pretending he was in dire pain.

"Hospital, man. Hospital. I've been attacked by a butterfly," Mike teased, flopping across the counter before winking at Brenna.

Due to Brock's home project, Brenna spent many hours getting to know Brock's friends while they helped him work on the house. Although Mike was big and imposing, Brenna knew he was a teddy bear at heart.

"Let's get out of here, coffee girl. I've had about all I can take of this drama," Brock said, grabbing Brenna's hand and leading her to the door as Mike followed behind.

"Thanks for the party, Mike. It was really nice," Brenna said, stretching up to kiss his cheek when he bent down toward her. "I'm glad you liked the cookies."

"What's not to like about double chocolate chip loaded with nuts?" Mike asked, remembering Brenna hid a few for him in the cereal cupboard.

"Later, man," Brock said bumping fists with Mike as he escorted Brenna out the door.

Driving home, Brock and Brenna talked about who was at the party, how Ned and Jett seemed to enjoy finding things to argue about including a pretty redhead who was a co-worker of Mike's, and how nice it was to spend an evening with friends.

Brock started to turn down her street, but Brenna remembered her car was still parked at the store, so she asked Brock to take her there instead.

The only car parked on that stretch of the block, since all the shops were closed, was Brenna's. Brock gave her a few kisses that Brenna thought might melt the rubber on the bottom of her ballet flats before helping her out of his truck and walking her the few steps to her car.

"Thanks for the date, construction man. I really enjoyed it," Brenna said, leaning into Brock and absorbing his warmth and strength.

"Anytime, coffee girl. I'm glad you had a good time," Brock said, running his hands up and down her back as he held her close, inhaling deeply of her scent. Bending his head, he trailed kisses down her neck, nibbled on her ear, then gave her one more scorching kiss before watching her slide into the car. "See you tomorrow?"

"Absolutely," Brenna said, blowing him a kiss through the car's open window. "Love you."

"Love you, too, baby."

Brenna drove home in a dreamy state, not noticing the car that sat across the street from her parent's house or the man sitting inside. Parking her car, she got out and started up the walk when a she felt herself spun around. A hand on her mouth was the only thing that kept her from screaming loud enough to wake her parents as well as every neighbor in a three-block radius.

Recognizing her would-be attacker, she grabbed his hand and pinched it until he dropped it by his side.

"Will, you idiot! You scared me half to death. What's the big idea?" Brenna said, glaring at him in irritation.

"I need to talk to you and I get the idea you've been avoiding me," Will whined, rubbing the spot on his hand where Brenna pinched him. She felt like slapping him upside the head and kicking him a few times, too, but managed to restrain herself.

"Honestly, I have been avoiding you. I'm tired of telling you that I won't take you back and you don't seem to be getting the message. I'm not interested in dating you again. Not now, not ever. Why can't you just accept that and move on?"

"Because I love you," Will said, tracing his thumb across Brenna's cheek, causing her to slap at his hand. "You're my girl."

"For the last time, Will, I'm not your girl. I haven't been your girl for a very long time and I have no desire to ever be your girl again. What is it going to take to convince you I'm not interested," Brenna said hotly. If she hadn't been so mad, she might have been frightened by the odd look in Will's eyes. "You are the most thick-headed man I've ever met. I don't want to see you anymore. If you don't quit stalking me, I won't even be able to be your friend. Can you understand that?"

"But, Rennie, we're so good together and I ..." Will said, sounding weak and desperate.

"We were never good together. We were barely ever together at all," Brenna fumed, wanting to stomp her foot, preferably on top of Will's. "Just leave me alone."

"You don't mean it," Will said, grabbing Brenna roughly by the shoulders and pressing his lips to hers. Brenna struggled against him and was trying to land a kick to his shin when she felt herself pulled against something solid and warm. She took a deep breath and inhaled the scents of cedar, musk and Brock.

Will took a stumbling step back and fell to the sidewalk.

"Leave her alone," Brock said, quietly but dangerously. Brenna turned and buried her face against his chest, wrapping her arms around his waist.

Brock ran a comforting hand along her back while clenching his other hand in a fist at his side. He'd started driving toward his house when something urged him to make sure Brenna arrived home okay.

Turning around, he stopped at her house just in time to see a man grab her and pull her into an embrace. He was jumping out of his truck when Brenna started fighting against the man and Brock knew it had to be Will.

"You don't understand," Will said, getting to his feet and taking a step backward, away from the anger shooting off Brock.

"I do understand," Brock said, the muscle in his jaw twitching. "What you don't understand is that Brenna can get a restraining order against you. She can see your sorry backside sit in jail for stalking and harassment. You really need some help, Will. Now go."

"But I.."

"Go!" Brock said, raising his voice just enough to sound like thunder, although in truth it was still quiet against the stillness of the evening.

Picking up Brenna, Brock carried her to the porch and sat on the swing, holding her on his lap and letting her cry.

"It's okay, Brenna, he's gone. It's fine, baby," Brock soothed, waiting for her tears to stop. When she finally sat up and wiped her eyes with the backs of her hands, she gave Brock a watery grin.

"Once again, you come to my rescue," Brenna said, her tear-filled eyes turning Brock's insides to jelly. He'd do anything for the woman in his arms and he hoped she knew how much she meant to him.

"Anytime you need rescued, coffee girl, I'll be there," Brock assured her, hoping what he said would prove to be true. The way Will was chasing her had gone from annoying to crazy. Brock would die if anything happened to Brenna. "Did he hurt you? Are you okay?"

"I'm fine. He mostly scared me and made me mad," Brenna said, getting off Brock's lap and straightening her spine. Staring down the street, her gaze narrowed and Brock could see her temper flare. "It makes me so ticked to think of him skulking around following me.

How dare he?"

Brock kept his grin to himself. He knew Brenna would be fine if she was angry.

"I can see his problem," Brock said, wrapping his arms around Brenna from behind and kissing her temple. "I'd have a hard time resigning myself to letting you go, especially to a handsome, charming, stunning man like the one you've got now."

"You are the most conceited thing," Brenna said with a laugh. Turning in his arms, she hugged Brock and kissed him softly. "Thank you for saving me, for letting me cry, and making me laugh."

"You're welcome. Now get inside and don't give Will another thought. If you do want to file for a restraining order, you certainly can," Brock said, walking backward down the porch steps.

"I hate to do that, especially considering his dad and my dad work together and he's been a friend of Greg's for so long. Let's hope he learned his lesson and will leave me alone."

"Yeah, let's hope," Brock said, catching the kiss Brenna blew to him, watching as she went inside and locked the door behind her.

Grateful for the prompting that urged him to follow Brenna, he wouldn't let himself think of what might have happened if he hadn't shown up. Then again, knowing Brenna and her temper, she might have just taught Will a lesson right there in the front yard.

Now that would have been something to see.

Chapter Fourteen

"Are you girls ready? Tomorrow is the big day," Brandon asked as he passed a platter of grilled steaks around the table. They were having a celebration dinner the night before the store's big grand opening.

It was a family affair with Brandon, Letty, Avery, Greg, Brenna and Brock. Since they all considered Brock an unofficial part of the family, everyone expected him to join them and he was glad he could.

"I can't believe it's finally here," Brenna said, taking a helping of twice-baked potatoes before passing them to Brock. His knee bumped hers under the table and she gave him a secret smile. "I just hope everything goes well."

"You ladies have worked so hard, how can it be anything but successful?" Greg said, kissing Avery on the cheek.

"Here's to our girls and Trio Designs," Brandon said, holding his glass up in a toast.

"To our girls," Greg and Brock echoed.

As they finished the meal, Avery looked at Greg and asked for everyone's attention.

"We've got a little announcement we wanted to share and tonight seems like a good time," Avery said.

"What's that, honey," Brandon asked, looking at his oldest daughter with love and pride.

"Well, by Christmas, we'll have one more addition at the store," Avery said, looking at her mom, then

Brenna.

"Addition? You're not remodeling again are you?" Brandon asked, looking from Letty to Avery. When Avery nodded at her mother, Letty let out an ear-piercing scream that had Brenna scrambling out of her chair and running around the table to hug her sister.

As the three women hugged each other and bounced around in a circle, Brock and Brandon looked at Greg for an explanation.

"Not remodeling at the store, Dad," Greg said, with a knowing grin, "but we might need Brock to come do some work at the house. We'll be needing a nursery."

It took a moment for the words to sink in before a smile lit Brandon's face and he gave Greg a hearty slap on the back. Brock got to his feet and extended his hand to Greg across the table with an enthusiastic "congratulations."

The women had stopped dancing and crying, regaining their seats.

"I propose another toast," Brandon said, holding his glass up again. "To our new baby."

Brenna smiled at Avery. Her dad's reference to the baby belonging to them all was accurate, because they would all stake a claim on the little one when it arrived.

Later as Brenna and Brock sat outside on the porch swing in the warmth of an early June evening, they talked about Avery's news.

"It's going to be hard to top that," Brock said with a grin, holding Brenna's hand to his heart with his arm wrapped around her shoulders.

"I don't think anything tops first grandbaby," Brenna said, learning into Brock and enjoying the quiet moment of sitting in the twilight with him.

"You girls certainly know how to pack a lot of excitement into a very short period of time," Brock teased. "As if the grand opening of your shops isn't enough, I bet you three already have the nursery planned, the names selected and are deliberating on what preschool the kid will attend."

"We haven't gotten to the preschool, yet," Brenna said with a saucy smile. "I can't wait for the baby to arrive. It will be extra fun if she arrives before Christmas."

"She? I don't know much about babies, but I didn't realize Greg and Avery already knew they're expecting a girl," Brock said, continuing to rock the swing as they talked.

"They don't," Brenna said, then lowered her voice. "I just really want it to be a girl. They're so much more fun than boys."

"What do you know of boys?" Brock asked, looking down in Brenna's blue eyes, seeing mischief mingling with love there. "It seems to me you are sadly lacking in facts about little boys considering you only had one sister."

"I know they are ornery, smelly and messy, loud and obnoxious and…"

"Is that so?" Brock asked, pulling Brenna onto his lap and tickling her until she couldn't catch her breath. When he stopped, she wrapped her arms around his neck and kissed him so passionately, he didn't know how he'd ever let her go and say goodnight. Finally, she grabbed his wrist and looked at the time.

"We've got a big day tomorrow, so I better make this goodnight," she said, getting to her feet and leaning against the front door. "I love you, Brock, so much."

"Even if I'm a messy, smelly, ornery boy?"

"Especially because you are," Brenna said, giving Brock a look of sweet enticement.

"I love you, too, my lovely coffee girl," Brock said, kissing each eyelid, her nose, and chin before giving her one last kiss that made her knees weak and her head spin. "Save me a cup of coffee in the morning. I'll be there cheering you on."

"I know you will, Brock, and I thank you for all you've done to help make my dreams come true."

"You tell me the dream and I'll do my best to make it happen," Brock said in a husky voice as he walked down the steps, waving before climbing into his truck.

Brenna would have spent more time mulling over Brock's words if she didn't need to get up at four the next morning to get everything ready for her opening day at the bistro.

Standing outside the shop long before the sun began to rise the next morning, she stopped for a moment and admired the new sign that said "Trio Designs." Avery, Brenna and her mom agreed it was the perfect name for the store. Lettering on the window explained they offered floral and gift designs, home interior designs and the bistro.

Turning off all thoughts except getting food ready for the day and making coffee for the hordes of customers she hoped would arrive, Brenna greeted the part-time helper at five-thirty when she came in the back door.

"Morning, Jen," Brenna said brightly. "I'm so glad you could come in early to help me today."

"I think it will be fun," the college-age girl replied, tying on an apron and getting started on the list of things Brenna needed done before they opened the doors at six-thirty.

When she went to unlock the door, a small line of customers had formed on the sidewalk including Brock, Mike and Levi.

"What are you guys doing here?" she asked, giving the two brothers a hug before kissing Brock.

"Everyone needs to eat breakfast," Mike said, walking with Brenna to a table. She handed them all a menu and soon returned with a cup of rich, dark coffee for Brock. She took the orders from the other two while Jen seated the rest of the customers and their day began.

Brock offered to stay and help, but she shooed him off, telling him to spend the day with Mike and Levi. She promised to call him when the breakfast rush was over and invited all three of them to come for lunch.

Brenna's plans were to be open from six-thirty to eleven for breakfast and then serve lunch from eleven to two. She'd close the bistro then, clean up and do prep work for the following day. Letty decided all three businesses should be closed on Sundays and Mondays, to give them two days of rest.

The bistro was packed when Letty and Brandon came in at eight to see how things were going.

"I never expected a turn-out like this," Brenna said, wiping moisture from her brow as she made another batch of breakfast quiche and popped it in the oven. At this rate, she'd have to order more product on Monday.

"Everyone knows you're a fantastic cook and there aren't that many places to eat breakfast in town, so of course it would be a big hit," Brandon said from the dish pit where Letty set him on dish duty. Letty and Brandon planned to just pop in to check on things but were quickly recruited to help Brenna.

"If it's like this every morning, we might need more help," Letty said, looking at the line of people waiting for a table. "This is so exciting, Rennie. I'm so glad you decided to do this with me."

"Me, too, Mom," Brenna said, kissing her mother's cheek in passing as she hurried out to a table with a large order.

Letty took over hostess duties, seating guests and taking their orders while Brenna cooked and Jen delivered plates and made coffee. Letty and Jen both bussed tables while Brandon did the dishes.

When the rush was over and the crowd cleared at a few minutes before ten, they all collapsed at a table and looked around.

"I guess I better get ready to open up my portion of the shop," Letty said with a tired sigh as she got to her feet. Brock installed decorative hooks that held velvet roping across the entrances into both Avery and Letty's portion of the store. It was easy to remove them when they wanted to be open and fast to put them up when their areas where closed.

Avery and Greg waltzed in and looked around in surprise at the weary faces.

"Did things not go well?" Avery asked as she sat down by Brenna, patting her on the back.

"No, they went great. We're just worn out and waiting for our second wind," Brenna said, moving her feet from a chair so Greg could sit down. "I had no idea to expect so many people in such a short time."

"Well, you'll have a better idea going forward," Letty said, rolling the shoulders that Brandon rubbed. "At least we'll have tomorrow and Monday to rest. You probably won't be quite so busy on a weekday."

"Probably not, unless the commuters stop here instead of waiting until they get to the freeway. Mike and Levi said they'd spread the word with anyone they know who drives down this direction," Brenna said, getting to her feet and surveying the tables to make sure they were all clean. "I better get ready for the lunch crowd."

Lunch service was every bit as busy as breakfast had been. Mike, Levi and Brock showed up at noon, took a look at the crowds and lines and immediately jumped in to help. Mike bussed tables, Levi helped with the dishes and Brock took orders as well as helped with the seating. Jen did the waitressing while Brenna filled the orders as fast as her fingers could fly.

When two rolled around, the last customer left and Brenna sank into a chair, resting her head on the table.

"Brenna?" Brock asked squatting down beside her, rubbing a comforting circle on her back. "You okay, baby?"

"Never better," Brenna said, lifting her head and smiling through her exhaustion. She was coated in food, flour dusted both cheeks and her curls had long ago escaped the confines of her bun, but she looked happy. "Thank you all for your help."

"No problem," Levi said, helping himself to a big sandwich and a plate of battered fries. Mike snitched a fry then went to fill a plate of his own.

"Eat anything you want, guys, you more than earned it," Brenna said in a tired voice.

"You sure you're fine?" Brock asked, continuing to rub a hand on her back.

"I'll be fine, just out of shape is all," Brenna said, leaning her head against Brock's shoulder. It felt so strong and wonderful beneath her weary head.

"I, for one, am rather fond of your shape," Brock whispered in her ear, making her blush.

"Enough of that, you two," Mike said, taking a bite of the sandwich he made to go with his fries. He wiggled his eyebrows at Brenna, making her laugh.

"Have you eaten?" Brock asked Brenna as he got to his feet.

"No. I haven't had time," she said, starting to rise from the chair.

"Sit," he ordered as his hand kept her from getting up. "I'll be right back."

He returned with sandwiches and chips, since Mike ate the last of the fries. He went back to the kitchen and retrieved a pitcher of lemonade and a plate of brownies.

Letty was busy with her own customers and Avery made Greg stay to help her handle her own flood of new business, so Brock fastened the ropes that separated the bistro from the rest of the store before sitting down and enjoying his lunch with two of his good friends and the girl he loved.

Talking to Brandon a few weeks ago, Brock was assured he had his permission and blessing to ask Brenna to marry him. They'd been so busy, though, he just hadn't found the right time. He was hoping once the grand opening was over and things settled into a routine, he could find a special way to pop the question.

Looking at Brenna nearly falling asleep over her lunch, he smiled to himself, knowing today would not be the day to have her undivided attention.

Resting for a few minutes, Brenna finally mustered the energy to go back to the kitchen and clean up before going home and taking a nap.

She shooed the guys out the door, promising to be at Brock's for dinner later.

She made it home and in the door before collapsing on the couch in the living room. Hearing bells, she realized the doorbell was ringing and since no one else was home she managed to pry open her eyes and stagger to answer it.

"Delivery for Brenna Smith," Greg said, smiling around a huge bouquet of beautiful summer flowers.

"What's this?" Brenna asked, no longer feeling so tired as she carried the flowers into the house and set them on a table near the door.

"I guess someone thinks you're pretty special," Greg said, smiling at her. "It sounds like you had a gangbuster business today."

"I did. And a lot of extra hands that pitched in. I'm definitely going to have to hire more help," Brenna said, digging the card out of the bouquet and opening the envelope. She smiled as she read it:

My lovely coffee girl,
Congratulations on your first day of business. I knew you could do it and I'm so proud of you!
Love you,
Your construction man

Brenna looked at Greg with teary eyes and sniffed.

"If you're going to get all emotional and sappy on me, I'm out of here," Greg said with a quick step toward the door.

Laughing, Brenna swatted at his arm. He gave her a one-armed hug and ruffled her already messy hair.

"We're all proud of you, Rennie. You did great today," Greg said. "And in case it comes up, I think Brock is a great guy who'll make you very happy."

"Thanks," Brenna said, swiping at the tear that trailed down her cheek. "Now get out of here. I'm sure Avery has you running errands along with deliveries."

"She's a slave-driver, for sure, but what's a guy to do?" Greg teased as he went out the door. "I'm not supposed to come back without a pint of salted caramel ice cream and a chocolate bar."

"And so it begins," Brenna said, knowing Greg would do his best to supply whatever it was Avery craved during the next several months of her pregnancy.

Taking the flowers with her up to her room, Brenna sat them on her desk before falling back on her bed and going to sleep. She woke up to her mom giving her a little shake.

"Honey, are you okay?" Letty asked as Brenna finally opened her eyes.

"Hi, Mom. I'm fine. What are you doing home early?"

"I'm not early. It's almost five-thirty. I thought you were going over to Brock's for dinner. Did you decide to stay home?" Letty asked, noticing the flowers on

Brenna's desk.

Brenna jumped up from the bed and glared at the clock.

"I slept much longer than I planned. I'm going to grab a quick shower then I'll be out the door," Brenna said, pulling clothes from her closet and tossing them on the bed.

"Nice flowers," Letty said with a knowing grin.

"You'll never guess who sent them," Brenna said with the impish look her mother loved.

"Let's see. Could it be Brock? The man who makes lovey-dovey eyes at you during dinner and kisses you a lot longer than he should on my porch swing?" Letty asked, then laughed as Brenna grinned and shooed her out the door.

Ready in record time, Brenna grabbed a pie she'd made yesterday and stashed for the dinner tonight. Planned ahead, she assumed she wouldn't have the time or energy to make anything this afternoon.

"Don't wait up for me," she called as she hurried out the front door and drove to Brock's.

She wasn't sure who would be at Brock's for dinner, but was glad to see only Mike's truck at his house.

Running up the front walk, she didn't even pause before going in. The house was quiet, so she hurried down the hall to the kitchen and left the pie on the counter before going out the back door.

Brock was grilling something that smelled wonderful while Mike and Levi played with Mutt, taking turns tossing a stick for the dog to chase. When he saw her, Mutt barked and ran her direction.

"Down, Mutt," she said with a laugh before the dog could jump on her. She was wearing a new blue floral sundress and the last thing she wanted on it was paw prints. She took his scruffy face in her hands and whispered in his ear, making the dog's tail wag with excitement. Rubbing his head affectionately, she gave him a final pat and said, "go play" which sent him back to chasing his stick.

"Hey guys," Brenna said, waving at Mike and Levi before walking over to Brock and kissing his cheek. Lowering her voice, she stood on tiptoe and placed her lips close to Brock's ear. "The flowers were gorgeous. Thank you so much."

"You're welcome," Brock said, turning his head and giving her a quick kiss. "You look lovely, as always."

Brenna blushed. She busied herself pouring a glass of iced tea before sitting down next to Mike.

"I can't thank you guys enough for jumping in to help today. You all were lifesavers," Brenna said, leaning back in her chair and looking at the two brothers.

"Glad to be of service," Mike said, throwing the stick for Mutt to chase. "It looked like you had your hands full."

"Anytime you need help, just let us know," Levi said, leaning around his brother to better see Brenna.

"Thank you for that offer. I decided I need to hire a busser and a dishwasher, then I think we can handle everything just fine. Since you jumped in and saved me today, though, you guys have an open invitation to eat at the bistro anytime you like on the house," Brenna said, taking a sip of her tea, watching as the dog brought the stick back to Mike. Sitting forward, she gave the dog's ears a good rub before reclining in her chair.

"You don't know what you've done, coffee girl," Brock teased from his spot at the barbecue. "They'll be in there every Saturday eating up your profits, scaring away the customers. Bad move on your part. Very bad."

"You, be quiet," Mike said, pointing at Brock with Mutt's stick. "This wonderful lady knows exactly what she's doing, so you stay out of it. In my opinion, she's a smart business woman who obviously cares about keeping her favorite customers happy."

"Coming from you, I think that's a great compliment," Brenna said, giving Mike a gracious smile.

"Don't say I didn't warn you," Brock cautioned as he put grilled chicken on a platter and took it inside. Mike and Levi washed up then helped set the table while Brock grilled some bread and Brenna made a green salad. They sat around the dining table teasing and laughing until the sun set and the pie was gone, then Mike and Levi headed home, leaving Brock and Brenna to clean up the dishes.

Brock could tell Brenna was still tired and walked her to her car much earlier than he wanted or planned. He pasted on a smile to hide his disappointment at not spending more time together.

"You did great today, Brenna. I knew you'd be a big success," Brock said, holding Brenna to him as he leaned against her car, inhaling her fresh scent.

"It was definitely a team effort. Thank you for coming to the rescue again," she said, wrapping her arms around his waist and nestling her head against his chest. Closing her eyes, she soaked up his warmth, breathed in his scent and found herself not wanting to leave the circle of his arms to go home.

"Anytime, coffee girl." Brock tipped her chin up and planted a soft kiss to her lips. Despite her exhaustion, Brenna found herself caught up in the turmoil of sensations that descended upon her anytime Brock held her close.

Sliding her hands up around his neck, she pulled his head down and deepened the kiss. Brock groaned and drew her closer until there was no space left between them. He pillaged her lips with his while his hands wove a magical trail of tingling sensations along her back and around her sides. With languid limbs, she clung to him, no longer able to stand on her own.

"Brock," she pleaded, not sure what she wanted, but knowing whatever it was, Brock was the only one who could provide it.

Looking into her eyes, which were now glowing from an inner fire, Brock let the heat penetrate his gaze before kissing Brenna again with barely restrained passion. Finally, he released her lips and let out a shaky breath.

Bringing his forehead to rest against hers, he felt her shiver against him.

"Are you cold?" he asked, gently rubbing his hands along her back while her arms still encircled his neck.

"No," Brenna whispered, unable to look at him while her stomach continued to flutter uncontrollably. His last kiss had nearly been her undoing and she was unable to think of anything other than the heat that sizzled between her and the man she loved. "Hot. Extremely hot."

"Brenna," Brock said, taking a step back. He had to put some space between them or he was going to completely ignore what his conscience was yelling at him and Brenna wouldn't be going home tonight. Taking another step back, he opened her car door. "You're going to get in this car, drive home, and go to bed like the good girl that you are."

"Maybe I don't want to be a good girl right now," Brenna said, drunk with exhaustion and the very essence of Brock. Her voice dropped seductively and she seared Brock with a blatant look of wanting. "Maybe I want to stay right here."

"No," Brock said, drawing on every ounce of inner strength he possessed as he waited for Brenna to get in the car.

"Maybe you need convincing," she said, pressing a

hot, wet kiss to the pulse that was beating wildly in his neck.

"Brenna," Brock said, his voice low and raspy as he struggled to hang onto what little was left of his composure. "In the car right now."

"But, Brock…" Brenna said, putting a hand on his chest.

"Now," he ordered, pushing her into the car and closing the door before leaning in the window and kissing her cheek.

"Go home, coffee girl, before you make me do something we'll both regret," Brock said, mustering a smile to soften the commanding tone of his voice.

Brenna gave him a withering glare as she started the car, knowing he was right, but wishing he wasn't.

"I love you, you little tempest," Brock teased, making her smile.

"I love you, too, you bossy man."

Chapter Fifteen

"You asked her yet?" Andy asked as he helped Brock hang the last door in the master suite. The beautiful room was finally finished.

The inspectors were satisfied and he'd even talked to Letty about ordering a new bedroom set that arrived last week and now sat on the newly carpeted floor.

Airy and spacious, the walls of the room were a mellow shade of tan that accented the rich tones of the solid oak furniture. Light filtered in from the big picture windows highlighting a great view of the side and back yard.

The door they were hanging opened into a large walk-in closet that featured a variety of rods, shelves and brackets, sure to please any woman and guaranteed to please Brenna. A second door led to a spa-like bathroom complete with a walk-in shower, garden tub and double vanity sink.

Brock could hardly wait to show it to Brenna now that it was finished and the furniture was in place. He hoped she would choose window treatments and the bed linens because Brock could care less about what covers went on the bed. His interest was wrapped up in the thought of Brenna eventually sharing it with him.

"Well, did you?" Andy asked, pulling Brock from his musings with his question.

"Asked what?" Brock said, playing dumb to his uncle's questioning, holding the door in place while

Andy tightened the screws in the hinges.

"Son, that isn't going to work with me," Andy said, tightening the final screw. Brock stood back and Andy worked the door a few times to make sure it functioned properly then grinned. "I thought you got a ring and were ready to pop the question."

"I did. I do. I was," Brock said, trying not to show his frustration to his uncle as he gathered up the tools and put them in his tool box. "The timing just hasn't been right."

Andy laughed and slapped his back. "If you wait for the timing to be just right, you'll be sitting here alone when you're my age. Suck it up and get it over with, boy."

Brock glared at his uncle as they moved into the kitchen where Brock poured them both tall glasses of lemonade and set out a plate of cookies Brenna had given him that morning when he stopped by the bistro for breakfast.

Since it was Saturday, they were planning to go to a movie tonight, but he didn't think that was a special enough way to propose. It's not like he could drop the ring in the popcorn and hope she'd find it before she choked on it or broke a tooth.

Proposing to Brenna demanded something special. Something unique. Something wonderful. Something unforgettable.

"Any suggestions?" Brock finally asked as he and Andy went out to the backyard where Mutt was chasing a squirrel between trees. The squirrel chattered at the dog sounding irritated which made Mutt bark and yip and run in wild circles, trying to get to the squirrel. The game between the two had been going on for days and neither Mutt nor the rodent seemed to have tired of it.

"Nope. Just do it. The longer you wait, the longer you're depriving yourself of the pleasure of her company," Andy said, winking at Brock. "From what I've seen of the two of you, she seems to like you just fine. It'd be a shame for that beautiful new bedroom you just finished not to be put to proper use."

"I can't just hand her the ring and ask 'what day?' I want to make it special," Brock said, releasing a sigh. He wasn't a guy given to a lot of flowery, romantic thoughts, although they did randomly strike him on occasion. The few times he'd surprised Brenna with a little romance had been completely spontaneous, so he wasn't sure how to approach planning a proposal. "How did you propose to Aunt Liz?"

"I threw the ring at her and asked 'what day?' and lucky for me she said 'yes, a week from Thursday'," Andy teased.

"You did not," Brock said, unable to keep from grinning, knowing his aunt and uncle had a very traditional wedding, which would have required time and planning. "Come on, Andy. Don't hold out on me now. How did you propose?"

"I took her out to dinner at a fancy little restaurant in Portland that has long ago closed its doors. After an amazing meal that cost more than the suit I was wearing, we strolled along downtown, staring in the store windows. When we got to the jewelry store, I had already arranged for them to have the ring in the window with a card that read 'Marry me, Lizzie?' When she saw it, she looked at me and smiled with her heart in her eyes and I've had forty years of spending every day with my sweetheart. You don't want to miss out on that Brock. You're already thirty and time waits for no man."

"Wow, that's a great story," Brock said, picturing how thrilled and surprised his aunt would have been. Brock was surprised that Andy had it in him to be such a romantic. Maybe there was hope for him to devise some way to dazzle Brenna.

"Take my advice, son, and don't wait too long. I'll eat my drill if she turns you down," Andy said, getting up and walking around to the front yard and his truck.

Mulling over what Andy said, Brock spent the rest of the afternoon making plans. When he picked Brenna up for dinner, he tried to act normal.

They'd decided on a casual date of pizza followed by a movie. Brock had a hard time paying attention to the movie because his thoughts kept churning around the best way to propose.

As he walked her up the steps to her parents' home later that evening, she put a hand on his arm and smiled at him.

"Are you okay, Brock? You seemed a little distracted tonight. Is everything good with the new construction job?" Brenna asked, concern shining from her eyes.

"Everything's fine, coffee girl. No need to worry," Brock said, pulling her close and savoring the feel of her in his arms. Uncle Andy was right. He was wasting time by not asking her to marry him. If he'd asked her when the idea first came to him, they could already be married. Instead of dropping her off at her mom and dad's house, he'd be taking her home to his house, sweeping her up in his arms and carrying her back to the new master suite's big bed. As heat flooded through him with those thoughts, he tamped down his longing and kissed Brenna good night, barely keeping his passion in check.

"Do you still want to go on the picnic after church?" Brenna asked opening the front door once she regained the ability to speak after Brock's wild kisses.

"You bet I do," Brock said, giving her one more quick kiss. "I'll see you in the morning."

"Night, Brock, love you."

"Love you, too, Brenna."

Watching Brock walk to his truck, Brenna wished

he would tell her what was bothering him. Despite her hectic schedule with the success of the bistro, she paid enough attention to realize something was causing Brock to not act like himself.

After the night he practically shoved her in the car and ordered her to go home, they both had been careful about how far they let their passion run away with them but this was something beyond that. Something that she hoped wouldn't eventually drive him away. Brenna couldn't bear the thought of a future that didn't include Brock.

~◇~

"Sit still," Brenna whispered, giving Brock a reproving look as he squirmed on the pew. He'd never, even as an antsy boy of six, had this much trouble paying attention to a church service before.

He gave her an apologetic glance before forcing himself to quit jiggling his foot or shifting his weight. Finally the minister ended the service and the closing hymn was sung.

"You stand on an ant hill this morning?" Brenna teased as they walked toward the back of the church hand in hand.

"No, I did not," Brock answered, wondering when his tie had ever felt so tight. For that matter the buttons on his shirt were about to choke him.

"You most certainly have ants in your pants," Brenna said, swallowing a giggle as they shook hands and chatted with other members of the congregation. "I thought your uncle was going to reach back and smack you."

"I sure thought about it," Andy said from behind them. He winked at Brenna and gave Brock a firm thump on his back. "What are you kids planning today?"

"We're going on a picnic and then visiting The Oregon Gardens," Brenna said, her eyes shining with excitement as she studied Brock, wondering what had gotten into him. She'd seen preschoolers sit with more decorum than he seemed to be able to muster during the service. Turning to his aunt and uncle she smiled. "Would you two like to join us?"

"Wouldn't that be just lovely, dear," Aunt Liz started to say, but Andy cut her off. "As nice as that sounds, Brenna, we'll have to pass today. Thank you for the invitation, though."

"Maybe another time, then," Brenna said, watching Liz stare at Andy like he'd lost his mind.

"Another time would be perfect," Andy said, hustling Liz toward the door with an encouraging nod of his head in Brock's direction.

Once they were outside the church, Brenna waved to her parents, along with Avery and Greg, as they all left for home. Brock took Brenna's hand as he helped her into his pickup.

The bright blue dress she wore made her eyes look even bigger and bluer today and the sun seemed to dance around her golden head. Brock didn't know when she'd ever looked as lovely.

Driving south of town, they parked at the gardens and while Brenna held a thick quilt over her arm, Brock carried the cooler with their picnic. Staying in the designated picnic area, Brenna chose a quiet spot beneath a tree and spread out the blanket. Brock helped her set out the food and they enjoyed the lunch as well as the beautiful summer afternoon.

Once they repacked the food, Brenna kicked off her shoes and leaned back on her elbows while Brock placed his head on her lap. They talked about happy summer memories from their childhood, discussed plans for some fun things they wanted to do before fall arrived, and argued about the shapes of clouds.

"Only you would say that cloud looks like a hammer," Brenna teased. "It's obviously a fairy wand."

"I'll fairy wand you, smarty," Brock said, turning over and tickling Brenna. She finally begged for mercy and he stopped, finding himself poised above her with his lips just inches from hers. Golden curls spilled all around her on the blanket and her eyes glowed hot and brilliant.

When her lips parted, it was more invitation than Brock could deny.

"Brenna," he said in a voice deep with emotion and wanting. Burying his hands in her hair, he took her lips in a demanding kiss, losing himself in her arms.

Sure she would dissolve into a molten mass just from the look in Brock's eyes before he kissed her, Brenna gave herself over to the moment, savoring every touch of Brock's lips to hers. Putting her hands around his neck, she pulled him closer when he took a breath and drew back. In the instant their gazes connected, she smiled at him and raised her lips to his for another kiss.

She felt his mouth on her neck and, finally, a long hot breath as he stilled.

"We need to … not do this," Brock said, sitting up and pulling Brenna beside him. "You're too much temptation for me today, coffee girl."

"I'm sorry. I…" Brenna said, fully realizing what Brock said. She gave him a shy smile as she blushed, pleased by his words. "Maybe we could go walk around the garden a while."

"I think that is a great idea," Brock said, getting to his feet and helping Brenna to hers. She put her wedge sandals back on then Brock helped her fold the quilt. They returned the cooler and quilt to the truck before strolling through the garden, holding hands.

Due to the warmth of the day, Brock had removed

his jacket and tie right after church. His shirt sleeves were rolled well above his elbows, revealing his muscular arms. Brenna had a hard time not admiring the way he looked, especially when they passed a group of college girls who kept glancing back at Brock and whispering. Brenna knew she was a lucky woman to be the one he chose to love.

Reaching the rose garden, Brock pointed to a bench and suggested they sit down to rest for a minute. They admired the blossoms and Brenna talked about the roses Brock could plant in the arbor he recently repaired across his front walk.

"You should plant them," Brock said, when Brenna pointed to a pretty yellow climbing rose that she said would look perfect greeting his guests.

"You really want me to plant roses for you?" Brenna asked, resting with her head against his chest as his arms encircled her from behind.

"I do, but only if you take care of them for me," Brock said, trying to keep his voice steady.

"You know I wouldn't be there during the week, but I could take care of them on the weekends," Brenna offered.

"No, they need more care than that. You'd need to be there every day. We could make that work," Brock said, not able to hide the smile on his face. If Brenna could have seen it, she would have known he was leading up to something. "I guess you'll just have to marry me and move to my house so you can take proper care of them."

"Brock McCrae, you know I won't move in with you. I'm not that..." Brenna spluttered, suddenly realizing exactly what it was Brock said. "Did you just ask...do you really mean..."

"Yes, I do," Brock said, gently pushing Brenna away from him and getting down on one knee. He pulled a ring from his pocket and held it out to Brenna.

"Marry me, Brenna? I want to wake up every morning to see those beautiful blue eyes and fall asleep every night in your sweet arms. Please, marry me, coffee girl."

Unable to speak, Brenna threw her arms around Brock and nodded against his neck.

"Is that a yes?"

He felt another nod.

"I love you, Brenna," Brock said, holding up her hand and sliding the ring on her finger. He kissed it when it was settled in place, pleased that it was a perfect fit.

Brenna looked at the ring, then at Brock, trying to take in the fact that her dream of spending forever with Brock was about to come true.

"Oh, Brock, I love you so, so much," Brenna said, brushing at her tears as Brock pressed his lips to hers then lifted her off her feet and swung her around.

"I can't wait to marry you, to finally make you mine," Brock said, lavishing kisses on her face and neck.

"Let's not wait too long," Brenna said, giving Brock a heated look that was filled with temptation and longing. "How fast can we pull together a wedding?"

"Not nearly fast enough," Brock said grinning as he swung her around again.

~◇~

"Someone left this for you on a table, Brenna," Jen said, handing Brenna an envelope with her name across the front.

"Thanks, Jen," Brenna said, setting the envelope on a shelf out of the way while she cleaned up from the lunch rush and started the baking for tomorrow. "Is the lunch crowd gone?"

"Yes. It was a busy one, today, wasn't it?" Jen said, helping put things away. Brenna added a dishwasher and a busser to the staff and between the four of them, they made it through the rush periods without too much trouble.

"It seems like it's that way every day," Brenna said with a big smile. She never dreamed the bistro would be so popular.

With tourists in town for the summer and the great location of the shop on one of the main streets through town, Brenna had almost more customers than she could handle some days.

Avery's business was flourishing as was their mother's. In addition to the home interiors, Letty was now doing custom orders for furniture and window treatments.

"Everyone says the bistro is the best place in town for breakfast and lunch. I'd have to agree," Jen said, with a big smile as she handed Isaac, the dishwasher, the last of the dirty dishes.

"Thanks for all your help today," Brenna said as Jen removed her apron and signed out her time card for the day.

"You're welcome. See you tomorrow," Jen said with a wave as she went out the side delivery door. Isaac and Nell, the busser, finished up their work and soon left.

A couple of hours later as Brenna cleaned up the last of the mess from her preparations for the next day's menu, she remembered the envelope. Taking it down from the shelf where she stashed it, she opened it to find a typed note. Assuming it was from Brock, she smiled.

I've got a surprise for you. Meet me out on the patio at five.

Brock had written her a few little notes during the course of their courtship so she was surprised to see the note and envelope had been typed instead of handwritten.

Staring at her ring, her heart going all soft at thoughts of her charming fiancé, she decided she didn't care how she got the note, she looked forward to seeing Brock soon. Glancing at the clock on the wall, she realized she wouldn't have time to run home and change before five if she wanted to get a few more things done at the bistro.

Resigned to wearing her chef uniform when Brock came, she went to the computer she kept on a small desk in the pantry area of the kitchen and placed her order for next week's supplies, planned out specials for the following two weeks and browsed through websites for a wedding gown. She and Brock both wanted to get married as soon as possible, so they'd decided on the second Saturday in July, just a few weeks away.

He knew there was no possibility of her leaving for a honeymoon right now, but they both thought they could wait for an extended trip after Christmas. His business was typically slow in January, Avery and Greg would have welcomed the baby and Brenna hoped by then to have a part-time chef and assistant manager for the bistro.

With just a few weeks to plan, Brenna wanted a simple outdoor ceremony. It seemed perfectly fitting for them to exchange their vows right where he proposed, among the roses at The Oregon Gardens. Their close family and friends would join them for an intimate afternoon wedding.

The pastor of their church would perform the ceremony. Mike and Levi were going to stand up with Brock while Kat and Avery served as Brenna's maid of honor and bridesmaid.

Avery was in charge of the flowers, Letty would oversee decorations, and Brenna was making her own cake.

She just needed to find a dress. Seeing a few that she liked online, she printed out the pages and slipped them into a folder she'd started of wedding ideas. Avery and her mom promised to go with her to Portland the following Monday to find a dress. Kat said she'd take a day off work and meet them, so it promised to be a fun-filled day.

Noticing that it was now a few minutes after five, Brenna turned off the computer, made sure all her equipment was turned off and walked through her mom's part of the store to the back patio.

Expecting to see Brock, she was surprised to find a single red rose in a vase with a small gift bag and another envelope with her name typed along the front sitting on one of the patio tables.

Opening the envelope the note said:

Put this on and wait for me.

Opening the gift bag, Brenna pulled out a sleep mask, the kind that blocked all light. Thinking it was odd but not wanting to spoil Brock's fun or his surprise, she sat down at the table, sniffed the rose then slipped on the mask.

Leaning back in the chair, she breathed deeply of the summer air, hoping to catch a whiff of Brock's enticing scent. Instead, all she smelled were the flowers that were blooming in the patio pots.

Brenna didn't have long to wait before she felt a warm hand on her arm, urging her to her feet.

"Hey, Brock, what's all this?" she asked, turning to give him a hug, but felt herself pulled along the patio behind him toward the side of the building. From the lack of sunshine giving warmth, she knew they were in the alley that led to the front of the store.

"Surprise," she heard in a whispered voice that sounded raspy.

"Are you okay? You sound like you've got a sore throat."

"Fine," the voice said as the hand patted her arm reassuringly.

"Where are we going?" Brenna asked as she was carefully helped off the curb. Reaching out, her hand brushed the roof of a car.

"Surprise," the voice said again. "Keys?"

"Oh, you need my keys? We're taking my car?" she asked and felt a hand squeeze hers.

"Yes."

Brenna pulled her keys from her pants pocket and held them out. She felt gloved fingers brush her hand as the keys were lifted from her palm.

"Why are you wearing gloves?" Brenna asked, knowing Brock always took them off to drive because he didn't want his steering wheel to get all dirty from his work gloves.

"Surprise," the voice whispered.

Brenna heard the car door open and found herself being helped inside. The gloved hand directed her fingers to the seat belt and she fastened herself in.

Brock had never asked to take her car anywhere. She drove sometimes, but if he was given a choice, they went in his truck. It was odd that he wanted to drive her car today. He was certainly acting strange, and not in a fun surprise kind of way, either.

As the car backed out of her parking space and pulled into traffic, Brenna tried to relax, deciding to sit quietly if Brock wasn't in the mood to talk. Breathing deep, she anticipated a whiff of Brock's scent. Even after a day on the job, he still smelled like cedar and musk and virile man.

The odor she inhaled immediately sent alarm bells clanging in her head.

Will.

All she could smell was a scent that made her think of the heavy, overpowering cologne Will always favored.

Pretending to sneeze, Brenna took a quick peek from beneath her mask to see that it was Will in the car, not Brock.

Panic threatened to choke the air from her lungs, but she forced herself to remain calm. She began chatting about her day at the bistro, hoping to keep Will distracted as she mentally followed their route through town. In a few more blocks, they'd be at a stop light. If the light was red, she may have a chance to hop out of the car and make a run for it.

Forcing herself to relax while keeping up her one-sided conversation, she tried to gauge where they were at, realizing the light must have been green and Will was still heading straight. If Will continued on this course, he'd come to a stop sign in about half a mile and Brenna planned to hit the ground running.

Not wanting to contemplate what Will had planned, Brenna liked to think he wouldn't actually hurt her. He had been gentle with her so far, so she hoped that would work in her favor. She'd certainly find out when she took the opportunity to escape. Sending up a prayer for help, Brenna waited for the car to stop moving, silently sliding her hand to the handle of her door.

~◇~

Sitting at the stoplight impatiently waiting for it to turn green, Brock was in a hurry to get home, shower, and go to the Smith's for dinner. They were going to work on finishing up the wedding plans this evening.

It was hard to believe that in less than two weeks, Brenna would officially be his wife. Thinking back to the first time he saw her, looking so sweet yet impatient at the coffee shop, he had no idea the freckle-nosed woman with a love for Chai lattes would soon be his bride.

Brock thought of all the decisions they made in the past few weeks as they selected everything from wedding invitations to the towels for the bathroom.

Remembering one discussion they had about the proper way toilet paper should hang made Brock grin as he tapped his fingers on the steering wheel. He could care less which direction it rolled, but arguing with Brenna was so much fun. Especially the making up part after the arguing.

The grin slid from Brock's face like ice cream left too long in the sun as he watched Brenna's car slowly drive through the intersection. Brenna was in the passenger seat with a blindfold over her eyes and that psychopath Will was driving her car.

Fear wrapped icy fingers around his heart and he regretted not being more forceful with Brenna about Will having some very real mental problems. He should have made sure Will understood Brenna was not his for the taking. He should have been more insistent that she get a restraining order against Will.

Dialing 9-1-1, Brock relayed what information he knew then gunned his pickup as soon as the light turned green. Whipping around the corner, Brock raced after the car. If Will hurt even one hair on Brenna's precious head, he was going to regret ever being born.

Wondering how Will had got her in the car, acquired her keys and put a mask on her, Brock filled with a rage unlike anything he'd ever known. He wasn't a violent man, but he would rip Will into pieces if

Brenna wasn't safe.

Following the road, Brock drove around a curve and slammed on the brakes. Brenna, still dressed in her chef's coat and pants, sprinted down the street with Will close behind her, screaming her name over and over. Brock jumped out of his truck, opened his arms and braced himself as Brenna ran right into them, trying to catch her breath, her eyes wide in fear.

Setting her behind him, Brock watched as Will approached, a glazed look in his eyes. When he tried to reach for Brenna, Brock raised his fist and popped Will once hard in the face, knocking him to the ground. While he was down, Brock rolled Will over and pulled his arms behind his back, pinning him to the asphalt with his knee until the police arrived.

Will yelled and sobbed that he just wanted to talk to Brenna, to convince her that it was him she really loved, despite the duct tape, rope and a hunting knife they found in his backpack that hinted otherwise. Brenna waited in Brock's pickup, tears streaming down her face, trembling with the fear of what might have happened if Brock hadn't miraculously arrived when he did.

Once the police came and put Will in their car, Brenna told Brock she realized right after she got in the car that it was Will and started thinking of a way to escape. When Will pulled up at the stop sign, she jumped out of the car, yanking the mask off as she ran.

"You came to my rescue, again," Brenna said, leaning into the safety and solid security of Brock. She didn't know what would have happened if Brock hadn't been there. Didn't want to think about it.

"I told you, Brenna, I'll always, always be here for you," Brock said, kissing the top of her head, grateful that his coffee girl was fine. The enormity of what Will could have done to Brenna made him feel weak-kneed, so he turned his thoughts to the fact that he got there in time, Will was going to get the help he needed, and Brenna was safe in his arms. Where he always wanted her to be.

Epilogue

Three Years Later

"Look, Brock, the roses are blooming," Brenna said, pointing to the soft yellow blooms that arched over the front sidewalk, as she and Brock walked down the front porch steps. Taking a deep breath, she smiled. "Can you smell them?"

"Yes, I can," Brock said, thinking the smell of the roses didn't hold a candle to the fresh, sweet scent of Brenna. Her fragrance, her very essence, would forever make him think of spring and sunshine.

The roses were the same variety as the ones she admired in the rose garden the day Brock proposed. As a wedding gift, he'd tracked down four rose bushes and carefully planted them, two on each side of the arbor. This summer was the first one that the canes arched all the way to the top of the arbor and delicate, fragrant blooms greeted their guests at the front gate.

Mutt ran around them barking as they strolled across the lawn and Brock plucked a blossom, handing it to his wife.

She smiled and held it up to her nose, looking over it at him with big blue eyes that still made his heart pound anytime he gazed into their bright depths filled with warmth and love.

Resting his hand on her rounded belly, he smiled thinking about the baby who would join their family in a few months. Avery and Greg's little girl Megan was a spirited handful they all spoiled and loved while her brother, Kevin, was too little at three months old to get into any trouble.

Standing in the yard with the dog bounding around their feet, the worrisome widows waving from down the street, and his hand bouncing from the kicks of their unborn child, Brock knew a feeling of contentment that filled him with an unimaginable joy.

His thoughts turned to the dream that used to haunt his nights up until the day he married Brenna. It came to him clearly now and he realized for the first time the woman in the dream had been Brenna all along. All those years of being plagued by that dream, he knew it had always been Brenna standing beside him. It was her beloved face he gazed into with such rapture.

"It's you," he said, staring at Brenna with a look of surprise. "It's always been you, coffee girl."

She glanced at him with an indulgent grin. "Of course it's me. How many other pregnant women do you stand with in the front yard, waving to our nosy neighbors? Have you been out in the heat too long today? Maybe we better go inside for a while."

Brock laughed and engulfed her in a hug. "I never told you this, but I used to have this dream. I was standing in a yard, this yard, with a mangy mutt running around barking and a beautiful woman in my arms. I'd reach down and put my hand on her belly and feel this amazing sense of love as our baby kicked my fingers. I could never see the woman in my dreams, but I just realized it was you all along. I know it sounds crazy."

"Not crazy at all," Brenna said, kissing her husband before taking his hand and leading him toward the house. "I used to have my own dream of a broad-shouldered, dark-haired man who would love me like no other man ever would. He smelled of cedar, musk and coffee, and I could feel the strength of his arms around me. Then one day I was standing right over there with you…"

###

Banana Bread

Once in a blue moon, when I have a bunch of overripe bananas, I get inspired to bake banana bread. Captain Cavedweller is pretty excited when this happens and will eat half the loaf, still warm from the oven, if I let him. *(Have you ever tried stopping a hungry man from eating warm bread? Not an easy task, I assure you!)* This recipe isn't hard to make and always turns out well.

Banana Bread

1 3/4 cup flour
2/3 cup sugar
2 tsp. baking powder
1/2 tsp. baking soda
1/4 tsp. salt
1 cup mashed ripe bananas
1/3 cup butter or shortening
2 tbsp. milk
1 tsp. vanilla extract
2 eggs
1/2 cup nuts
1 tbsp. cinnamon

Preheat oven to 350 degrees.

Mix one cup flour, sugar, baking powder, baking soda, and salt. Mash two to three ripe bananas (or overripe bananas, the riper the banana the stronger the flavor) to make one cup. Add banana, butter, vanilla and milk to dry ingredients. Mix on low until blended then beat on high for two minutes. Add eggs and remaining flour, beat until blended. Fold in cinnamon and nuts. Bake 55-60 minutes or until golden brown and starting to pull away from the edges of the pan. Let cool, turn out of the pan, slice and enjoy!

Available Now!

Savvy Autumn Entertaining - Ideas for fall party themes, tips for bringing autumn into your home and yummy fall recipes are included in this quick and easy guide for savvy entertaining at home!

From Savvy Entertaining's blogger, this book includes her favorite fall tips!

Coming for the 2012 Holiday Season!

The Christmas Bargain - As owner and manager of the Hardman bank, Luke Granger is a man of responsibility and integrity in the small 1890s Eastern Oregon town. Calling in a long overdue loan, Luke finds himself reluctantly accepting a bargain in lieu of payment from the shiftless farmer who barters his daughter to settle his debt.

Philamena Booth is both mortified and relieved when her father sends her off with the banker as payment of his debt. Held captive on the farm since the death of her mother more than a decade earlier, Philamena is grateful to leave. If only it had been someone other than the handsome and charismatic Luke Granger riding to rescue her. Ready to hold up her end of the bargain as Luke's cook and housekeeper, Philamena is prepared for the hard work ahead.

What she isn't prepared for is being forced to marry Luke as part of this crazy Christmas bargain.

Coming Fall 2012!

The Cowboy's Autumn Fall - Brice Morgan thought love at first sight was some ridiculous notion of school girls and old ladies who read too many romance novels. At least he does until he meets Bailey Bishop at a friend's wedding and falls hard and fast for the intriguing woman.

Bailey Bishop attends her cousin's wedding with no intention of extending her brief visit to Oregon. Married to her career as a paleontologist, Bailey tries to ignore her intense attraction to her cousin's best friend, Brice. Ready to return home to Denver, Bailey instead accepts the opportunity to explore a new dig site not far from the family's ranch in Grass Valley.

Can she keep her feelings for Brice from derailing her plans for the future?

As the autumn season arrives, love falls on willing hearts at the Triple T Ranch.

THE COWBOY'S AUTUMN FALL

by
SHANNA HATFIELD

An excerpt…

Chapter One

"He who would not be idle, let him fall in love."

Ovid

"Disgusting. Absolutely disgusting," Brice Morgan muttered to himself as he made his way through the crowd gathered for Trent and Lindsay Thompson's wedding reception.

If he had to watch one more couple gazing dreamily at each other, Brice thought he might be sick. Enduring about all the romance he could handle for one evening, he sat down next to his sister Tess at a large table beneath one of the white canopies. Leaning back in his chair, he shook his head in irritation and sighed.

"Maybe you need to work some moves like that into your routine, man," Travis Thompson said, leaning around Tess and slapping Brice on the shoulder. Travis and Brice, just days apart in age, had been best friends since they were old enough to push each other down.

Following the direction of Tess' pointing finger, he watched Travis' adopted six-year-old niece Cass dance with the wild abandon of a happy child next to her uncle and his new bride. Arms flailing, red curls bouncing, Cass spun around and around giggling with giddy excitement.

"That would definitely get you some attention," Tess teased, offering Brice a sassy grin. "I'm sure all the girls would be lining up to dance with you."

"Definitely," Travis said, nodding his head in agreement. "Anyone under the age of ten or over the age of seventy would be putty in your hands."

Before Brice could form a snappy comeback, Travis leaned over and whispered in Tess' ear, making her blush.

Rolling his eyes, he realized sitting next to Travis and Tess, basking in their newly declared love for one another, wasn't the best choice if he was trying to get away from the evening's love fest this wedding was turning out to be.

Travis' older brother Trent was goofy in love with his bride of a few hours. If that wasn't bad enough, Travis' oldest brother Trey and his wife Cady were sitting across the table from him whispering sweet nothings to each other and looking more in love than a couple wed eight months had a right to.

Brice sighed again and swiped a hand over his face. All this talk of love and romance was ridiculous. It was the stuff that kept school girls twittering and old ladies and love-starved women buying romance novels. In his opinion, it was a bunch of mush perpetuated by florists, candy companies, and sappy-minded idiots.

"You okay, BB?" Tess asked, calling him by the nickname she'd given him when she first learned to talk. Less than a year apart in age, Tess couldn't quite say "baby" so the name BB stuck.

"Just great," Brice said, trying to hide his annoyance as Trey stood and took Cady's hand in his, kissing her fingers.

"Cady, darlin', will you please dance with me?" Trey turned on his charm. He gave his wife a pleading look, one that everyone knew inspired Cady to do whatever Trey wanted. "I know you're pooped and you shucked off your shoes half an hour ago, so you can waltz out there barefoot for all I care, but come dance with me. Please?"

"I'd be honored, boss-man," Cady said, getting up from the table and stuffing her tired feet back into her high heels, letting Trey pull her toward the dance-floor.

Swallowing down another sigh, Brice supposed he should be used to the Thompson brothers and their romantic tendencies by now. It was practically legendary in their small community of Grass Valley, Oregon.

Growing up nearby, Brice, Tess, and their brother Ben spent as much time here at the Triple T Ranch with the three Thompson boys as they did at home on the Running M Ranch. That was before Trey, Trent, and Travis were all love struck.

Sitting back in his chair and looking around, he had never seen the Triple T look quite so nice, especially in mid-August. From the fresh coats of paint on the outbuildings to the flowers blooming profusely in every available corner, the ranch looked like something you'd see in a home and garden magazine.

The big yard was now set up like a fairyland with billowing tents, enough white lights to line the landing strips at PDX and a portable dance floor where he could see Trey drop Cady into a dip while Trent twirled Lindsay in his arms.

The only reason Tess and Travis weren't out on the dance floor was due to the pair of torn hamstrings Travis received the previous month when he rescued a little boy windsurfing. Only able to walk for short stretches without crutches, dancing wasn't on Travis' current list of activities approved by his physical therapist, who also happened to be Tess.

"I hate for you to miss all the dancing, honeybee," Travis said, rubbing his hand across Tess' shoulders. "Why don't the two of you go show them how it's done?"

Tess kissed Travis' cheek and gently patted his leg. "The only guy I want to dance with is you, Trav. I'm fine sitting on the sidelines tonight."

"Give me a break," Brice muttered under his breath, again rolling his eyes. If those two kept this up, he might even regret the extensive efforts he made all summer to get them together.

"I heard that," Tess said, leaning closer to Brice and smacking his arm. "What's gotten into you tonight, grumpy britches? You're usually the life of the party."

Brice shrugged. His sister was right. Usually the first one on the dance floor and the last one to leave, Brice loved to have fun, be the center of attention, and keep everyone entertained. Tonight, he just wasn't interested. Maybe it was because he was here all alone.

"Excuse me," a soft voice said next to Brice and he turned to look into the face of a lovely girl. Petite with honey-blond curls cascading down her back and sparkling blue eyes, a dimple popped out in her cheek when she smiled at him. "Would you like to dance?"

"Absolutely," Brice said, getting to his feet and taking her hand as she walked toward the dance floor.

"You must be related to Travis' girlfriend," the girl said as they settled into the rhythm of a moderately fast dance.

"Tess is my sister," Brice said, smiling at his dance partner, admiring her well-shaped form and beautiful face. "How do you know Travis?"

"He's my cousin," the girl said, bringing her dimple back out of hiding with a big smile. "I'm Sierra Bishop. My mom and Denni are sisters."

"Nice to meet you. I'm Brice Morgan and I've known the whole Thompson clan since I was born," Brice said, admiring the way Sierra moved on the dance floor while casting teasing glances his direction. She was not only a very good dancer, but also an accomplished flirt. He had met a few of the Thompson boys' cousins, but obviously they'd been holding out on him with this branch of the family tree.

Deciding the evening had just gotten a lot more interesting, Brice asked Sierra for the next dance and they both grinned when Travis limped onto the dance floor, pulling Tess behind him.

The band played Blake Shelton's *Honey Bee*, thanks to Trent and Trey's prompting, drawing the interest of all the guests. Most everyone knew the song was the inspiration behind Travis' nickname for Tess. As they the crowd clapped and cheered, Tess' cheeks turned bright red but she buried her face against Travis' chest and kept on dancing.

"Do you think there'll be another wedding soon?" Sierra asked, eying the couple as they became much more involved in sharing loving glances than dancing.

"Quite possibly," Brice commented, glad to see both Tess and Travis so deliriously happy, even if it was a little nauseating.

As the song ended, Brice walked Sierra over to the refreshment table and handed her a glass of sweet tea. They were standing there talking when a young woman came up beside Sierra and whispered something to her before pouring herself a cup of punch.

Studying the two of them, Brice could see a resemblance although the girls didn't seem to share much in common. Where Sierra was short and bubbly, the other girl was older, taller and had an aura of self-confidence. Her hair, the same honey-gold shade, fell in short curls above her shoulders and Brice would have guessed her to be about five eight or so if she'd kick off her incredibly high heels.

When she turned and looked at him with eyes the same intense turquoise shade of blue as Trey Thompson's, Brice thought he'd been struck by lightning when an electrifying jolt shook him from the top of his head right on down to the toes in his polished cowboy boots.

Half expecting smoke to billow around him, Brice forced himself to stand still.

"Brice Morgan, this is my sister Bailey," Sierra said, putting a hand on the arm of the woman Brice decided in the last dozen seconds he was going to one day marry.

Brice leaned forward and offered his hand which Bailey took in hers. Ignoring the snap of heat that shot up her arm at his touch, Bailey studied the lean, muscled man before her and liked what she saw.

"A pleasure to meet you Mr. Morgan," Bailey said in a smooth voice that made Brice think of something silky and rich. Her hand in his felt soft and so right, he hated to let it go.

"The pleasure is all mine, Miss Bishop," Brice said, reaching to doff a hat he forgot he wasn't wearing. Quickly recovering, he gave her his most charming smile. "May I ask you for a dance?"

"You may," she said, handing her cup of punch to Sierra and placing her hand back in Brice's as he led her to the dance floor. Bailey glanced over her shoulder and caught the look of surprise on her sister's pretty face. This was the first time any member of the male species chose Bailey over the perfectly perky Sierra.

Looking into the bottomless depths of her eyes, Brice realized he had never, in his twenty five years of living, felt this way about another person. While his heart pounded wildly, the rest of the world suddenly disappeared, leaving him with his attention completely focused on Bailey.

Trying to maintain his composure, Brice was glad the dance was a slow one. It gave him time to start a conversation with the woman in his arms.

"Welcome to Grass Valley, Miss Bishop," Brice said, keeping the formal tone of their introduction.

"Thank you, Mr. Morgan. We've been here a few times over the years, but it's always fun to visit," Bailey said, glancing up at Brice. He was taller than her, about six feet, she would guess. He had lush brown hair that was cut short and styled with a spiky wave in the front.

Eyes the color of root beer held a spark of mischief and his teeth gleamed white when he smiled. Deciding he was definitely handsome, she smiled back at him. "Please, call me Bailey."

"Bailey," Brice repeated, liking the sound of her name on his lips. What he'd like even more was the taste of her lips on his. He supposed that was pushing things a bit since they'd just met a few minutes ago.

Carrying on a conversation about generalities, they were oblivious that the tempo changed as they continued to dance the next three dances in each other's arms. Finally, Brice asked Bailey if she'd like something to drink and escorted her back to the refreshment tent. Sierra was long gone, so Brice poured Bailey another cup of punch and fished a bottle of water out of an ice-filled tub for himself.

Bailey finished her punch in a few swallows and refilled it while Brice was looking around for an empty table where they could sit and chat.

Taking her elbow, he walked her to a table where her aunt sat visiting with his parents.

"Bailey, honey, I see you met our Brice," Denni Thompson said when Bailey sat down beside her. "This is Mike and Michele Morgan, Brice's parents."

"How lovely to meet you both," Bailey said, suddenly feeling a little light headed. She probably needed to eat something, since she'd missed eating her dinner, distracted by some work details she'd received. Sierra told her to put away her phone and have some fun, so she of course ignored her sister and responded to three text messages. By that time, her plate had disappeared and she was left watching Sierra work her charm on the single male population attending the wedding.

Denni put her arm around Bailey and gave her a hug as they all visited for a while. Bailey felt oddly detached from herself, being chatty and carefree. Normally she was quiet and reserved, much preferring to sit back and analyze the conversation going on around her than actively participate in it. She assumed her behavior was due to the fact they had flown in from Denver that afternoon and she was a little punchy from the excitement of the wedding.

"Brice, why don't you go get us all some cake," Michele said, looking at her son as he gazed adoringly at Denni's niece.

"Sure, Mom," Brice said, getting to his feet, hoping Denni wouldn't let Bailey escape before he got back. "Coming right up."

Brice soon came back trying to balance five pieces of cake on flimsy paper plates and managed to get them all on the table without dropping one. Seeing Bailey's empty cup of punch, he went to get her a refill and poured himself a glass of tea.

Finishing up their cake, Bailey seemed interested in spending more time with him, so Brice asked her to dance again. He nearly bore a hole through his brother Ben with his cold glare when he cut in. Knowing he ruffled Brice's feathers, Ben returned Bailey to his keeping at the end of the dance with a wiggle of his eyebrows.

"Your brother seems nice," Bailey said, watching Ben walk away, surprised at how much the two brothers looked alike. In fact, if there wasn't a definite age difference between the two, it would have been easy to think they were twins.

"He has his moments," Brice said, pulling Bailey a little closer into his arms. When she didn't offer any resistance, he ran his hands up and down her back, fighting the urge to kiss her.

Observing her as they danced, he realized she wasn't the most beautiful woman he'd ever seen. Her nose was a little too wide and a gap between her two front teeth would keep her from being considered magazine cover quality, but she had a heart-shaped face and skin that looked like smooth porcelain.

Although her mouth was small, her lips were moist and inviting. She had long legs, a nice curved figure, and apparently worked out by the toned muscles visible with her sleeveless dress. The most important thing Brice noticed was how absolutely perfect she felt in his arms.

"I enjoyed meeting your parents," Bailey said, glancing around like she was looking for someone. "Mom and Dad are around here somewhere. I'll introduce you if I can find them."

"I'd like that," Brice said, knowing it was hard to find anyone in the crowd of hundreds of guests filling the Triple T ranch yard. Since it was getting late, some of the guests were starting to leave. It wouldn't be long before Trent and Lindsay tossed the bouquet and said their goodbyes, then the cleanup process would begin.

Brice promised to help tear down the tents after the crowd cleared out, so he hoped to spend the next few hours with Bailey. He suddenly wondered if she was staying at the ranch or elsewhere. "Where are you staying?"

"Here at the ranch," Bailey said, enjoying the feel of Brice's arms around her. It had been a while since she had allowed herself the pleasure of being close to a man. This particular man was doing funny things to her ability to reason as his warm, leathery scent kept teasing her nose and his engaging smiles kept drawing hers out in return. "I have some business to attend to Monday and then I'll head back to Denver with the family on Thursday. We all want to make sure we have time to visit with Nana."

Brice smiled as he thought about Ester Nordon, grandmother to the rowdy Thompson brothers. She had the same brilliant blue eyes as Trey and Bailey and was known for her gentle yet formidable spirit.

"You definitely don't want to miss that opportunity. I've had my ears boxed by your Nana more than once," Brice said with a grin.

"I'm sure you did nothing to deserve it," Bailey said, smiling at Brice and finding herself wanting to kiss the mole that rested at the edge of his bottom lip. Shaking her head to rid herself of the notion made her dizzy, so she leaned forward and pressed her cheek against Brice's. She felt his arms tighten slightly around her and let out a contented sigh.

Brice had never been so enraptured by a woman before. Usually one to take things slow to keep girls he wasn't all that interested in from getting the wrong idea, Brice felt like he'd been hurtling headlong down an unchartered course since his eyes connected with Bailey's.

"Bailey, I know this sounds crazy..." Brice started to say, but was cut off by cheers and clapping when it was announced that Lindsay was ready to toss the bouquet. Turning with his arm around Bailey's waist so they could watch the fun, Brice cheered when Trent shot the garter in a high arc and Travis captured it by sticking one of his crutches up in the air.

The crowd went wild with applause when Lindsay tossed the bouquet straight to Tess. Someone hollered "two down, one to go," causing Tess' face to turn a bright shade of red. It seemed to be a fact of general agreement that there would be another Thompson family wedding in the near future.

"That is perfectly splendid," Bailey said, leaning closer to Brice. "I didn't realize Travis was that serious about your sister."

"He didn't either until a few weeks ago," Brice said, taking Bailey's hand and leading her along with the crowd as they followed Trent and Lindsay out to where a carriage waited to whisk them away. Given the lateness of the hour, Trent and Lindsay were going to spend the night at their cute little cottage down the road then leave in the morning for a week on the Oregon coast. The carriage would drive them the few miles from the Triple T to their house.

Waving as the carriage rolled down the long driveway, the guests began saying their goodbyes. It didn't take long for the crowd to depart and the remaining family and friends to begin the massive undertaking of taking down the fairyland and picking up the debris left from the celebration.

Brice and Bailey helped clear off tables, fold linens and carry gifts into the house where Trent and Lindsay would open them upon their return. Bailey was uncommonly thirsty and drank three more cups of punch while she helped move the gifts inside.

Noticing that plenty of help was making short work of the mess, Brice caught Bailey's hand and tugged her away from the chatter of the others down to the pond where Lindsay and Trent exchanged vows earlier in the evening.

Hundreds of white lights illuminated the area, hanging in the trees and draped over shrubs. It was beyond lovely and Bailey stopped at the bottom of the hill where the trail ended to take it all in.

Brice watched Bailey and smiled, wondering if she enjoyed evenings like this in Denver. Frogs and crickets created a soft serenade and a slight breeze cooled the warm summer air. In addition to the twinkling white lights around them, a canopy of stars twinkled overhead.

"Wow," Bailey said, tipping her head back to stare at the night sky. She wasn't sure if she moved or Brice did, but she found her head resting against his shoulder and his arm around her waist as they stared up at the stars. It was one of the most romantic moments Bailey had ever experienced.

Feeling completely unlike herself, she spun around, throwing her arms around Brice's neck and putting her lips to his.

Brice's surprise rapidly gave way to acceptance as his arms went around her and he pulled her closer, deepening the kiss.

Sure her lips were on fire, Bailey was torn between wanting the kiss to end immediately and go on forever. Tremors rocked through her and her heart felt like it might take flight from her chest in its frenzied beating.

"Brice, I…"

Lips moving insistently on hers kept her from saying more. It was probably a good thing since she couldn't remember what it was she was going to say. Brice worked his way from her lips down her neck and back up to her ear, which made her moan and bury her hands into his thick hair. She tipped her head back to give him better access and he pulled her flush against him.

Suddenly he released his hold and took a step back as reality crashed down on him. What was he doing? This was Travis' cousin and from all appearances, she wasn't the kind of girl to get embroiled in a passionate encounter upon first meeting someone.

"I'm sorry, Bailey," Brice said, trying to catch his breath and recapture some small degree of sense.

"Don't apologize, Brice," Bailey said, leaning against him, even though she knew she shouldn't. She should be offended, annoyed and angry.

Only she wasn't.

She was, however, lightheaded, emboldened, and more interested in the good-looking cowboy standing in front of her than she had ever been with a man before.

Brice took a series of deep breaths, started to say

something, stopped and swiped a hand over his face. It would be way too easy to take advantage of this situation and he wasn't going to let it happen.

Finally, he took her hand and turned them both toward the house, urging her up the trail. "I think we better get back to the house. We both seem to be under some sort of spell."

"Spells can be good," Bailey said, casting him a look that filled him with renewed longing. The heat in her intensely blue eyes made Brice trip. He had to take a few hurried steps to catch himself, making Bailey giggle.

"Bewitched is more like it," Brice muttered under his breath. He was doing some fast thinking as they walked back up the hill. If Bailey left Thursday that only gave him about ninety-six hours to convince her she was the woman for him and to stay in Grass Valley permanently.

"You can't be bewitched, I can't wriggle my nose," Bailey said in a breathy voice, turning her face to Brice. "See?"

"Yes, I do see," he said, trying not to kiss her again with her face only an inch away from his. Actually, he was finding it difficult to see anything except the alluring woman who was standing next to him, warm and willing for his attentions. Gently pushing her forward, they continued walking.

Cresting the hill, it looked like the work was done and those left behind were either going to the bunkhouse, the ranch house, or getting in their cars to go home. He watched Travis limp beside Tess as she walked to her car and whisper something in her ear that made her smile. Brice knew he'd have a few minutes before he needed to leave since Tess was his ride home and she obviously wasn't quite ready to tell Travis goodnight.

Leading Bailey around the corner of the ranch

house where it was dark and quiet, he put his arms around her and let her warmth seep into him. He never imagined holding a woman would make him feel like he was finally complete, but that is exactly how he felt with Bailey.

"Can I see you tomorrow?" Brice asked as Bailey rested against his chest, melting against him while melting his restraint.

"Umm, hmm," she said, eyes closed and face upturned to his. Feeling weightless and wonderful, she grinned. "But you better kiss me goodnight first."

"Yes, ma'am," Brice said, dropping his head to hers and giving her a kiss that made bright lights explode behind his eyes and his gut clench with heat.

Bailey wrapped her arms around his neck and was leaning so far into him, he was all but holding her up.

"Oh, Brice, I think I just love you," she said with a giggle followed by a hiccup. She toyed with the wave of his hair that fell across his forehead and was nearly purring in his ear. "You're so sweet and sexy."

Pulling back, Brice studied her, trying to determine if she was sincere in what she was saying. Bailey had been somewhat reserved and quiet when they first met. As the evening progressed she became more and more relaxed and now she was quite … uninhibited. If he didn't know better, he'd think she was drunk, but all he'd seen her drink was punch.

Rolling his eyes, Brice realized the punch must have been spiked. Thinking back, he saw the rotten Bradshaw boys hanging around the punch bowl when no one else was around. They were famous for their ability to spike just about anything in liquid form.

"Punch, Bailey. How much punch did you have, sugar?" Brice asked, gently untangling her arms from around his neck and helping her walk around the corner of the house.

"I don't know. Five or nine or eleventy-three cups," Bailey said, knowing she sounded stupid, but unable to keep her mouth shut. Feeling flushed and dizzy, she was having the most difficult time simultaneously holding open her eyes and moving her feet forward. Despite that she felt completely light and without care. She giggled again and leaned against Brice's arm. "It was yummy."

"I'm sure it was," Brice said dryly, trying to keep her walking upright in her high heels.

The third time she stumbled, Brice sighed and picked her up in his arms. Hurrying up the back steps, through the mud room and into the kitchen, he wasn't surprised to see a few people milling around. Sierra was there talking to an older woman who looked enough like her, he assumed she was her mother.

"My gracious, is she hurt?" the woman asked as Brice tried to set Bailey down and she refused to let go of his neck.

"No, but she's probably going to have a humdinger of a headache tomorrow," Brice said, bending his head and sliding it out of Bailey's grasp. He set her down on her feet, but her legs were wobbly and she tilted dangerously to the right.

"I hate to ask, but would you mind? I'm her mother, Mary Bishop" the woman said, pointing toward the great room. She tried to hide a smirk behind her hand. "I can't believe she's snockered."

"No problem. Just point me in the right direction. South or North Wing?" Brice said, happy to help as he picked Bailey up, enjoying the feel of her body close to his, even if she was drunk.

"South," Mary said leading the way. Knowing the house well, Brice followed Mary and Sierra through the kitchen and dining area, past the great room and down the hall to the south wing of the house. "I'm Brice Morgan, a good friend of Travis'."

"Thank you, Brice. I hate to meet you under this embarrassing circumstance, but it's our pleasure. My apologies for Bailey," Mary said, sounding more amused than distraught over Bailey's drunken state. "I can honestly say she's never been drunk before. I don't know what inspired her to do so this evening."

Brice laughed and both Sierra and Mary turned to look at him. "It's not her fault. I think the punch was spiked. Here I thought she found me charming and clever. Guess it was only the liquor talking."

Sierra, who was glad to see her sister show some spark of interest in a man regardless of how drunk she may have been, smiled.

"Oh, she liked you, Brice, or she would never have danced with you in the first place. She's not much of a socializer," Sierra said, sharing a knowing look with her mother.

Brice carried Bailey into the room that was Trey's during his growing up years and gently placed her on the bed. When she reached up looking like she would kiss him again, he turned his face so all she got was his cheek. It wasn't that he didn't want about a thousand more kisses from her, he just preferred she be sober without her mom and sister watching.

"Well, isn't that something," her mother said, observing the way Bailey was clinging to Brice.

"I told you, Mom," Sierra whispered, having already informed her mother about the cowboy who swept Bailey off her feet. "Now do you believe me?"

"Yes, I do," Mary said, watching as Brice kissed Bailey on the forehead and told her goodnight.

He turned and gave them both a grin before walking toward the door. Mary put a hand on his arm with a warm smile before he stepped into the hall.

"Thank you, Brice. I hope we'll see you again before we leave the ranch."

"I'd like that," Brice said, tipping his head to both Sierra and Mary. "I look forward to seeing the lovely Bishop ladies soon."

Rather than retracing his steps through the house, Brice walked to the end of the wing and went out the door, hurrying around to the side yard where Tess was parked. Seeing Travis with his hands buried in Tess' hair, Brice grinned.

"I think you two have done more than enough of that for one evening. Come on, Tessie, let's head home," Brice teased as he walked up to the car.

Tess jerked away from Travis, giving her brother a stern glare that only made him laugh.

"Thanks, dude," Travis said, shaking his head at his friend. "Don't think we didn't notice you saying goodnight to Bailey a minute ago."

Brice stopped the snappy retort he was going to give Travis and instead climbed into Tess' car.

Watching his sister blow a kiss to Travis, he felt compelled to blow one as well and bat his eyelashes theatrically, which earned him an elbow in his side from Tess.

Heading down the driveway, Tess was quiet while she seemed to pull her thoughts away from Travis. When he glanced at her again, she offered him a teasing smile. He was going to have to be careful or Tess would give him a hard time about his attraction to Bailey.

"You like Bailey, don't you?" she asked, already knowing the answer.

"Maybe," Brice said trying to sound uninterested.

"She's quite pretty with all that honey colored hair and those intense blue eyes. I wonder how come she and Trey are the only ones to inherit Nana's eye color?"

"Don't know. Just the way genes work I suppose."

"I happened to notice you two getting pretty friendly out back a little while ago. Don't you think that is kind of pushing the limit considering you just met her?" Tess asked with a raised eyebrow.

"I would say yes, except I figured out she was drunk."

"Drunk! How'd she get...oh, the punch," Tess said, turning off the road to their driveway.

"So it was the punch," Brice said, slapping his leg. "Let me guess, the Bradshaw boys?"

"I assumed so," Tess said, parking the car and turning off her lights. "Travis said they asked a couple of their hands to keep an eye on the punch bowl, but there were a few minutes when it went unguarded. I guess we should have thrown it out, but Travis didn't think the boys had time to dump anything into the bowl."

"Well, apparently they did," Brice said, keeping a hand on Tess' elbow to steady her as they walked through the gravel to the back sidewalk. "I mistakenly thought Bailey was completely taken with my undeniable charm and dashing good looks. Instead it was just the punch talking."

Tess laughed as they went in the back door.

"Maybe, but I hope it at least had something good to say."

Brice grinned. It definitely had something to say. Something along the lines that love at first sight wasn't such a far-fetched crazy notion after all...

SHANNA HATFIELD spent 10 years as a newspaper journalist before moving into the field of marketing and public relations. She has a lifelong love of writing, reading and creativity. She and her husband, lovingly referred to as Captain Cavedweller, reside in the Pacific Northwest with their neurotic cat along with a menagerie of wandering wildlife and neighborhood pets.

Shanna loves to hear from readers:

Blog: shannahatfield.com

Facebook: Shanna Hatfield's Page

Pinterest: Shanna Hatfield

Email: shanna@shannahatfield.com